CAITLYN CAN'T DIE

THE SERIAL SURVIVORS
BOOK 1

LIZ HAMBLETON

EDITED BY
BETH HUDSON INK

COVER DESIGN BY
K.B. BARRETT DESIGNS

LIZHAMBLETONBOOKSLLC

To my beloved book club—
Great books, good wine, plenty of laughter, delicious snacks, and, most of all,
precious friendship.

CONTENT WARNING

Before you read…

Caitlyn Can't Die contains adult subject matter that may not be for everyone. If you are uncomfortable with explicit on-page romance, this book is not for you.

Although not described in great detail, there are mentions of attempted sexual assault and idealizations of ending one's life.

Be mindful when you read.

CHAPTER
ONE

CAITLYN

Tips for surviving the apocalypse.

DON'T.

The end of days has been dragging on forever, and I'm stuck in its never-ending loop. This has to be the worst time of my life, and that's not something I say lightly.

I'm not an overdramatic woman who thinks every job setback or broken heart means the end is near.

But this time, the end came and didn't take me with it.

Which, right now, seems like the worst-case scenario.

I'd rather be anywhere but here, barely alive and fighting to survive in this hell on earth. I'm beginning to think that death is the better option.

From the moment I open my eyes, I count down the minutes and hours until I sleep, dream about my life before, and pretend I didn't survive this nightmare.

I'll wake up in the morning and realize I'm still in this hellscape, a survivor amongst the millions dead.

And why?

Is it my fortitude in the face of adversity?

Is it my strength and quickness of mind?

Was I part of a survivalist family that trained for this, ready for the inevitable end?

Uh, no.

Hell, no.

Dumb, stupid luck got me here today, and every sunrise, a small part of me, *a part growing larger by the day*, regrets my existence. Countless souls would have given anything to make it this long, but I'm not one of them.

I'm not sure what keeps me going, preventing me from sealing my fate by jumping off a high-rise building or running straight toward a group of bloats.

Bloats.

The most disgusting anomalies that some virus from hell dreamt up. They are sacks of dark goo that once resembled a person. Just the thought of them induces bile to rise from my stomach.

There's no other way to say it, so I'll admit the truth no one alive would dare speak out loud.

Surviving is a nightmare.

There's no way I can go on like this forever, but to become a bloat… that doesn't sound great either.

Becoming one of those monsters means going into convulsions and foaming at the mouth while your blood thickens and squirts from your veins. Stiff walking like a robot to find a fresh victim may be worse than death.

But in my low moments, like right now, I wonder if the grass is greener over there with the bloats.

In reality, the grass is braindead and therefore, doesn't care that it's walking on a broken ankle with dark goo seeping from its open flesh.

Braindead people aren't happy or sad. They just *are*, and sometimes, I wish I could feel nothing.

Even if it means sludge for blood.

Even if it means my life ends.

What's left for me anyway? Brian? I can't just leave him alone in this wasteland. He'll never make it by himself.

Fuck, I hate being a nice person.

So here I am, very much brain alive and scavenging a flooded grocery store in search of tampons with a man I've been on two and a half dates with before everything went to shit. Our third date was cut short by the apocalypse, so it's only a half-date. Come to think of it, most of our dates ended early and at my place having sex.

Sex isn't something to live for, but it certainly helps our situation. Too bad I'm cramping to the point of debilitation and my uterus is about to explode.

It's just like clockwork and the only calendar I've been using. Isn't stress supposed to stop menstruation or at least slow it down?

One's period during the apocalypse is a complication I never planned for, not that the end of days was on my schedule.

"This would go a lot faster if you would help," I hiss at Brian.

His shoulders rise to his ears, and even in the dim light, I notice how his cheeks flush. "Come on, Caitlyn. I don't know what to look for. I don't know about this… stuff."

"Feminine hygiene products," I huff at him. "Pads. Tampons. Menstrual cups."

"Menstrual… cups?" His voice rises in question, and I'm honestly not sure which word confuses him more. He seems like someone who cringes at any sign of blood, let alone a woman's period.

Hell, he's grimacing knowing how my uterus is about to throw up all over my already filthy clothes. When I told him the dam was about to burst, he couldn't hide his distaste for the situation.

I'm the only woman left within a hundred miles, so it's not like I can ask a friend for a tampon. He's going to have to wo-*man* up.

"You made it thirty years without ever hearing of a menstrual cup?" I sneer. "Just look for pink boxes with happy females doing yoga or laughing with friends. Those have something inside that can help me."

"It's just weird that the word for your… monthly thing, starts with the word 'men' is all. *Menstrual.*" He draws out the word, sounding it out like a child. "It's a female thing."

"You're not a connoisseur of languages, I take it."

His eyebrows knit together as I wade through packages of diapers, hoping something bobbing to the top of this flood can save me from ruining more clothes this week. I scowl at the dirty water and keep looking.

The grocery store we've climbed into is empty but mostly under-water. Why someone built this place half-underground, I'll never know. I had hoped I wouldn't find a lake in the aisle with the tampons, but I guess all my luck was all used up keeping me alive.

Brian turns and climbs on top of a shelf, continuing the search despite his confusion. He maintains the bewildered look of a little boy, but at least he's looking.

His mother did him a disservice shying away from any period talk, not that I ever met her. I knew Brian for all of two weeks before the world fell apart. Now we're practically common law married, spending every waking moment together since it happened.

Three months and going on three periods.

Brian picks up a pink box of baby products, studies it, then tosses it to the side. It's insulting that tampons and diapers are in the same aisle. I'm unnerved by the fact, as if women are just children who need help to handle their bodily functions.

Well, I do, but that doesn't mean I belong next to the diaper cream. Tampons should be with books or journals, something more adult.

"Menstrual comes from the word menses, which means month," I sigh.

He looks back, a can of formula in his hand, and nods. This guy might be the literal last man on earth. I can't let him stay stupid.

In the murky water, an image of women jogging on neon green and pink boxes catches my eye, and I groan.

"Hey, look at that," Brian beams. "You found them." He jumps from the shelving and grabs a few boxes, holding them high in triumph.

"They're wet." I slap one box away, and it smacks back into the water.

"Okay. You think that's not… hygienic or something?"

I raise my hands to my head and rub my temples, a feeble attempt to stop myself from ripping all of my hair out. "Brian, what do you think a tampon does? What is its sole purpose?"

"It's for your menses?" He smiles but I can tell he's unsure. He has no clue how a tampon works, and I'm too exhausted to explain.

He's not a bad guy, but he's not my guy. Not that I've ever had a successful relationship, hence my being stuck with Brian. My career was my partner, and it kept me fulfilled and satisfied. That and a device by my bedside.

The sound of a door opening saves him from my wrath. I freeze, holding my breath, my heart jumping into my throat. Brian might not be the smartest, but he isn't a coward. His arm wraps around my middle, his hand covering my mouth to muffle the chance of a scream leaving my lips.

I may hold the intelligence in this duo, but I'm easily startled. We learned this early on, and even though I've seen thousands of bloats, they still terrify me. This fear worsens when they catch me off guard.

Who wouldn't run for the hills screaming at the sight of a human with black liquid dripping from their mouths, grey eyes that stare at nothing, and involuntary tremors that jerk their limbs in all directions? Their irregular walk and the mess they leave behind make my stomach churn. They move at almost a crawl through the deserted earth, trails of dark liquid in their wake.

Unless they're running.

When they run, nothing about them is unsteady or spastic. They're like sharks gliding toward their prey. When I see them, I squeal or sprint, both of which aren't ideal for survival. I'm like an opossum, jumping up into the car headlights instead of running off the road.

Maybe that's because I want to leave this nightmare, even if it's in a body bag.

What am I talking about?

No one uses body bags around here.

Even though I'm coming to terms with my inevitable death, my dense friend is more optimistic, and I hate to ruin his apocalyptic optimism.

"Caitlyn, do you hear me?"

I didn't. The sound of blood rushing in my ears blocks out Brian's whispers.

Shaking my head, his lips touch the curve of my ear. "They are at both doors. We need to back up and get under the water."

I roll my eyes but don't argue, not that I can get a word out with his sweaty palm pressed against my mouth.

The sounds of their footsteps sloshing through the flooding grow closer, and Brian drags me with him, water rising to our waists.

This entire supermarket is sinking on one side, and the rain for the past week has created a lake on aisles fifteen through thirty. We're wading in the cesspool around aisle eighteen, square in the middle while bloats pour in from either side.

There's a part of me that thinks about releasing Brian's arm from my waist and walking up to the beings that used to be human, giving them a little wave before one touches me and sends the pulse of whatever infects people rippling through my limbs.

It would be quick, or it looks like it would. No one speaks afterward to confirm how terrible it is or isn't.

But Brian would be alone.

As much as I want this all to end, I can't do that to him. Sure, he can't find a tampon or talk about them without blushing, but he's a decent person. A loyal person. We've been through some shit, and he never shies away from helping others. Returning the favor the only way I know how, I exhale, my warm breath hitting his palm, and decide to hide.

We'll try to live one more day.

Why?

I don't know anymore.

Cold water makes me shiver as it slides up my arms and touches the lobes of my ears. The groaning and gargled sounds from the bloat's speech grow louder as Brian's arm tightens around my waist.

They're communicating somehow, the steady garbles back and forth in a foreign rhythm, unlike anything a human would make. It's nothing but noise to me. A language that doesn't take a breath, all of it coming in constant streams, and their talking grows louder as Brian pulls me closer, his chin resting on my shoulder.

I hate this place.

"Stay quiet and they'll move on," he says. His hand slips from my mouth leaving me free to scream and alert them to our presence. He trusts that I'll follow his lead, stay quiet, and for some reason, try to survive another day.

My hair floats on the water's surface, tickling my cheek. I move it away trying not to splash, pulling it into a ponytail with my fist, ready to dip below.

"Steady breaths. Deep breaths," he reminds me.

For a man who can't handle menstruation, he's calm in the face of death. It should shock me, but nothing surprises me anymore. People are weird, and so is the planet these days.

A door slams on one side of the store, and I jerk, startled by the noise. Dirty water touches my lips as Brian clutches me against his torso, my heart beating rapidly against his forearm. One bloat makes a series of sounds while others stop sloshing around the flooded market. They listen to whatever message it delivers while we wait in the freezing water.

The sun that once hovered at the skyline dips, the room darkening from the loss of light. The shadows change as the bloat speaking steps forward, and I make out its outline.

It's not facing us, and it's naked. Most bloats don't bother with new clothes when theirs inevitably shed off with time, but by that point, they don't look human anymore.

Once fully turned, the veins full of muck run through them, puffing and stretching the skin, making them distorted versions of what's left of a human. Hence, my thought out and scientific name, bloat. There aren't any news outlets to confirm what we are calling these monsters.

Except this bloat is something new.

It's a woman I surmise from the curve of the hips. Her hair cascades down her back, swaying from side to side while she speaks to her cohorts. Another bloat comes into view, this one more misshapen, but still recognizable as a person. I think they are talking to each other, but they are quieter than the others. They remain side by side and full of whispers, not that I could understand them anyway.

I wonder if I knew her.

After months of survival, we haven't moved far from home. It's possible she was a teacher, a nurse, someone's mother or sister. She might have been someone I saw every day, a person I loved and cared about.

She could have known my mother.

Everyone did and everyone loved her. My mom's voice creeps into my mind during long walks in the woods and cold mornings when I refuse to lift from the hard ground. I can't shake her presence even after she's been gone for years. It's a constant nagging, telling me not to give up yet.

It's with me now, urging me to keep going.

It's incredibly annoying.

I'll admit that when I'm dead, everything about her will be gone forever. The memory of her laugh and the stories she would tell about her childhood. It will all vanish into nothingness once these monsters get a hold of me. The thought of every part of my mother being gone forever makes my heart ache, but some things are outside my control.

Like what this bloat-woman is going to do to us.

I lift to my toes, Brian fighting me but not wanting to make any noise. I want to see her as they speak to one another but he slowly, carefully, pushes me back down.

"No." His words are soft but firm, and I concede, my chin sinking into the water. He's thinking the same thing, wondering if the woman in front of us was a friend or neighbor. How could he not? It's been weeks since we've seen anything one might recognize as human.

The bloats' moaning noises stop, silence filling the space except for the steady trickling of water.

The woman turns to look over her shoulder, but I can't see her. It's too dark and the others crowd my view.

I take in a slow, deep breath, holding it in my lungs, and we sink beneath the surface.

CHAPTER TWO

CAITLYN

My chest burns as seconds turn into minutes and I know my oxygen is running out. We need to make a move.

Brian bragged about being captain of his high school swim team, so he's holding steady, but the most athletic thing I've ever done was fall down the bleachers during a football game without breaking a bone.

A fracture is technically not a break.

I turn to face him. He can't see the panic in my eyes, but he has to know it's there. This is someone who doesn't understand the basic workings of a uterus, but we've been under for too long. Our teenage years were a long time ago, and the man needs to breathe at some point.

I motion under the water, and I think he nods before pressing my back up against a fallen shelf and tilting my neck.

My mouth rises to the surface, and when the cool air touches my lips, I do my best not to gasp for it. Oxygen slides down my throat with its sweet relief. I grip the fabric of his shirt, feeling the stitching rip with my hold. I want to lift my head higher and look around, but I resist the urge, fighting for each breath that might be my last.

Even though life sucks right now, being a bloat has to be worse. Every time I see one I'm reminded of their awful fate, and although I'm not sure I want to keep going, I don't want to end up like that naked woman.

Another inhale, my final breath before I dip back below and change places with Brian. He loosens my fingers that still clasp at his shirt before he lifts to the surface, his back arching when he takes his chance for oxygen.

He's quick about it before he dips back under, moving me once more into a position to breathe. I can't hold my breath as long this time, already growing panicked at the thought of no air. Thinking about drowning, about my life ending, is far different from the act. There's still the instinctual part of me that refuses to die, that inner voice that fights for survival even though it's hell. He tilts my chin up, higher this time, and I flutter my eyelids open.

It's already darker inside the store, the sun now completely below the horizon. One ear crests above the water before I dip back under. Their noises are louder and so close that I almost gasp in a mouthful of dirty water.

Brian must hear them and pulls me away from the shelf where the water runs deeper and my feet don't touch. He's taller than me by a good six inches, but even he struggles to reach his feet to the ground here.

He holds me against him, keeping me hidden, my lungs burning and panic rising.

Their sounds grow so loud I hear them all around us, and I wonder if this is it. All that work and worry. All those arguments about my period, and I'll die in a diaper aisle next to some guy I met online.

A wave hits us both, an undercurrent in the water that pulls me to his side, and he tightens his grip around me, desperately trying to hold us both in place. I feel its movement, something or someone that dove into the black pool with us. I've survived this long, so long a part of me thought I might be invincible. A superhero that doesn't realize they have powers until there's a knife sticking out from their gut.

Except I'm not special. I'm exceedingly average, and this will be a very normal way to die. Millions have been murdered in grocery stores all over the world on a random Tuesday while they were shopping for tampons.

Do we keep trying to run when there's nowhere to go?

I'm so very tired.

Brian decides for us, pulling us to the surface for all the bloats to see. I choke on the air, dirty water sliding into my lungs as all their heads, or what used to be their heads, jerk in our direction. More splashes spray water through the darkness as bloats dive in after us.

Panic, fear, and acceptance all hit me at once. I don't know his plan, but it seems I'm along for the ride.

Their talking stops, all of them focused on the new targets that made themselves seen. Brian grabs the fabric of my pants, pulling me with him to shallower water. He's attempting to flee toward a break in the group, but there are over a hundred of them, and this escape is futile.

My feet drag from wet clothes, stumbling behind him as he yanks us toward the gap just as the bloat that still resembles a human comes forward with more of her kind fanning out around her.

Our feet hit dry ground. It's pitch black except for a sliver of moonlight that beams on her skin revealing thin lines of black crawling across the flesh. She's almost beautiful compared to the things on either side of her, but it's also been months since I've seen a woman, so my standards are low.

We're surrounded, our backs against the wall. Brian reaches for a baseball bat on an end cap. I almost laugh at the memory of Joaquin Phoenix swinging away. That was one alien, not a hundred… or whatever the fuck these things are.

It's over.

It's so over.

I square my shoulders, grabbing a fire extinguisher from the wall and waiting for them to overtake us. Going down fighting seems like the right thing to do even if I'm over this entire existence.

Why aren't they charging?

The naked, somewhat human woman makes eye contact with me,

which I have to say is a first. Most bloats don't have human eyes anymore. They have swollen masses of grey orbs streaked with black veins where eyes used to sit. Those who do, the ones living in a purgatory between being something that was once a person and is changing into something else, they don't look at you.

They look past you.

People are objects. They're in the way of whatever mission the neurons still firing inside their brains tell them to do. Non-bloats are destroyed or changed, but discarded either way.

She looks right at me, her arms outstretched, as if her crooked fingers are pouring out an order to freeze time. She makes a gargled noise somewhere between their language and ours. It's a groaning version of English, and the beings around her don't charge us. Their limbs jerk at their sides, vibrating with want, desperate for permission to take us.

"Leave me," I tell Brian. I don't think about the words when I say them, but I know I'm slowing him down. This is his chance to survive, even if it's alone.

I know I bring delightful wit laced with pessimism to the table. Who wouldn't miss that? I also have a vagina which he enjoys, but someone needs to be the sacrificial lamb.

Even if I'm the worst kind of company, and he doesn't want to be alone, two of us won't make it out of here. I'm the one who doesn't want to keep going, to keep fighting to live. He has to know that, to feel the truth of it somehow.

I shut my eyes tight, not wanting to look, and Brian shoves me behind him, his body acting as a barrier that will last maybe three seconds before we're mauled.

"Leave me, please," I beg.

My pleas go unanswered, and the woman grunts again, guttural noises from bloats surrounding her the only response.

Turning might not be that bad. My worries and fears will cease to exist. They seem sort of peaceful in a gross and terrifying way. I'm lying to myself because I know this fate was unstoppable no matter how long we stayed alive. Maybe it's merciful that there are so many of them and this will be quick.

"The fire extinguisher!" Brian yells. "Get it ready."

I react, opening my eyes and pulling the pin on the red canister before pointing the hose at the group, hoping whatever plan he's thought up saves him and him alone.

"Now!" he yells, and I react.

Shattering glass hits my shoulders as I release the pressure of the canister, the puff of white reflecting in the moonlight. The spell breaks, all of them storming toward us as I'm lifted, my feet leaving the ground while I kick and fight. A sharp pain along my arm makes me cry out and drop the extinguisher, my screams stopping when I hit the cement pavement.

"Run!" Brian screams as my head bounces on the gravel.

Fuck, that man doesn't listen.

It's brighter outside, the moonlight illuminating the parking lot filled with cars that haven't been driven in months. I turn back to see Brian halfway out of the broken window of the grocery store, and I stand up and reach for him.

It's useless, his body ripped back inside before our fingers even touch. He screams, grunts a few times, and then there's nothing.

They're changing him, and I can't go back.

I'm running before I realize my legs are moving and leading me toward a treeline ahead. This wasn't what I wanted, and now some instinctual part of me is back to fighting to survive once more.

The forest is safer, but nothing will keep me hidden for long.

It should have been me.

My arm throbs as I push my body faster, sprinting into the thick woods where the moonbeams don't penetrate. I slow down, my eyes needing a moment to adjust, and when I turn around, I spot a glimpse of her through the foliage.

The woman stands below the window, bloats pushing through the broken glass to follow her. They pour out one by one, but they aren't running after me. I can't decide if I'm relieved, and I walk backward, staring at her, wondering if she'll see me and meet my eyes.

Wrapping my arms around myself, I feel the warmth on my skin. A sticky liquid that's thicker than rainwater or sweat.

It's blood.

A lot of blood.

Her head jerks from side to side and she stops, deciding if I'm worth the effort perhaps. One thing about bloats is out of sight, out of mind. They don't hunt, they only react to the prey they come across.

My breath catches when Brian climbs out from the window, his pale face looking up at the sky. One solid dark line stretches from his hairline, down his face and neck, dipping below his wet shirt.

It's started.

The change has already taken hold, and I can't do anything to help him.

This is bullshit.

I almost trip over tree roots, my back slapping against a trunk, and I stop, watching as they turn and circle the grocery store. More bloats gather outside, their bodies jerking while they wait for instruction.

I don't want to be one of them, but I don't want to live like this either.

Could I really end things?

I fought for air when I thought my lungs might burst and sprinted from the store once I knew Brian was gone.

Death terrifies me when I stand at its doorstep.

My soaked shirt catches on the bark as I slide downward. Sitting in the dirt, I watch and wait for their next move.

I watch Brian, how his movements are smoother than the others, but so unlike him. He had the grace of an athlete, and I'll miss him, even if his mind wasn't exactly that of a scholar. His thoughts are nothing but what they want now, and he'll kill me given the chance. I've seen it happen before.

My head feels light as I situate myself to lean back against the tree. Dark liquid seeps all around me, creating a puddle where I sit. My hand reaches out to touch the sticky blood mixed with the dirt.

My blood.

My fingers curl into the earth, a sliver of fear pushing my heart to beat faster. I touch my arm with my free hand, sliding my fingertips down the skin, feeling the shard of glass still wedged inside my muscle.

Years of watching medical dramas tell me I shouldn't pull it out. I could bleed to death in the woods.

No one to help.

No antibiotics.

No clean wraps for the wound.

I'm still at death's doorstep, but this time, I'm alone. No one needs me, and there's nothing but my inevitable end in sight.

Wiping my fingers against my pants to dry them, I take in a breath and hold it, reach up, and rip the shard from my arm. The scream of agony doesn't come. Instead, I cough, my eyes flooding with tears, the earth spinning before I drop the glass. My wound burns, sending a jolt of pain throughout my body, and I'm suddenly aware of my pulse.

It's everywhere, thudding in my ears and throbbing through my limbs. Warm blood trickles from the gash, and I rest my head against the tree, letting my arms dangle at my sides, watching as a hundred bloats make their way to the abandoned highway and begin their unsteady march.

I smile to myself.

It's over.

It's all over.

I don't know where they're going, what unspoken voice tells them to keep moving toward something. Some virus with an innate need to increase its numbers.

That's rather human of them.

It might be the only human part left.

The last of them is out of sight, Brian hidden somewhere in their ranks when my vision blurs. I spread my fingers out in the dirt, steadying myself, embracing the feeling of floating as I let out a slow and even breath.

"Sorry, Mom," I mumble, closing my eyes and picturing her face. Damn, she was pretty.

Maybe I'm being a coward, but I don't have any more to give. The world is too brutal, too cruel to keep going. She would tell me to pick my battles, but I'm always at war with these bloats, myself, and my uterus. I made it this long, and wherever she is, hopefully, she's proud.

Yes, this is the way to go. I'll fall asleep and never wake up. Never suffer their fate.

I'll never have to search for tampons again.

I'd laugh at the thought if I had the strength. Exhaustion washes over me, and my head lolls to the side before I pass out, hopefully never to wake up again.

CHAPTER
THREE

"Is she dead?"

"No more than the rest of us," I answer Landon.

His eyes dart around the woods, nervous and unsure. He's always like an animal prepared to step into a trap, but he has reason to be afraid. People have used women as traps before and lured men with the promise of a feminine touch before they strike.

What do they do with the bodies? I don't stick around to find out.

This one though… her pulse is too weak to fake her injuries.

"So, she's alive?"

I don't bother to answer Landon, instead wondering how I got stuck with this fool in the first place. He's not helpful, constantly disappearing at any sign of trouble, and always needing to be told what to do. He repeatedly asks where we are headed, and seeing as how I never invited him along in the first place, I don't think *we* are going anywhere. I am headed toward Canada and if he wants to follow me, I won't stop him if he's not in the way.

All I tell him is, "North." He might wander off in another direction someday. That or die. The latter is more probable, but that's true for all of us.

Leaves cover the woman's thighs, the dead brown foliage shrouding her from the night winds. When I brush them aside, I feel congealed blood coating a few and peel them away. Her arm, caked with a thick layer of the dark smudge gapes open, and the sliver of glass at her side must be the culprit.

Her first mistake was removing it from the wound. It's a miracle she lived through the night. Considering her decision-making skills, I'm surprised she survived this long. There are no other scars on her body, unlike me. The glass could have fallen out while she ran, and knowing her fate, she sat down to bleed out.

"She's from the store back there," I say mostly to myself.

The puzzle pieces come together while I survey the scene. An abandoned store, half-flooded and streaked with the infected's slime, a trail of white powder from a broken window. The same speckles coat her shirt and pants. The fire extinguisher left behind was a good weapon, but I thought the user escaped. Looks like she didn't get far.

"How could she outrun the infected?" Landon asks.

He's not praising her. He's curious, always concerned with his survival over anything or anyone else. That's not abnormal considering the world's become nothing but death and running, but how the fuck should I know how she got here.

We have the same two eyes, dumbass.

My hands move over her body, checking her airway as best I can and feeling her pulse. She's propped up against a tree, so I'm guessing there aren't any spinal injuries, but I hate being unsure. Assumptions and laziness get people killed.

"Ask her when she wakes up," I answer Landon.

His mouth gapes open while his eyes dart around the trees. They're gone, but he's still that nervous animal, always waiting to be captured. It's not my job to reassure him or babysit a grown man.

I remove my backpack, setting it down and away from the pool of blood at her side. It's got to be a few liters, but I can't be sure. Her heart still pumps inside her chest, and that's something.

"What are you doing?"

I don't answer Landon while he paces instead of offering to help.

"She could be dangerous," he muses, his voice weakening as he hears himself and how ridiculous he sounds.

Everything is dangerous, but a woman barely breathing is not high on the list of things to look out for in the apocalypse. I'm worried about wild animals, illnesses, and injuries, but not her.

She's nothing to fear.

The thought makes me uneasy, my inner voice warning me to be careful, but I quiet the noise, knowing that my mind is made up.

I'm helping her.

A blanket freshly washed in the river a few days ago will do the trick. It's not a necessity. A man doesn't need a covering to sleep, but it felt nice while it lasted.

So much for that.

Folding it over a few times, I stretch it out on the ground and tie the ends into knots for a better grip. This will have to do, but I'll need to fix her up a bit before we go.

Landon's bag has the medical supplies, but he hasn't moved an inch to get them. Everything we need is in there, recently stolen from the store where she fled. I usher him over, flip him around, and unzip the bag. He wants to protest, looking over his shoulder, starting a sentence he never finishes.

"Riley, I..." His jaw closes, knowing this is one argument he can't win.

My decision is final. There's nothing he can say to stop me, and he knows better than to try. I'm twice his size, and he needs me far more than I need him. Landon's a parasite, leeching himself onto something else to survive. I'm not one to judge another, though. Parasites have a place in the world. Without them, population explosion would kill us all.

I'm acutely aware that the infected may be an over-zealous pathogen or parasite, ridding the earth of humankind. We are the worst thing to happen to this planet.

Except a parasite wants to keep its host alive, depending on it for survival. That doesn't seem to fit here. I've watched infected people grow so large their bodies pop until there's nothing left but a black river of ooze.

I hadn't noticed any weaknesses before a few of them exploded, none that I could use against them, and I'm unsure if that's the fate for all of them.

We can only hope.

I take out the gauze and suture kit, grateful I insisted on grabbing one. Landon can restock while I patch her up.

"Go back to the store and get more of these." I turn him around, waving what I'm taking in his face. "Grab ethanol if you can. Whiskey works, too. More water bottles. As many as you can carry. I'll use all we have."

He wants to object but thinks better of it, his jaw tightening while he weighs his options. His shoulders slump while he adjusts his pack, knowing I won't take no for an answer.

"What about medicine?" he asks.

Focusing back on the woman, I set the supplies on top of my pack. "Someone already cleared the place of antibiotics and anything else useful. But you can check again." He won't find anything, but I want him out of my sight for a damn minute.

Landon nods, still unsure why we are helping her, but goes back to the dilapidated grocery store. He walks with trepidation, uncertain on his feet, and I curse to myself that he better not fuck up this simple task.

Sitting up, she's in a good position to clean the wound. I uncap a few water bottles, squirting soap inside and shaking them up. Washing my hands first for a few minutes, I watch Landon disappear through the woods, and I take a deep breath. She might wake up, but I can handle that. I've had unruly patients before.

Pouring the soapy water from a few bottles over her arm, the grime and dirt wash away, leaving behind a wound that, lucky for her, missed any major arteries. The gash likely happened when she crawled through a broken window, wedging a piece inside the muscle. Even though removing the glass was stupid, it won't kill her as long as she doesn't get an infection.

I take what whiskey we have and disinfect as best I can, guessing that's what Landon will return with. He'll swallow a few shots of whatever he finds before coming back.

She doesn't wake up, and her pulse remains weak, her body almost comatose while it tries to heal itself. By the time I start stitching, his footsteps come crunching through the dead leaves of the forest floor.

Landon throws down what he's carried back, his face flushed and sweat across his brow. Sure enough, he's brought back whiskey with a ridiculously high proof. He uncaps the top, pouring a swig into his mouth without his lips touching the rim.

"That was stressful," he admits. I don't answer, not wanting to waste the energy. "Do you need the gauze?"

"Don't touch it. Your hands aren't clean."

He raises his palms in surrender and plops down on a mess of leaves, still holding the whiskey.

"We need that."

"I need it," he argues. Whatever he drank gave him some liquid courage. "I don't know how you can be so calm all the time. Especially after what we've been through."

We haven't been through anything. During our last run-in with those monsters, Landon vanished into thin air. Flight or fight is real, myself being on the fight side and Landon firmly on flight, but he acts like we were brothers in arms.

"I don't understand why you worry about things you can't control," I groan.

"Everyone worries about that," Landon huffs. "That is what consumes most people's thoughts. You're a freak of nature is all."

"Seems to work for me."

Landon shrugs. "You need any help?"

I wrap the bandage so her arm is secure across the front of her body and won't drag when we pull her.

She's been on the run like me. There's a slight sunburn on her face from the past few days when no clouds filled the sky. Her hair, brown at the roots, the rest of it blonde, sits in two messy braids down her head. Dutch braids, my sister would call them. I would guess she's my age, maybe thirties. She's young enough to run but old enough to know she can't run forever. It's horrible to have self-awareness, especially in the apocalypse.

"I'll need you to help me drag her. We need to find some plywood if we can from the store. There's probably something in their storage."

"I can stay with her," Landon offers.

I can't explain why, but I don't want him alone with her. He hasn't said anything to make me concerned, but I feel it in my gut, a gnawing of distrust. Most men have a few demons when it comes to women. Landon strikes me as someone with more than a few.

"I can't do it alone. I need your help."

It's a lie, and Landon's face flashes with frustration. I hope it's because he doesn't want to go out into the open again, but we need more layers under her back, even if it's another blanket.

"Sure, buddy." There's a thin layer of anger laced in his words, but I don't care. We leave her there, bloody but bandaged, our packs at her side.

"What if she wakes up and steals our stuff?"

I'm not worried. Chances are she won't be able to walk for at least a day if she regains consciousness anytime soon. If she does awaken and find herself fixed up, surrounded by food and water, I hope she takes it with her.

I hope she survives.

Landon asks again, impatient with my lack of response. He's a child in some ways. In many ways. But he's another set of hands so I'll put up with it for now. We step over shards of glass I didn't notice before. They trail toward the tree line, her path of escape. She's tough to make it months and to run, injured like that, busting through a window.

That takes courage.

"If she comes to and takes our shit, then I wish her luck," I tell Landon. "I wish her all the luck left in this shitty world."

CHAPTER
FOUR

CAITLYN

Halloween is not my holiday.

That was certainly true about three months ago.

Why? Well, the days get shorter, I get wider, and all events on the calendar include forced servitude with a series of interrogations.

It's the catalyst of my seasonal depression, the downhill slide into sadness I can't escape. This year, that descent was about as gentle as jumping off a cliff.

Even with All Hallows Eve ringing the bell to the beginning of my least favorite time of year, I had moments where I could deny that I was going through the misery all over again. Avoidance in previous years meant I'd attend a haunted house to remind myself of how there were scarier things in this world. Little did I know there would be very real terrors in some nightmare forest this time around. What a way to ring in the apocalypse. That sounds theatrical, out of some television show, but it's historically accurate in this case.

I'm getting ahead of myself, so let's back up a little.

Deciding to bypass my annual depression, I downloaded some rent-a-dick app, or dating app as some people call it, and along came Brian.

He agreed to the odd date night choice because ninety percent of our few interactions until then involved asking each other where to eat or what to do, followed by me deciding... and sometimes paying. Getting to know each other consisted of veiled flirtations geared toward finding out how he could get me into bed. Based on how my year was going, the man didn't have to try that hard, but I appreciated the effort.

Before we connected on the app, I'd been dumped twice in the span of six months, but it was by the same guy. That makes me pathetic or downright tragic depending on who you ask. My mother had died before the second breakup, but she would never think I was anything less than fantastic. She left me on Mother's Day, and I swear the woman did it on purpose so I could be extra sad on the one day rather than stretch it out over two.

Turns out I miss her every day, so the joke's on her.

My life was bearable, but so is the apocalypse, so that bar is low.

All that to say when I met up with Brian, it was a given. If he could deliver a smidgeon of an orgasm, I would sit on his face without hesitation.

And I did.

Date night planning may not have been his strong suit, but he was a man of action. That might be why we survived that night and so many after. He was good on his feet, and when needed, I was good on my knees. Survival means using your skillsets, so he kept us alive, and I did what I could. There's a lot of free time when the world ends. It's not all being chased by monsters.

Running isn't my specialty, but when chased by a former human with black oozing veins, a dislocated arm, and an eyeball hanging out of its socket, well, I'm a damn Olympian. Halloween night, I leaped over bales of hay stacked two high when my flight mode was in the highest setting.

Jumped over it with what I envisioned as athletic grace like I was a damn hurdler. I can't even say the word hurdler properly, but there I was, side-by-side with Brian, leaping like a Russian ballerina. Call me Diana Vishneva. Or don't, because I can't pronounce her name either, but damn that woman can jump.

Halloween, the one night a year when everyone dresses up as a nightmare, makes it difficult to gauge danger. Bloats weren't the hot outfit flying off the shelves, but they were terrifying and fit the bill that October.

We survived hiding inside the roof of a barn, staying still and quiet, listening to people line up and walk into the slaughter. I thought about screaming out to the headlights parking in the distance, but they would have cast me off as drunk or playing a part. People walked into the cornfield toward the cries without a second thought.

I'm not judging their ignorance. It was Halloween at a haunted house, after all.

Brian held me against him, begging me to stay silent. Yelling out meant murdering him, too, and I couldn't have any of it on my conscience. It's also important to note that he did offer more than a smidgeon of an orgasm. The man was worth saving.

The next morning, hungry and scared, we thought we would find help. That was months ago. We'd been wandering around ever since, looking for food, water, shelter, and the occasional orgasm. I was sure to always find the latter. There's not a lot to look forward to when the world ends except a few moments of pleasure where nothing else matters.

Brian had an amazing dick and tongue, and now both are gone forever. I want to remember something more about him, a piece of Brian that his mother would be proud of or words that could be etched into a tombstone.

Despite our months of quality time together, I admit I didn't get to know Brian very well. That's typical for me. My cousin, a therapist who would diagnose anyone if a drop of wine hit her bloodstream, told me I shut myself off from the world after Mom died.

No shit, Rachel. You paid two hundred grand to point out the obvious. The checkout guy at my local grocery store mentioned how I never chat him up anymore, and he's making minimum wage.

I search my memory for something substantial about Brian. Nothing else comes to mind, but what man wouldn't love *orgasm-wielder* as his legacy?

Here lies Brian, *I forget his last name because I've lost a lot of blood and some strangers are dragging me on a blanket through the forest.* His dick was bliss.

My eyes fly open, cold air making them water. I blink several times and make out the tops of leafless trees.

I'm alive.

The ground underneath me rubs across my sore back, and my arm won't move. It's strapped to me, my fingers cupping my shoulder with a bandage wrapped from elbow to knuckles.

What the fuck?

"H-hey," I croak out. I try to wiggle but I'm a turtle on its back, tied down at the waist with one working arm and maybe a liter of blood left. How much blood do I need? How much did I lose? How the fuck am I still alive?

My head weighs a thousand pounds, and I'm dizzy from trying to lift it. "Hey!" I'm screaming at them in my mind, but dry leaves crunching beneath me drown out any sound.

My head pounds inside my skull, and the occasional rock they drag me across isn't helping matters. I reach out my free arm, feeling for a tree or root I can hold onto to make them stop and catch sight of my rescuers.

Or captors.

It's too soon to tell.

Two men trudge onward, not speaking to one another. They are opposite in height and stature, but alike in their mission.

Men.

Another danger of the apocalypse is anything with a dick. Yes, Brian's was a gift and I'm glad I had it when I did, but there isn't a woman alive who wouldn't feel a twinge of fear in my predicament. All eighty of us women left would agree that this could end badly for me.

That's a generous guess.

I'd speculate maybe fifty women left.

Does that half-bloat woman count?

Fifty-one.

My hand bumps along the ground, dirt collecting under my fingernails with my grip too weak to grab hold of anything.

"Hey," I say again, but I think the voice is only in my head. No sound escapes my dry throat.

Why didn't they leave me to die? I'm slowing them down and making a lot of noise as they drag me through the forest.

The possibilities run through my mind as I try to grab onto a passing tree trunk. My fingers can't close fast enough to grab hold, and I feel a splinter pierce through my palm.

They are taking me back to be their sex slave.

They want to eat me. Meat is hard to come by these days.

They are Jehovah's Witnesses and can't help themselves. Maybe I should have been nicer to those door-knocking fuckers and I would have been beamed up with Jesus when this shit started.

The sun hangs low in the sky which means I've been out for almost twenty-four hours, or maybe it's been days. My stomach churns with hunger, and the only chance of them stopping is if it growls loud enough for someone to hear.

The edge of a rock passes by, and I can't do anything but let it slip from my weak grasp. I decide on another tactic, cupping my hand along the ground until it's filled with dead leaves and dirt. It takes all the strength I have, but I lift my arm and throw.

Muck spreads across one man's back, and he flinches, stopping in his tracks.

Bullseye.

The other one grumbles, dropping the edge of the blanket, and turns to set his gaze on me. That trickle of fear turns into a river, and I swallow hard, hoping my face doesn't give me away.

A large scar stretches from his hairline and down his left cheek. It's terrifying, his face reminding me of a button-down shirt, except they missed a button. His skin knarls on the one side, the tissue burned and red. My tiny obsession with Phantom of the Opera makes him kind of hot, but fear overshadows that feeling.

Fuck.

"What's wrong?" the man next to him asks. I can only see this one's profile, and I wonder if they're a matching pair and someone sliced and diced his face as well.

"She's up," scar-guy grumbles.

Now they're both staring at me, and all I can do is wave with my free hand. The argument starts from there in hushed, hissing whispers.

"I told you she'd make it."

"Fucking great. Another mouth to feed."

"You don't have to be here."

"Maybe I don't want to anymore. I'm tired of looking at your ugly fucking face."

I cringe and avoid looking directly at scar-guy. We're not checking ourselves out in mirrors every day, but damn, that comment wasn't necessary.

"Then go. I don't know why you're tagging along, anyway." Scar-guy's words are strained. He's holding back from clocking his friend in the jaw.

"Tagging along? To go where, mother fucker? Do you have some plan you want to share?"

"You can go East then, and I'll go North."

"There's nothing alive East."

"There's nothing alive anywhere." Scar-guy looks down at me. "She's barely alive."

"You can just let me die, you know," I chime in, my voice barely over a whisper.

"What?" no-scar-guy says. "What did you just say?"

I need to get names for these two.

They both pause, the only sound rustling leaves and their steady breathing.

"You both patched me up, and that's nice, but, uh, I was kind of resigned to the idea of, well…" I struggle to finish the sentence. They used valuable supplies to fix me up and dragged me along for who knows how long. I may not want to live anymore, but I'm not an asshole. "I came to terms with dying back there, and I'm okay with that. If you… wanted to just leave me. Go your own way."

"You're bleeding," scar-guy says.

I manage to loosen the tie around my waist and sit up, every muscle in my body aching with the effort. Looking over the beige bandage on my arm, I don't see any blood seeping through. I do my best to lift it and check around the wound. The pain has set in, a dull ache you get when the adrenaline of an injury wears off, but it's patched up so tightly that I'm not in agony.

"I'm not. I'm fine. The bleeding's stopped."

Scar-guy walks around me and crouches down, his face inches from mine, and I hold my breath. If I want to kill him, I can always exhale. I haven't touched a toothbrush in days. He lets out a sigh, and even with the scar, I can discern his expression.

Annoyance.

He points down and gives my thigh a few gentle taps. I flinch from his touch and he sees it, notices the fear in my eyes, but doesn't offer any words of reassurance.

"You're bleeding," he repeats, placing his palm behind my neck and moving my head.

I look down and… I'm bleeding.

"Oh, shit. Well, it's just my period," I grumble.

His friend's eyes grow wide. "Will that… attract them?"

Scar-guy stands, his hand twitching to hit his friend. "They aren't sharks, you dumb piece of shit."

Both me and scar-guy give him a look of disgust. I might be immobile, but both of us think he's a useless idiot. That's saying a lot, considering only one of us can walk.

"What's your name?" I ask the dumb one.

I watch his chest fill with a large inhale, fighting the urge to defend himself. He has to realize that was a stupid question.

"Landon," he says. "I just meant, you know, for our protection."

"Periods are terrifying for so many reasons," I huff. "They may not attract bloats, but bears are drawn to menstrual blood."

Landon looks to his friend, whose eyes give him away. He wants to laugh, but won't budge as much as a smile.

"And velociraptors, too. That's what you really have to look out for. One sniff and the pack goes on the hunt."

"You're fucking with me," Landon groans.

"I am."

Scar-guy shakes his head. "What's your name?" he asks.

"Caitlyn Alice Tarton. Yours?" I'm a bit sarcastic with the full name, but he can't scold me for following directions.

"Tweedledee, and he's the dumb one."

I laugh, and it hurts. Scar-guy's face softens, and he looks me over, his eyes stopping at the pool of blood I can't do anything about.

"You call them bloats?" Landon asks.

Incapable of shrugging, I sort of nod and stare up at the sky. "What do you call them?"

"Just… them, I guess," he trails off.

"And what do I call you?" I ask the scar-guy once more.

He exhales, shoots Landon a look, and grabs both sides of the blanket in one fist. "I'm Riley, and I'm going North," he announces as his friend fights him for one corner of the fabric. "And you aren't dying in wonderland today, Caitlyn Alice. Not after I lugged your ass for the past day."

They squabble a bit before resuming their hike, back to marching in silence. Before I fall asleep, I chuckle to myself, my morbid thoughts spiraling in my head. Poor Landon wasn't too far off.

Brian died because of my period.

CHAPTER
FIVE

Riley

Landon proves to be more of an idiot every day.

Do periods attract the infected? Bloats, Caitlyn called them. What a fucking moron.

Mother Nature didn't weed him from the pack, if these monsters came from nature at all. My work makes me uniquely qualified to know more about people's bodies, but it's clear this guy never had a sister or a serious relationship. If I had to guess, Landon was one of those men who didn't have to keep a job through college, his mother hovered over him while he ate in case he needed a salt shaker or pat on the back, and he finds menstruation gross.

Like it or not, Caitlyn's stuck with us now, and I suppose we're both stuck with Landon. He's the gnat that won't go away no matter how many times you swat at it. His one redeeming quality is he's helping pull her along. She's not heavy, but lack of food makes the task increasingly difficult, especially when we have to change direction and go around rocks or other things that might bruise her.

Caitlyn has survived in impossible circumstances, just like us, and I understand resigning yourself to death. A part of me wishes I never walked out of that grocery store a few weeks ago with Landon trailing at my side.

When my eyes open each morning, I think of Maisie. Before I sleep, her face flashes in my mind. Peace won't come anytime soon, but I don't deserve a dreamless sleep, one where I don't see her slipping away… running away. I failed her, and the knowledge won't ever leave me. When my mind isn't occupied, it fills with thoughts of how I let her down.

When they killed her, some part of her soul stuck to me, and I can't shake its presence. A part of me doesn't want to, but if I'm honest with myself, a darker part of me wants to leave this world and join her.

"Hey," Landon pipes up.

I grunt in response.

"Who would be okay with dying?" he asks. "I mean, people are supposed to try and survive. People want to live."

I look back at Caitlyn. She's passed out again, her body limp and rocking gently as we walk. "Not all people," I grumble.

"She has a tattoo of a bible verse on her back. Wouldn't religious people want to live?"

My chest tightens at his comment, curious when he had time to explore her body and find a tattoo that I hadn't noticed.

"Tattoo where?"

Landon's demeanor changes and worry creeps up my spine. I've been with her every minute. He didn't undress her on my watch.

"The back of her neck, man. Don't growl at me. When we were moving her onto the blanket, her shirt pulled down."

It sounds innocent enough, but the feeling of concern doesn't dissipate, and I trust that my body is telling me something I need to know. Instincts are all we have left out here, and since October, mine have been on full alert. The animalistic side of me springs to life when forced, and I'm grateful. Better to overreact than not pay enough attention.

"Some people just like a phrase," I point out. "It doesn't mean every part of the bible is something they agree with."

"For do not fear, I am with you," Landon recites.

I assume that's the verse, but I won't verify for myself. It's her body, and I'm not going to go snooping around unless it's medically necessary.

"She doesn't seem afraid," I say.

"Right," Landon huffs. "And she should be. She's near death, and those things are always on our tails. Someone who reads the bible is ready for suicide. That's nuts."

"She didn't say she was ready for suicide," I point out. "She said she had come to terms with death, and who wouldn't be a little disappointed to wake up in this hell on earth? You know there's a famous bible verse about how everything has a season. A time to die and all that. Maybe she thinks it's her time."

Landon lets go of the blanket, and she jerks to the side, her body partially rolling from the sudden movement. I mutter curses under my breath. The last thing I need is him running off. She's too heavy to keep pulling alone when all I've had is a packet of Ramen today.

"Why are we helping her? Hear me out."

Like I have a choice.

"She doesn't want to be here, and what good is she to us? I mean, unless she gets a lot healthier and more grateful." He chuckles to himself, giving me a wink and nudging me on the shoulder.

"What?" I ask, even though I know exactly what he means.

"It's just she's a woman and… weren't you traveling with your sister? When was the last time you were with a woman?"

My fists tighten around the corner of the blanket because if I let go, he's done. He doesn't get to talk about Maisie, not after he vanished when trouble came near. And he certainly isn't trying to bargain to keep Caitlyn around for his dick's sake.

Landon's face softens, and he brings his hands to his hips, looking down at the dirt. "It's just that it's hard enough to survive out here. She doesn't want to live, and if a pack of, what did she call them, bloats? If they come around that corner right now, what's our plan? We need to be on board with what to do."

My grip loosens a little, and I look over at Caitlyn, watching her breaths so shallow and weak. She's lost a lot of blood, and I'm worried about infection, but I think she'll make it if she has a few more days to recover. This conversation is pointless. If bloats come, he's running for it and leaving us in his wake.

I remind myself that doesn't make him a terrible person. We don't know each other and neither of us knows Caitlyn.

"You do whatever you need to do. I'll stay with her," I answer. "Now help me. We need to walk until dusk at least. Then we can camp for a few days."

Landon eyes her, a small smile forming on his lips. "She sure was eyeing your scar."

I stiffen, not wanting to bring up this topic again. He's asked a dozen times why half my face is melted off, and I'm not giving him the satisfaction of knowing.

"Chicks dig scars," he says, reaching for the corner of the blanket.

My scar is not attractive, and considering we bathe once a week at most, and Landon didn't think deodorant was a necessary item to pack in his bag, neither of us is impressing her.

Before we continue, I right her on the blanket, centering her body so she doesn't slip off. She's floppy, lifeless from my touch, and my stomach drops, dread seeping into my veins. She needs an MRI. There could be bleeding in her stomach or on the brain. Her bloodwork would show infection if I could pull it, but none of that is available to us. We have to wait and see.

She has to live. Why else would she fall in our laps like she did? The chances of finding her out in the woods were slim to none. I'm not superstitious or religious, but a part of me knows things happen for a reason. There is a series of events here that can't be ignored.

I touch her forehead, feeling for fever, but she's cool. She might be too cold, the temperature more frigid near the dirt. I shrug off my jacket and wrap it around her chest, tucking it underneath her. I'm hot from the exertion, anyway.

Standing, I wait for Landon's snarky reply, something about how beautiful she is or how it's too bad she's on her period. Thankfully, he shrugs and says, "Fine. You ready to keep going? Sooner we get there, the sooner we can sleep."

I exhale, grab the other corner, and trudge forward. Hours pass in silence, a much-needed reprieve. We typically talk about sports teams that no longer exist or ponder where our hated politicians are stashed away. Are they in some bunker, safe in their cowardice? None of it matters, and as much as idle chatter would pass the time, I can't stop thinking about Maisie and how I can't fail Caitlyn like I did her.

We make camp near another store where we can scavenge for some throw-away items. I grab a laundry basket to wash in and tear up some shelving for a fire. Landon makes a bed for Caitlyn and lays her close to the flames, packing blankets on her other side to keep her warm.

It's almost nightfall when he speaks again. "Did you want to die? Do you… want to sometimes?"

I'm making our food, hoping the smell might awaken her. She needs to eat and give her body something to keep fighting. His question is oddly insightful, unlike him from what I've learned so far.

"Yes," I admit.

Maisie's face flashes in my mind, and I hear her laughter as if she were standing next to me. She always giggled at my dry humor, wrapping an arm around me and leaning her head on my shoulder when she was happy.

"I don't want to die," Landon says. His voice is shaky, and he wrings his hands, looking around the woods again.

I know this. He ran like the wind instead of helping others when we first met. He's someone who will always look out for himself first, and because of that, I need to keep an eye on Caitlyn. She's my responsibility, not ours.

"None of us are dying tonight."

"And tomorrow?"

"Tomorrow, you make the best decision you can in the moment, and we'll see."

Landon's face hardens, and he looks over at Caitlyn, her face lit up from the flickering flames. He's deciding something, and if I ask him, he'll lie. That gnawing feeling in my gut returns, and it's not hunger.

It's a warning.

CHAPTER
SIX

Caitlyn

The heat of the fire licks my right side as Landon lifts me, holding the lip of a bottle against my lips. "Wake up. Have something to drink."

My body responds to the idea of hydration, my dry mouth desperate for it. I try to lift my hands and grab the bottle, but one arm remains strapped to my chest. He chuckles, tipping the liquid inside my mouth, and I gulp it down.

"Slower or you'll get sick," Riley barks.

I turn my head to the side and see the mayhem of a campsite. There are empty water bottles tossed to the side, some chocolate bar wrappers, and other varieties of leftover Halloween candy. It's still prominent in the stores, our lives forever frozen in that spooky season.

Landon gets me situated so I'm sitting up on my own and walks over to the fire where Riley cooks. His boots crunch over the familiar orange packaging of chicken ramen, and he passes by what looks like first aid supplies, and oh, hell yes.

"Did you get me tampons?"

Riley looks up from a fire he feeds with small sticks. There's a pot sitting over the flames with the tag still hanging from the handle. They must have found a store while I was out and had better luck stealing than Brian and I ever did.

Is it stealing if the owners are dead? Or if the owners were turned to goo and still walk the earth, which I suppose is more likely.

"Yes," Riley growls. He jerks his head at Landon who stops, notices the stack of supplies for me, and grabs them before coming back to my side.

"We got you more than that," Landon tells me. He's like a puppy wanting a pat on the head for his good job.

Down boy.

"Oh? What else." I look at Riley when I ask, knowing he's probably the one who handles any period necessities. Landon would be too afraid of the Raptors.

"I got you tampons, pads, panties that come five to a pack with pink fucking polka dots, and this."

Riley tosses something my way, and Landon reaches out to catch it. The feeble attempt to move my arm reminds me I'm still at a loss for strength and down quite a bit of blood. I chuckle when he turns the bottle to face me.

"Midol. You're a saint."

"Don't fall in love with him too quickly," Landon jokes. "He's really an asshole when you get to know him."

Landon helps me up, letting me lean against him as I stand on shaking legs. I nudge him away once I take a few steps, painfully aware that I stink. Blood trails down my legs, and I groan, but there's nothing I can do but try to clean up.

"Are you sure you're okay?" Landon asks. He's back at my side, which is odd considering my state of cleanliness. Riley may be the asshole, and that scar on his face might be proof of that, but Landon's looking at me like a meal.

"There's a bucket over there." Riley points to a large tree behind him. A beach towel hangs from its limb, creating a makeshift curtain to hide behind.

"There's soap, and we boiled some of the bottled water so it isn't ice cold," Landon adds. "You'll need your bandages changed, but do you want to get cleaned up first?"

I've been gifted tampons and a bath. Are these guys trying to woo me? This is akin to wine and roses before the world turned to shit. Mom always said she liked people who saw what you needed instead of needing to be seen. I thought she was complaining about social media again, but now I get it. It would have been nice if, in her final years, some of her so-called friends and family did that for her.

"Do you want me to take your bandage off first?" Landon asks. "I can help you."

"I got it," I say, walking toward the striped beach towel on wobbly legs.

"You've been out for almost two days. You haven't eaten. What if you pass out?"

"She's ten feet away, dipshit," Riley interrupts. "Here."

He hands me some kind of cereal bar as I pass by him, the kind that tastes like cardboard if you don't eat it with a gallon of water. Right now it looks like a perfectly cooked, juicy steak, and I rip the packaging with my teeth and take a bite.

"Bottled water's back there. Sip it."

"You're bossy," I huff.

"And you're attracting monsters. Go clean up."

I swear there's a hint of a smile before he disappears out of sight, and I duck behind the towel curtain. Landon whispers something to Riley that I can only guess is him needing another confirmation that my period is not going to attract bloats, bears, or raptors.

"Can you bring—"

A hand holding a plastic package of panties reaches around the curtain before I finish the question.

"Thanks."

"And this," Riley adds, handing me sweatpants and a hoodie. The fabric is so soft in my hands that I almost cry.

"You're amazing."

He grumbles in response, and I set down the clothing, reaching into the plastic laundry basket full of warm water. It's perfect and I rip my clothes off before it cools.

"Do you need help?" Landon offers.

My clothes are almost falling off of me, so I don't. The shirt I had must have ripped when Brian pushed me out of the window, and my pants are toast, caked in blood and dirt, and two sizes too big to begin with. They used to fit, but I've been missing my favorite fast food for months. I kick them as far away as I can and use the tree as support before I step into the laundry bucket.

"No," I call out. "I've got it."

The tub is wide enough to sit inside and soak my aching body. Lathering the soap in my one good hand, I scrub from head to toe. I pick at the bandage with my fingernail, avoiding ripping it away from the sore skin too fast. They wrapped it well, and when I get a loose end and unwind it a few times, tears prick my eyes. Blood oozes from the wound, slow but steady, and I know it needs more attention.

This wouldn't have happened if I died, but they just provided me with food, water, clothes, and a bath. It would be rude to ask if I can go jump off a cliff.

The soap burns against the gash, and my inflamed skin hurts so much that I bite my lip to keep from whimpering. Once it's clean enough to wrap up, I rinse myself, rise from the cooling water, and do my best to get my period situated before I step into clean pants.

Holding the sweatshirt against my chest, I step around the towel to find Landon waiting with bandages in hand. His eyes dart over my body that's barely covered with the sweatshirt. I'm shaking, the cold seeping its way into my bones.

"I didn't want to put it on and get blood on it."

"Right," Landon says, his eyes fixed on my bare skin.

"You need more stitches," Riley says, and I simply nod in agreement. "Sit."

I shuffle over to where Landon stands and watch as Riley unpacks some medical supplies. His kit is professional, full of syringes and gloves, and hopefully something to numb me.

"There's no lidocaine."

"Fuck," I groan.

"Maybe you'll pass out," Landon offers. "Alcohol is over there." He points in the distance, and Riley goes to fetch it.

"I couldn't find any saline to flush it out," Landon says.

"She'll be fine," Riley barks as he walks off.

I turn back to Landon who seems more reasonable and less of an asshole. "And if we don't pour straight alcohol into my open wound, and it gets infected, would that kill me?"

"Well, yeah," Landon says with his eyebrows scrunched together.

"How bad of a death is that? Are you in the medical field or something?"

"I was in car sales, but I know it's pretty fucking bad. Fevers, you lose your mind, organ failure. Not a great way to go."

I weigh my options, shifting my body side to side, observing Riley who comes back with the bottle in his hand. He looks like he wants to kill someone right now.

"This won't hurt so bad that you want to die," Riley says. "No more than usual."

"You still don't want to be here?" Landon whines.

I shrug, not wanting to get into the discussion. I'm too tired and barely standing up straight. This isn't the time for a debate.

"Everyone left is trying to survive," Landon argues with my silence, his face contorted in frustration. "You're safe now. We've got you. You don't have to wish for death. Now let's clean your wound."

I nod, knowing this isn't the time to admit survival sounds awful right about now. Staring at the bottle of alcohol, I swallow the lump in my throat as Riley crouches down and puts on gloves.

They won't get it, and I can't blame them. I'm wired differently, too practical for the end of the world. I've always been this way, and the past few years haven't helped.

I was usually the one tending to wounds. Helping my mother rotate so she wouldn't get bed sores. Massaging her muscles and managing her pain. It's odd to be on the other side of things, especially when I'm not all that happy with surviving thus far.

She would be disappointed if I refused their generosity. That's all she wanted in the end. Someone to help me care for her, to visit her, talk to her. It would be a real slap in her face if I said, "No thanks, boys. Let me die a horrible and painful death." Not that one can slap a ghost, but still, not nice.

Landon tries to wrap an arm around me, but I flinch. Riley notices, his eyes narrowing at us both. They saved me, dragged me through the forest for days, and then offered me the joy of tampons, but I can't relax.

"She was asking if she would die if we don't do this," Landon tells Riley.

"She might die even if we do this," he answers.

Riley's waiting for permission to use a sewing needle and pull the gaps of my ripped skin together, but I can't.

"It's just that I don't know if this is the kind of life anyone wants. Sometimes survival isn't living is all, and I just don't know if going on is worth it. Is that so crazy in these circumstances?"

Landon says yes just as Riley answers no. They both stare at each other, annoyed with one another's response.

"Do you want to live today?" Riley asks with a sigh. He's fed up with the conversation, ready to get started. "We're only talking about today."

My mouth hangs open, but words don't escape. This is a simple answer. A no-brainer, but I don't know what to say.

"She hit her head, maybe," Landon muses. "She's not thinking clearly. What can we do about that?"

"Nothing. It's simple, Caitlyn. You want to live, then get more stitches and a new bandage. You want to die, then don't. It's your life."

"Or death," I whisper.

"You can't just die," Landon clutches me against him, the blood in my arm seeping out at a faster pace. The desperation in his voice makes me uncomfortable, and he's squeezing so hard he's pinching my skin. "We did all that shit for you—"

Riley continues grabbing things from the kit, his proficiency a bit unnerving. It looks like he's worked with this stuff before. "What the fuck do you care?" he says to Landon. "Another person to trip us up – to feed."

Gee, thanks.

Landon doesn't budge, and my arm aches, the tips of my fingers going numb with his hold. I look up at him, and there's a flash of awareness in his eyes, followed by regret. He lets go, raising his hands in the air.

"I'm sorry. I don't want you to die."

I don't know why he cares. Dragging me across a forest isn't fun, and I understand the desire for company, to have someone to talk with. Brian had his quirks, and well, sometimes the conversation was lacking, but he was a person. A living and breathing human who walked beside me.

Riley pauses, holding the open bottle of alcohol in one gloved hand. I exhale, my shoulders dropping in defeat.

"Can I have a swig of that?"

He nods, dropping the liquid into my mouth. It burns going down, but the warmth hits my nearly empty stomach, and it calms me a bit.

"This will hurt," he says.

"Will it hurt you more than it hurts me?" I ask. The joke falls flat, my body shivering with the knowledge of what's about to happen. I clutch the sweatshirt to my chest, bringing up a sleeve to bite down on and muffle my screams.

I've decided. I'll live another day so my mother's ghost doesn't come and lecture me.

Riley shakes his head. "I think you know the answer to that."

When the liquid slides into my flesh, the stinging burns so hot my body breaks out into a sweat and vibrates in pain. I wonder if Riley suffered worse from the looks of his face, but it's not a good time to ask.

Landon rubs my back, and I want to shake him off. When you're in this much pain, being touched is the last thing you need. Maybe he could hold me down because every cell in my body wants to run from them both.

"Less than ninety seconds," Riley says.

Before it registers what he means, I feel the needle and scream into the fabric of the sweatshirt. Landon tries to hold me, and I push him away with my free hand while tears pour from my eyes. The sweatshirt slips down, exposing me, but I don't care.

"Sixty seconds."

I count backward in my head, trying to say Mississippi after each second. I know I can do this, we're over halfway, but I still don't know why I'm doing it.

Riley has a purpose. He's going north. I don't know what I'm doing, and if I'm honest with myself, I haven't for years.

"Forty."

Landon stands, pacing in front of us both.

"Go check the soup," Riley barks at him.

He rushes off, unable to handle the bloodshed and screaming.

"Thirty seconds. Pour those soup cans into the Ramen."

I didn't know men could multitask.

The fabric falls from my mouth, wet with drool, and I cry, a loud and pathetic sobbing that I hate myself for letting escape.

"Ten seconds, Caitlyn."

The string tightens, the opening of my wound pulling together. Before a final scream escapes, Riley's hand moves across my mouth to muffle the sound.

"It's done. I need to tie it off. I think we're safe but you need to quiet down."

I consider slapping him with my good hand, but instead, I choose to pull my sweatshirt back over my naked chest.

He removes his palm, and I somehow stay silent, except for in my mind where I'm cursing him incessantly.

When he's finished, the world spins, and I almost topple over. Riley grabs my torso, lifting me enough to wedge me against a backpack. "I'll wrap it in an hour. I need to make sure that will hold."

It needs to work because I can't go through that again.

Landon's focused on the fire and the giant pot of whatever he's stirring. I see the packets of Ramen and opened cans of soup. Is Riley a master chef or a surgeon? I want to pick a fight with him, argue about something trivial to forget the agony that slowly dissipates from my body.

Landon cracks a can of Campbell's and adds it to the pot.

"She lives another day," Riley snips.

He saunters to the fire, opens another pack of noodles, and tosses the garbage to the side. Noodles plop into the boiling water and if I had the energy, I would lecture him about overcooking it, prove to him I'm worth keeping around.

The ability to properly cook Ramen doesn't make me an asset, and I know in my heart that Riley's words were right. Cruel, but right. I'm another mouth to feed, and that's all.

Considering I'm still too weak to run or find food, company is all I can offer. Brian didn't get my sarcastic wit and dark humor, but something tells me Riley already has me figured out.

I rest my head back, watching the trees sway overhead and counting the seconds until the pain subsides. When the seconds turn to minutes, and my skin grows cold from the sweat, I make a move to get the sweatshirt over my head.

"Do you need help," Landon asks.

Riley crouches in front of me before Landon finishes the question, pushing the sleeves of the shirt over my hands and pulling it over my head. He doesn't look at my bare chest which I find surprising. Landon, however, cranes his neck to spot a nipple.

"Thank you for saving me," I tell him. "Ready to die or not, it was a nice thing to do."

"I can hear your stomach growling," Riley says, pulling me forward to tug the sweatshirt down my back. "If you want to live, eat something so we don't have to pull you around for another day."

"Because you won't?" I ask. "You'll leave my worthless ass to bleed out in the woods."

I'm joking, but there's a chance I'm right.

He rises, opening his mouth to answer, but stops himself.

If he let himself speak, I worry he might have said yes.

If I let myself be honest, I might tell him to leave me here.

Instead, I ask for the soup.

CHAPTER
SEVEN

Caitlyn

I go to sleep with a throbbing arm and a full belly, my eyes opening at dawn when the sun breaks over the horizon. Riley bandaged me up after we ate, and the relief mixed with exhaustion allowed me to rest deeply for the first time in weeks.

Someone's boots tromp over the autumn leaves and twigs, cracking them with every step. My vision comes into focus, and I see a sleeping Landon resting beside me with his mouth open, a slight snore escaping with every inhale.

"Making enough noise?" I croak to Riley.

"Maybe we'll be stormed by bloats and die. You'd like that."

"Valid point."

The fire already roars to life, and I wonder if it ever died out. The nights have grown colder with winter around the corner. I kept track of dates in the beginning, but I'm not sure how much time has passed, only that I'm on my period. I'm as reliable as the sunrise so it's not a terrible system.

"Sometime in December," I mumble to myself.

"December seventeenth," Riley responds.

I didn't ask, but I don't have to with this guy. He's in my head, and

I can't decide if it's unnerving or a relief. Brian had to be reminded how to hold his dick when he peed.

Maybe it wasn't *that* serious, but I certainly mothered him a lot.

Riley grabs a water bottle and chugs it in a long and steady stream. Landon stirs and sits up, motioning his hand for Riley to toss him one. He picks it up with a subtle eye roll and chucks it at him a little too hard.

I can't figure out the friendship between these two. Men have odd mannerisms when it comes to relationships. They can be in a fistfight one minute, and leave the bar a few hours later like brothers, swearing a blood oath of eternal friendship in the parking lot.

And they say women are complicated.

"So, how did you two come together in this mess?"

"The mess with you?" Riley asks. His tone picks at my nerves, but I don't take the bait.

"No, I mean… Were you two friends before and made it this far together?"

"I met him a few weeks ago," Landon answers. "Maybe nine or ten days. It's hard to keep track."

"It's December seventeenth and you hitched your wagon to my ass on December ninth," Riley spits.

Not besties, then.

"You would have been dead ten times if it wasn't for me," Landon argues. "Don't you forget that?"

"How can I forget something that never happened? Do you want me to imagine the history you wrote and then burn it into my memory?"

"They would be eating your brains in the bakery aisle if it wasn't for me."

Riley shakes his head and grits his teeth, his words barely audible as he spits them out. "The fact that you were hiding by the cupcakes… That says a lot, man." The way he says hiding, stretching out the word, makes me wonder what happened there, but I don't want to listen to their argument. I'm in enough pain as it is, and I don't want to add a headache to the mix.

Landon rises, looking like he's ready to take a swing. Instead, he kicks the dirt and grabs a few pieces of wood for the fire, throwing them in and making the flames lick up the sides of the pot.

"They don't eat brains," I say, breaking the tension.

Both men turn to face me.

I shrug and raise my lips in a half smile. "Well, they don't."

"They do enough damage," Landon huffs, poking at the fire with a stick.

I secretly hope he's cooking something delicious because I'm hungry again. Surprisingly, Clam Chowder Ramen didn't disappoint, but I'm salivating over the idea of food. It's been mostly Halloween candy stuffed in our pockets for weeks.

Our pockets.

A wave of sadness hits me when I remember Brian is dead.

Well, worse.

He's a bloat.

I don't know if I'm bothered because of what he has become, or that I'm still here, arguing with strangers about brain-eating monsters and the manhood of those that hide behind baked goods. I'd give anything for a pumpkin roll right about now.

"Have you seen what they do?" Landon asks, jostling me from my thoughts. "Up close?"

"Why ask her that? Especially when you haven't?" Riley interjects.

"How do you know that?"

"You're not one to look."

Another dig at Landon. If these two were friends at one point, they aren't anymore.

"What's for breakfast?" I ask. "Since we can agree that the three of us don't eat brains. More Clam Ramen?"

Something flashes in Riley's eyes, and I know he finds my comment funny. He wants to laugh but won't. I take this as a challenge, or better yet, a positive distraction. The man must find me more agreeable than Landon.

Not that I care.

"I'll get back to cooking," Landon mocks. "It's Beef Ramen today. I threw in a can of some fucking soup."

"That sounds great," I tell him with a smile, and he exhales, letting the argument between the men die.

I sleep a little before Landon wakes me to eat. The sun doesn't warm us much under the cover of trees, so we sit close to the crackling fire. Not wanting to sit between these guys, I position myself by Riley's side and listen to the sounds of animals scurrying around the campsite. That's a good sign. They run from groups of bloats, so even though a bear attack would be catastrophic, I'd take that over what else is out there.

"That might be a decent way to go," I mumble.

Riley hears me but doesn't ask which I find deeply unsettling. Landon's in his own world, his eyes shifting around the woods.

"Of all the ways to die…" I trail off.

Riley only huffs.

I inhale more beef ramen and clear my throat. "But I don't know. What if we were only injured?"

"What?" Riley gives up and asks. His shoulders reach his ears, and his eyes don't meet mine.

Pulling my legs closer to my chest with my good arm, I rest my head on my knees. "I was thinking about how a bear attack would be a better way to die than turning into a bloat."

"Bears don't come near fire. Not wild ones. Bears in urban areas might, but they're docile. They know the food source is in a garbage can."

I'm undecided if I'm relieved or not. This might be considered an urban area, but I don't see the tops of any buildings above the trees. After they dragged me for days, I truly don't know where we are hiding out. With Brian, we stayed relatively close to home, always moving in a circle to avoid the bloats.

"What about other animals?" I ask.

"What about them?" Riley growls.

"You seem smart about these things. I mean you must be to survive this long." I'm overacting with the sarcasm, toying with him too much, and Landon notices.

"I think what she means," Landon interjects.

"She means to know all the ways to die so she doesn't have to be here," Riley says. "I am smart. It helps more than being a defeatist with luck on your side."

I sit up straighter and slurp what soup remains in my bowl. Turning to face him I plaster a smile on my face, doing my best to make it genuine. "Well, if you're so smart… what other animals should we worry about if say, we wanted to live?"

"Coyotes and foxes will come around, but they don't attack. They pillage."

I turn my head and notice Landon avoiding us on the other side of the fire, a strained look on his face. Maybe he's remembering what happened at his grocery store. I know I'll have nightmares about mine.

"Anything else we should know for our survival?" I sigh.

Riley stills, and I wonder if he's done with me for the day. He seems the type to enjoy an Irish goodbye.

"Survival?" His voice is harsh, and I bite my bottom lip, ready for a debate. I've let the fact that he called me a quitter go for the moment. I'm sure he's lost people, and here I am, going down the roster of how to check out.

Not proper dinner conversation.

"Maybe you're right about dying," he admits.

"But…" I drag out my one-word question.

He pokes at the fire, throwing on another few pieces of wood, and I back up from the flames. Landon rolls over, pretending to be asleep but sensing the heat.

"But I don't care to discuss death with you right now. Not after I've spent days keeping you alive. You get that?"

I open my mouth to speak, but nothing comes out. His eyebrows raise as best they can with his scarring, and I offer a nod.

"We'll stay here for a few more days. There's enough food at the store to keep us for a while, and then we need to move."

He's changing the subject, and I'm grateful. Sometimes I push too hard. A lot of times, actually. I push and push until everyone's gone.

Based on the mangled skin that covers his cheek, Riley's a survivor. He isn't built to go down easily. The idea that I might want that, it's foreign to him. Even in our strange new reality, some things are beyond our grasp.

I sigh and rub the shoulder of my hurt arm, the skin hot to the touch from the flames. "Okay. That's not too long. They won't notice. Can I come to the store with you?"

"No."

"Listen," I grumble. "I appreciate the tampons. I really do. You know the guy I was with before…" I trail off, not wanting to speak ill of the dead or compliment Riley too much. "Anyway, let me go with you."

Riley faces me, his eyes boring into mine, and I feel uneasy under his gaze. It's threatening in a way that makes me shut up and listen.

"The guy before?"

I should explain, but I'm at a loss for words, unsure what to say about Brian. He thinks I'm running through the last available men to keep me alive. And well, he's kind of right.

"I want to help, and I'm an extra set of hands. Uh, hand."

"I said no."

"Bossy." He doesn't react. "I'm not scared of no bloats." Even though I sing it with the Ghostbusters tune, he doesn't crack a smile.

"It's unlikely there will be any bloats there," Riley says, tilting his head to one side and cracking his neck. "But if we're not the only ones looting the store, we could have a problem."

I wait for more explanation, watching the fire flicker in his eyes. We stare silently at each other, and then I understand.

The bloats aren't the only danger, especially for a woman.

My ass is staying at camp.

CHAPTER
EIGHT

Humankind fucking sucks.

I was never one to cry over heartfelt stories of kindness. Hallmark movies never appealed to me, and I never got weepy at a wedding or funeral.

Not even my mother's.

Life is harsh, and people are terrible. Despite the obvious, everyone has a story about some random miracle that gave them faith and proved that the world is fair and goodness wins.

But they're wrong.

Goodness does not win.

It doesn't even place or show.

Good people lost the court case because they didn't have enough money for a great lawyer. They stayed sick because insurance wouldn't cover their medicine, and never retired because they couldn't afford it.

Now evil… evil doesn't play by the same rules.

Evil gets away with things, stays rich, and makes others work. It's wreaking havoc all over the world every day, especially now. Yes, I'm bitter, but I'm also right.

Goodness dies.

Albeit with an honorable heart, but it's still dead, so who gives a fuck?

Deep down, I always knew people could be worse than bloats. I haven't seen anyone up close for weeks until Riley and Landon came along, but I know they're out there, looting just like us and willing to kill anyone who gets in their way.

It's not bears or coyotes that I'm frightened of when I go to sleep. Riley's warning spins in my mind, making me sick with worry, and I'm certain the sinking feeling in my gut is fear.

I'm not afraid to die, but how I'll go gives me nightmares. What if we come across a group of hungry cannibals? It's not overdramatic to admit there's a real possibility of someone eating me.

I'm easier to hunt than a deer.

When night comes and I drift off to sleep, my dreams are full of bears and bloats chasing me. Brian leads the pack, and he's right on my heels for what feels like hours. I awaken with a start, breathing hard, my skin misted with sweat.

Landon's there, his frame hovering over me, using a shirt to dab my forehead. I must have been thrashing around in my nightmare because I'm not in the same spot by the fire.

"What the – Oh, fuck," I sputter out, except that's not what I hear leave my lips. The words are a garbled mess, and I struggle to sit up. My body shivers from the cold, every droplet of sweat chilling my skin.

"The f-fire. We need to light the fire." It sounds like my mouth is full of rocks.

Landon pauses, trying to interpret what I'm saying before he understands. "It's lit. Here I'll show you."

He stands and pulls back the makeshift curtain that hangs in front of our bathing bucket. He points to the fire in the distance, and it takes a moment for the sight to come into focus.

Riley rests curled up on the other side of the flames, his large body visible through the flickers of orange. I try to stand, but my legs won't work properly, and I'm dizzy.

"Shhh, shhh," Landon says. "Go back to sleep."

"W-why… w-why?" I know the question I want to ask is, "*Why are we over here?"*, but my mouth won't listen to my brain. The things I want to do and the words I need to say feel out of reach.

Great, I have sepsis from this wound. At least anyone that eats me will die from the infection.

"You're covered in sweat. I think you might have a fever. I was trying to clean you up. Here. This will help."

Landon hands me a pill, and I go to grab it by instinct, but my hand feels numb and won't close around the small, white object.

"It's okay," he says, placing his fingertips on my jaw to open my mouth and setting the pill on my tongue.

I remember Riley's warning. It's the only clear voice in my head.

The bloats aren't the only danger, especially for a woman.

My stomach cramps, threatening to make me sick all over Landon, and I want that. I want to vomit across his lying, disgusting face because I know what's happening. I may not be able to say it or stop it, but every part of me knows.

I move the pill inside my cheek, careful not to swallow, making him think I'm obeying.

I'm a good girl Landon. Don't you worry. I'm here for your sick fantasies you pervert.

My mind is muddled, and all my ideas for an escape fizzle into confusion. I can barely sit up, and the realization makes my eyes well with tears. He may very well get his fantasy and then probably kill me. Throw me into some pit he's found in the woods. Then he'll tell Riley I went and killed myself, which sounds plausible given my big mouth.

"There you go," Landon says. His voice forces bile to rise in my throat. There's a slither to his every word, and it slides across my skin, spreading goosebumps over my body. "You'll feel better soon, just lay back."

His face blurs around the edges, and I turn my head to cough, spitting out the pill and hoping he doesn't notice in the darkness. If I'm lucky, none of whatever he gave me made it into my bloodstream, but the damage is done.

Something already festers inside me, crawling through my veins and making me weak and numb all over. I feel the tug of sleep, and I'm desperate for it. Landon lowers me, my eyes closing even as I scream at myself to open them. It's so cold away from the fire, and the thought of rest grips me, pulling me under.

It's the weight of Landon that wakes me back up as he lowers himself on top of me, sending a sharp pain through my injured arm. He wraps his limbs around my frame, holding me in place. I want to believe a lie, anything other than what's happening.

He just wants to comfort me.

He's been lonely.

He wouldn't…

But then I feel his hand go to the waistband of my sweatpants, and I take a deep breath before I do the only thing that may stop him. I'll only have one chance, so my stupid body needs to cooperate with my mind and scream loud enough to wake the dead.

To wake Riley.

When his fingertips slip below the fabric I scream. "Rile-"

His palm moves over my mouth before I can get another word out. It's not loud enough. It's not even his full name.

Maybe luck's kept me alive this far, but it won't help me tonight.

My body wants to fight him off, to wiggle away, but the ground and sky are spinning, and I can't make my limbs move. The branches that sway overhead blur together, and all the bright stars glide across the darkness in a foggy cloud. There are a million comets above my head, soaring through the night in streaks of light. I can't move or scream, only watch them whiz across my vision.

I'm high enough on something to feel like I'm walking through a Van Gogh painting, but aware enough to hear Landon unzip his pants.

Why, oh why, did Brian throw me out of that window?

Floating towards the spinning stars, I close my eyes, enjoying the weightlessness.

Maybe there are so many drugs in my system that I'll forget this happened, and tomorrow when I wake up this will be nothing more than a strange dream like the running bear-cannibals.

Or, I could die from the overdose. Hopefully before he gets his dick out and Landon becomes a necrophiliac. I wouldn't put it past him.

This is why I've stayed away from people these past few years, never giving them too much of myself. I was happy in my one-bedroom apartment with nothing more than casual dates and surface-level friends.

Most people want what they can take from you, never planning on giving anything in return. When you need them, when times are dire, like when someone's dying of cancer, they only think of themselves.

Good people, like my mother, spend years in bed alone because those so-called friends and family would rather go out to eat or drink at a bar rather than do what's right. To help, visit, and care for her, like she did for others all her life.

At least with bloats, you know their true intentions.

There's a grunt, and then I'm falling. This high feels like a roller coaster.

There's blazing heat at my side.

The fire.

I'm back by the fucking fire?

It's almost too hot on my skin, and something's not right. All of this is so wrong, but I can't get up and run away.

I struggle to open my eyes and force them to focus, but all I can make out are flickers of orange and red light. I'm certain I'm lying next to the fire again, the small sticks in the dirt digging into my skin.

Using my good arm, I check if my pants are still on and if my tampon is in place. It's not ladylike, but it's a decent system to check for rape. Everything seems to be in order, and now I'm questioning if I'm septic.

Doesn't sepsis make you crazy?

"Stop, please!"

Landon screams from somewhere in the distance. The sound makes my heart pound so hard that I feel it against my ribs. There's a steady *thump thump thump* between Landon's begging and gargling lies.

It wasn't a dream or me losing my mind. It happened, and Riley woke up.

"It's not what you think. She wanted it."

Thump.

"S-stop. You don't understand."

Thump.

"I care about her. I was helping her."

Thump. Thump. Thump.

I already know without seeing, and with each excuse he gives to Riley, another blow will follow.

It's music to my ears.

A dozen blows later, I find the strength to sit up, my good arm resting limply at my side from the effort. I try to make a fist, imagining it hitting Landon in the face, but my fingers won't listen.

Thump. Thump. Thump

With every blow Riley delivers, the ground beneath me vibrates, but I'm also enormously high so that could be an overactive imagination.

My head turns, almost sending me face-first into the dirt. Riley and Landon are too far away to make out, but I recognize the motion of a fist ramming into someone.

Again, and again, and again he hits. All the while, Landon begs for him to stop.

"D-donn… don't s-stoppp," I slur to myself.

He doesn't until Landon's pleas grow silent, and then Riley hits him a few times more. The slams sound wet, and there's a crack I surmise is Landon's face breaking. Maybe his scars will match Riley's, but I know that's not true.

He won't survive this.

Thump. Thump. Thump.

More silence after those last hits, minutes maybe. I'm still too dizzy to get up, so I sway where I sit and wait.

Footsteps crunch through the dead leaves, growing louder until Riley's there, standing over me with his chest puffing in and out. I want to ask questions, but all that comes out in my slurred speech is nonsense and drooling. Riley crouches down and when our eyes meet, his scarred face comes into focus.

A small tingle of longing pulls at my heart. I want to hug him, cry into his shoulder, and tell him how grateful I am that he's a brute with no qualms about fighting a monster.

His heavy breathing stops, and I want to keep looking into his eyes, but now there are four of him swaying in my line of sight. If I die from whatever drug courses through my veins, I'll do it happily knowing Landon got what he deserved.

I start to fall over, but Riley catches me, bringing me to his side. There's blood on him, and I don't think it's his.

He shakes a bottle in my face, small and orange with a white cap haphazardly sitting crooked on top. I can't read the label, but I feel its effects.

"Tizanidine," he says. "You'll be out for a while."

I stare at the medicine, knowing I've never seen it before. Riley doesn't offer more of an explanation. My drool makes a long stream of spit that falls to the dirt, and he wipes my mouth with his thumb. I notice his bloody knuckles, his swollen hand, and I smile. Or, I think I'm smiling.

Still so enormously high right now.

He grabs a few blankets before picking me up and lowering me atop the makeshift bed. My eyes grow heavy when another blanket drapes over me, but I don't fight the feeling this time.

He steps away, moving toward a dark mound in the earth.

Landon.

I see him lower over the body, making sure he won't bother us anymore before he comes back to my side.

Riley doesn't say goodnight, but I feel the steady motion of his breath on my cheek and the soft sounds of his sleeping at my side while the fire blazes on the other.

I drift off, hoping for better dreams this time.

CHAPTER
NINE

She'll think I'm a monster.

Maybe I am.

We're all discovering our inner demons these days. How you release them makes evident the kind of man you are. Are you a man who fights when it's necessary, or are you a coward who runs, hiding in the shadows?

There have been plenty of men I wanted to kill. Any man who tells you they don't think about that is lying. In the darkest parts of our minds, we imagine someone's blood on the floor after something like this. What deems a person deserving of death is another thing.

Before the apocalypse, no matter how much I wanted to, I wouldn't kill anyone. I was not judge and jury. That's not how the world worked, and I obeyed the rules. That's when rules had meaning and consequences.

Women would come into the hospital, injured again by some freak accident with a doting man on their arm. Bruises in spots easily hidden by clothing and we all knew the truth even when they would never confess. The lies would eat at me, drilling nails into my skull with every word.

She tripped on the stairs.

It was a little fender-bender last week. We had no idea the bruises would show up like this.

Oh, he didn't do anything. He would never.

I would think about taking the guy into an on-call room and beating him until he bled out, saving the woman from what would inevitably happen again.

Their eyes asked us for help, but unless they were willing to file a report and talk to the police, we couldn't do much. Pushing too hard might put them in more danger.

Those men I was ready to kill every time.

Men like Landon.

This time I'm judge, jury, and executioner, and I'm not wasting any more time asking questions. If it wasn't Caitlyn, it would be someone else. A person like Landon can't hide who he is for long. Given the chance, he'd do it again, and what if he was successful?

He didn't do it.

I got to her first.

I'm scared to ask her. I know when I kicked him in the side, sending him rolling into the dirt, only his hand was in her pants. That's a violation, but he didn't rape her. I'm confident I stopped him before he got what he truly wanted.

These thoughts spin in my mind while we rest by the fire. I chastise myself for falling asleep too far from her. If she had been by my side, I would have woken up. He wouldn't have tried if I had been close to her before going to sleep.

I won't make that mistake again.

Moving nearer, I look over her bandage and any bare skin. It's not daylight, but I don't see bruises or bleeding from her wound, or anywhere else. I exhale, relieved she's not worse off.

She might be in the morning when she sees Landon's lifeless corpse. I think about moving it, but then I'd have to leave her alone.

Then I remember…

She may want to be alone instead of going north with me. She may not want to be here at all anymore. It's not as if she's been shy about her disdain for survival, and after what's happened, I can't blame her.

My heart hardens with the thought, and I steel myself to the idea. She's sarcastic and direct, qualities I happen to love, but the downside of that is I know she's honest when she says death may be a better option.

She's also not wrong. There's no guarantee we'll make it to Canada, and there's less of a guarantee that anything will be waiting for us when we get there.

I roll to my back, staring up at the night sky, and decide Landon can stay where he died. There's no funeral for bad men. No ceremony for rapists in this world.

Maisie's face flashes in my mind, and I swallow the lump in my throat. Would it have been better if she hadn't seen so much death? She died anyway, screaming and scared.

The sky is so bright without the smog and city lights dimming the stars. It keeps me awake while I think about Maisie and Caitlyn, going through the list of things I wish I had done, and things I should have said.

This world is harsh and unforgiving, but I know what kind of man I am. I'm not able to go down without a fight. If Caitlyn's willing, I'll protect her at all costs. It doesn't make up for Maisie, but it feels right. It's what Maisie would have wanted.

The images won't stop flashing through my memory, and I hate them and love them at the same time.

Maisie and I swinging on a playground, trying to beat each other in a silent competition. Our bottoms lift off the seat when we get to the very top, making our hearts flutter from excitement.

Our dad giving a standing ovation at our graduation, his large hands booming in claps, ignoring the ask to hold all applause until the end.

Maisie making a makeshift Thanksgiving dinner from canned everything, insisting we eat on opposite sides of a flimsy cafeteria table during our lunch break.

There are harder memories, but I push them aside, refusing to let them surface. She wouldn't want me to think of her that way. My sister brought something wonderful to this terrible place. A beacon of light amongst all the death, so bright that it warms you somehow.

Something about Caitlyn shines as well. I can't explain it, but when I saw her in the trees, I felt at peace.

There are people you find yourself around and something inside you stirs. A part of you knows they're not going anywhere. They're in your life, plain and simple, and it's as if they always were.

Caitlyn's not going anywhere.

There's no chance I'll sleep tonight, so when a sliver of light casts through the horizon, I rise. We need to move. Bloats circle the same areas, and if you stay in one place for too long, you're dead. We might have another day, but it's risky. There was a lot of noise coming from our camp last night.

There's obvious danger going North. We don't know their patterns or habits, and if we come across a group of them, there's no outrunning the herd.

It's still a mystery how Caitlyn made it out of that store. I should ask her and have a conversation about more than stitches and Ramen Noodles. It's an odd thought because getting to know her seems pointless. Chances are, our time together will end, so why bother?

But still, I can't help but want her to stick around, and not just because Maisie would want that. I want to protect her for as long as I can. Maybe I could keep her safe. Stranger things have happened, like… the apocalypse. No one saw this coming.

Maybe I'll get her to Canada, and we'll find civilization. There she can find someone less scarred on the inside and out. Someone who isn't a murderer.

I run my hand along my cheek, the pinpricks of pain shooting through the muscle. I've seen my face less than a dozen times, but I know how burns heal in the best of circumstances. It's not pleasant to look at, which is fine because I'm not a pleasant person. I make no apologies for my demeanor. It saves lives, even if that means taking them sometimes.

Caitlyn curls her legs closer to her chest, and I place my blanket over her, warming her for the time she has left to sleep.

I need to pack up what we will take with us, keeping in mind she's still far too weak to carry much. She'll want to help, though, so I need to make her bag as light as possible.

Medical supplies aren't too heavy, and I start there, seeing the orange bottle that I tore from Landon's pocket in our brawl. Tizanidine could have killed her, and she'll certainly feel the effects tomorrow and maybe the next day. He didn't care. All he wanted was for her to be compliant. Fists form at my sides, and I curse myself for my stupidity.

I sent him back to the store to get medical supplies and look for antibiotics again. He had the opportunity to steal an array of drugs, and then I remember he was in sales. There's no way someone in sales knows what Tizanidine does unless they've done this before.

The fury inside me grows, forming a pit of fire inside my gut, and I stomp over to Landon's corpse. He's stiff, curled into himself like a coward, his face looking worse off than mine.

Squatting down, I let myself feel the rage. It's not just about Caitlyn, but all those women who never got the justice they deserved. I would kill him all over again if given the chance.

I'll kill anyone who threatens Caitlyn.

"You deserved it," I hiss at his lifeless body. "You deserved worse."

CHAPTER TEN

CAITLYN

My head pounds. It doesn't ache. A head-*ache* stems from an annoying email, a bill you can't pay, or my downstairs neighbor who would slam a broom into her ceiling if I got up to pee after ten o'clock at night.

This pounding is akin to a hammer slamming repeatedly into both sides of my skull, and once again, I question why I'm alive to suffer like this. Dead people don't get headaches. Tears threaten to escape my eyes that refuse to open. Any sliver of light will cause me to convulse in agony, so I squeeze them shut and push my palms into the sides of my skull hoping it will give me some relief.

A hand rests on my shoulder, and I don't jolt away. I cling to it, complaining to its owner that this isn't just a fucking headache.

Memories of last night flicker in my mind's eye, fuzzy images of Riley hitting Landon, his cries for help, and then silence.

"Riley?" I ask, my voice barely above a whisper.

"Are you in a lot of pain?"

I nod, and the tears well up beneath my eyelids that still won't open.

"I think..." I pause, a giggle almost escaping my lips. "I think I'm dying. Really dying."

"You're not." His footsteps and the sound of him rummaging through a sack are knives to my skull. I rock back and forth, pushing each side of my temple as hard as I can. My arm begins to pulsate from the pressure I'm using, but I'm trading one pain for another.

"Here." His fingertips grab my chin, and he tilts it upward. The sun through my eyelids makes me groan, and then there's darkness, his shadow protecting me from the light. Sweat trickles down my back, a reaction to both the intense pain and sitting next to the fire. The air might be cold, but my body is aflame. I want to remove my sweatshirt and cool off. I need to. There are too many clothes covering my burning skin, and I'm on fire.

"Open up. This will help," he insists.

I pull away from him, the heat of the fire growing at my back. One hand slides around my waist, and he yanks me toward him.

"The fuck I will," I spit. "Last time I took a pill—"

"You didn't even know it," Riley stops me. "He crushed it up and put it in your food or water. I found the residue on the rocks by the tub."

I shake my head, no, but my resolve wanes. This pain is increasing by the second.

"Caitlyn," he growls, his patience running thin. "Open the fuck up or stop bitching about your headache."

"It's not just a head—"

The pill pops on my tongue, and I try to not choke, reaching for some water with my eyes still shut. He brings the bottle to my hand, wrapping my fingers around the plastic, and I swallow it down before throwing it to the side. I awkwardly strip off my blankets and get to work on my top, my skin sticking to the fabric from sweat. The heat from within my body needs to escape.

"The air is cold, and your nervous system is telling you that you're hot, but you need to keep your clothes on." He grabs my good wrist, my other arm still weak and bordering on useless. "No, Caitlyn. Your body temperature can't shift like that. It will pass in maybe twenty minutes. Drink more. Get it into your bloodstream."

"What are you, a doctor?" I lay back down and cover my eyes with my hands, the brightness overhead unbearable. Screaming will only make things worse, but I feel it bubbling inside me.

"A nurse."

There are no words in response, no witty banter to complain or argue. He's a damn saint, and if there was a moment to cry, it would be now. I growl in frustration instead.

"Okay, nurse Riley. How long—"

"Twenty minutes. Faster if you drink water."

His hand slides behind my back, lifting me against him as the lip of the bottle reaches my mouth. I drink until I hear the bottle crackle, almost emptying it in one continuous swallow. In our five minutes of arguing, the pain has diminished, the throbbing pressure lessening against my brain.

"Do you have more of those pain pills if I need them?"

"Yes, but you won't need more after today. He almost overdosed you. You're experiencing a slight withdrawal."

"Drugs aren't a terrible choice, considering our situation. I just would have preferred a say." I crack one eye open, the hazy sun covered by clouds isn't as bright as I thought before, but it still hurts.

Riley's warmth leaves, and I almost tip backward into the dirt.

"We have to leave as soon as you can walk."

I blink a few times, the tears I held in before now falling down my cheeks, and he comes into focus. His scar, so horrendous and fresh, must have happened after Halloween. There's no way it would heal that way working in a hospital.

"Your bedside manner is fabulous."

His only response is to slam a few open bags at my feet and throw things in while I wait for the medicine to do its job. Both packs are identical except for splashes of blood across one, and I'm reminded of last night's duel.

I stand and turn, my body feeling almost energetic now that the headache from hell is gone. My legs are a bit shaky, but I'm thrilled to be upright.

"He's dead!" I whisper.

Landon rests in a pile of lifeless limbs where our washtub stands.

Riley walks over, his head tilted to one side, hovering over him for a moment before he kicks at his shins. Landon's body moves in a stiff jolt. He's been dead for hours, possibly all night.

"Yes," Riley says, nodding. His eyes meet mine, and he waits for my reaction. I don't know what to say. I'm glad he's dead but a little scared that Riley looks so nonchalant about the fact. Seconds tick by while he waits for me to scream or run, maybe praise him.

Instead, all I can get out is, "Okay."

Riley breaks our eye contact and grabs a few bottles of water from around the washtub, checks the seals on them, and tosses them into one sack.

Landon's death doesn't bother him, and he doesn't care that he'll leave him unburied and covered in blood. They weren't friends. Not even a little. I wonder if, in the back of Riley's mind, he knew what kind of man Landon was, and what crime he would commit if given the chance.

"Can you carry that with your arm how it is?" Riley asks, pointing to a bag full to the brim with supplies. "Is it feeling better or worse?"

"It's not quite there but a lot better, and thanks to you, my vagina will be alright, too."

Riley freezes, his face hardening, and he clenches his fists.

"You're a nurse. You haven't heard the word vagina before?"

"I haven't heard anyone who experienced a trauma talk about it so soon. Most women I saw… They didn't bring it up so easily."

I wave my good hand around the sky. "This whole fucking place is trauma."

The words stick in my throat, but I'm good at pretending I don't care when people hurt me. They disappoint and betray us. That certainly didn't change after the end of the world.

Riley grabs the blanket at our feet, ripping it through the air in an angry thrust and almost knocking me over. "We can't stay here. Bloats are headed this way." He folds it into a messy ball and shoves it into a pack. "But, if you don't want to come, you'll certainly…"

"I don't want to die like that. Being turned into one of those things."

"It still might happen," he muses. "Do you want to keep going?"

He looks at the bottle of painkillers, pausing for a moment, and I know what he's thinking without saying the words.

"Are those for the pain? For the withdrawal," I ask.

His eyes narrow at the medicine, and it's silent, our conversation pausing with all the things unsaid.

"Too many and they could stop your heart," he admits.

"Are you giving me an option here?" I ask. "I'm confused."

I can't be sure, but I think Riley's jaw gives the slightest tremble. It's almost non-existent, but he pauses before he speaks, and when he does, there's something different in his voice.

"We always have a choice," he says, every word slow and purposeful. "I keep choosing to help you."

Without completely understanding why, I decide I don't want to take those pills and fall asleep, never to wake up again. I don't say that to Riley, though. Instead, I step back from the bottle and place my hands on my hips. Well, my good hand. My bad arm still hangs like a limp noodle.

I've caused Riley more trouble these past few days than he's dealt with in weeks, but if I owe him my life, I can let him have it for a little while longer.

It's more than that that keeps me from reaching for the bottle. Something draws me to this scarred man, and it started before he beat Landon to death for me. I can feel an easy friendship despite the façade of bickering. Some people stick to you, and it's been a long time since that was the case for me. Years I've spent avoiding getting too close to anyone, but with him, I'm struggling. I blame the apocalypse. Normal Caitlyn would know better than to start catching feelings for some guy.

Riley chucks the medicine into a bag, and pulls the strings taut, tying it shut.

"I'm not sorry about that," he says, his chin gesturing to Landon's body.

"Me neither," I agree. "You did the right thing." His actions baffle me. I'm another mouth to feed and more trouble than I'm worth. "Did you help me because you're a nurse, and you couldn't stop yourself?"

Murder is probably not in whatever code of ethics nurses abide by, but I have to ask.

"You think people shouldn't help others?" He answers my question with a question. "That we should let people get hurt and die? Just be alone. Every person for themselves and see who makes it?"

It strikes me that my cousin Rachel did in fact waste hundreds of thousands of dollars on her therapy degree. This man diagnosed me in a matter of days.

"I just… didn't understand why. I-I don't—"

"The fact that you don't get it says enough, Caitlyn. There are awful people in this world, but that's not a reason to give up. That's not a reason to be alone."

Riley flings one pack over his shoulder and grabs another bag of water bottles as he stomps off into the treeline. "If you're coming with me, grab a bag."

I'm speechless. He could have played hot potatoes with me all drugged up last night if he wanted a lay, but that's not what happened. Riley did the right thing, so why does it feel so foreign, so wrong?

His outline is almost out of sight, and my hand twitches for the bag. I've never been suicidal. Overly practical, yes, but in this case, it messes with my head.

I'm just so tired.

And scared.

Scared I'll be one of them, and part of me will still live on with my thoughts and feelings trapped in a bloat's body. What if Brian is still someplace inside one of those things, his soul stuck from whatever virus or curse he can't overcome?

The memory of my mother, frightened and alone, creeps into my mind. I'm scared I'll be forced to watch another person I care about die. And something inside my gut tells me I could care about Riley. He's a little harsh and pragmatic, but he's my kind of person.

That's terrifying.

My fingers curl around the bag strap and I lift it, still unsure about what future I want.

Riley stops up ahead.

He's waiting for me.

I know I want to go with him. What I don't want to do is slow him down or be responsible if something happens to him. I'm dead weight, and we both know it.

It's her sound that gets me moving.

A small cry in the thick woods straightens my back and sends me sprinting through the trees before I worry one more second about our survival.

CHAPTER
ELEVEN

I run through the trees, the sound of the woods surrounding me, making me disoriented as soon as I lose sight of our clearing. There's a crackling of fallen branches, someone sliding through the mud. It's Riley, or I hope it is, both of us sprinting around, listening for the sound of a small voice, a child's voice.

"Ba-ba-ba-ba." The baby is too young to talk. It's not crying, but he or she is clearly in some kind of distress. Hell, we're all in distress, and a baby unattended doesn't stand a chance.

"Hello!" I call out. "Where are you, kid?"

"Quiet!"

Riley's words startle me as he comes up on my left and throws his bag onto the ground. "Between you and her, bloats will find us in a second."

"Well, just leave if you're so worried about it, and I'll find the kid."

His expression is almost pained before he shakes his head and moves toward the child's noises, clipping my hurt shoulder in the process. I grunt, my hand swinging forward just as he catches it.

"Fuck. Did I hurt you?"

Our hands folding together catches me off guard, a warm sensation washing over me from the touch.

"I'm fine," I rush out.

I don't let go, and neither does he.

"Ba! Ba! Ba! Ba!"

Those nonsensical words break the trance, and we separate, both of us craning our necks right to look for her or him. They are screaming now, making their presence known to anyone willing to listen.

Could a bloat get to it first? Or, a bear?

"Oh my god a bear-bloat," I whisper. Luckily, Riley doesn't hear me as he runs toward the noise. I chase after him, the pain in my wound returning now that his touch is gone.

"There." He points, and I see a toddler ahead, falling down every other step. A girl who smiles at the sight of us. She's in a soiled dress that was white at one time, her hair is filled with crushed leaves.

My mother said children go through phases where they love everyone or hate everyone. I thought she meant my unfortunate teenage years, but I can see this child is in a loving stage. She's purely giddy in the presence of two strangers.

"Ba-ba?" she asks, her small hands turned upward.

"What does that mean?" we both say in unison.

I shoot him a look. "You're the nurse!"

"You're a—"

He pauses, knowing he's about to say something stupid.

"A woman. Like my tits will just translate what the fuck she wants?" I cover my mouth with my hand and murmur an apology. "Shit, I shouldn't say fuck around a kid. Or, shit. Oh, shit."

Riley's eyes widen, and I'm not sure, but I think a smile hides somewhere in his expression.

"Ba-ba," she says again, a frown forming, her eyes swelling with tears.

"No, no, no," I protest. "It's quiet time, okay. We'll find the ba-ba. Does it, um, go in your mouth?" I make a motion with my hands like I'm sucking a bottle.

"She's too old for a bottle," Riley says.

I whip my head around and glare at him. "Now you're a damn baby expert?"

"Nice language," he bites back.

"Ba-ba," she says again. Her small fist taps on her lips, and she makes a sucking sound.

"It's a…" I snap my fingers a few times, unable to come up with the word.

"A thing that—" Riley makes the sucking motion with his mouth, holding his hand out the same as mine, both of us at a loss for the word.

We are useless and ridiculous all at the same time, and this child is about to erupt into tears which will no doubt send death in our direction.

"There." Riley points in the distance, his face lighting up with excitement. Jumping over a fallen limb, he picks up a pink object and wipes the dirt away. The little girl squeals with excitement and claps her hands. She toddles over to him and reaches for the ba-ba.

"Don't you need to wash that off?"

He hands it to her and shrugs while she pops it in her mouth, spitting a few times to get the dirt off in between sucks.

We are not qualified for this.

"Pacifier!" Riley says, the word coming to him.

"Where's?" I ask a half question, turning in a circle and looking for the large person who is responsible for this small person.

"Your pack?" Riley asks. "Where's your pack?"

I sigh, knowing he's being practical while at the same time patronizing me with his words.

He turns me toward the clearing which isn't all that far from us. I'm surprised at my lack of direction. Another reason I should have died a long time ago. "Go get it, and I'll look to see if anyone else is close," he orders.

"What if she's a trap?"

We both go silent while looking around the barren woods. It's dead trees and what's left of the foliage is disintegrating into the dirt. The kid makes a squishing sound with her pacifier and watches us.

They left her.

"I don't think it is," Riley says. I nod in agreement, a sick feeling forms in my stomach from the thought. "But I'll look just the same. Get your pack if you're coming."

My eyes roll, but he's not wrong. I'm not sure what I'm doing, but I'll live today if only to get that little girl somewhere safer. Maybe two childless adults equate to one caregiver.

Jogging back, my body tires, the adrenaline seeping away now that we've found and silenced the little girl. I'm still a bit groggy, my thoughts fuzzy from whatever drug is leaving my system. I get to the camp and stop at the edge.

The area looks abandoned, our fire smoldering out, the washtub sitting with cold water, and the beach towel swaying with the wind. I listen for anyone or anything, but all that finds me is silence.

Landon's body rests in the same spot, curled into himself and impossibly still. The dead lie in ways that make you feel wrong. It's an odd sensation that seeps into your soul watching someone who doesn't breathe.

My pack is only a few feet away from him, and I should step forward and grab it, turn the other way, and run back, but something stops me.

I'm afraid.

He's dead, and there's nothing to fear, but it's there, sending pinpricks all over my body. He drugged me and tried to rape me, and if it wasn't for Riley, I would have been another victim no one cared about.

The thoughts of what could have happened hit me like a truck. He could have killed me, thrown me into a ditch, or off of a cliff. Waking up the next morning, he'd have simply said, "She ran off, man. You know she didn't want to live."

There's the sound of footsteps, someone I hope is Riley getting closer. I remain frozen, staring at the monster who hid in plain sight. I should have known better and protected myself. A hand touches my shoulder, and I take in a sharp breath, stopping myself from screaming when I hear his voice.

"I'll get it. Take her."

I reach with my good arm and a fumbling toddler clutches to my chest. She grabs at my hair, fans it out around my face, and tilts her head. A small hand finds my cheek and she wipes away the tears that I didn't know fell.

"No. No. No. No," she says.

Riley passes by Landon's corpse on the way to the pack, but he doesn't acknowledge him, merely grabs what he needs and turns back.

The baby rests her head on my shoulder, her legs wrapping around me, and I hold her up on one hip. Her dress is full of dirt, and I smell the earth in her hair.

"No. No. No," she says again.

"You're right," I tell her. "No tears over that piece of shit."

She giggles, and I take it as a win even though I've cursed in front of a child, yet again.

Riley lifts her from my hip, and I reach for the pack, slinging it over my shoulder with my good arm. He looks at my expression, and I want to smile or offer a witty joke, pretend this scene isn't hitting me all at once.

His eyes meet mine, and I wipe the tears away with the back of my hand and shrug. I open my mouth to speak but I just sigh. There's nothing I can say to make this better, and all I want to do is leave.

"You ready?" he asks.

I nod.

He looks at the baby, who turns her head from him to me, quizzically looking at us both, waiting for conversation.

"I won't let anyone hurt my girls ever again," Riley says to the toddler. His voice is full of warning, deep and rough, but she claps and laughs anyway.

He can't make that promise, and I'm certainly not his girl, but I can't deny it's good to hear.

Whether he means it or not, the weight inside my chest lifts, and I find the strength to turn around and leave this place, Landon, and all the bad memories behind.

CHAPTER
TWELVE

Caitlyn

We walk for the first few hours in silence. I had a small emotional meltdown in the clearing, and for some unknown and insane reason, I want to talk about that. I'm not the type of person who wallows. I panic, run, flee from danger, and then make a mockery of the situation if it comes up again. This is my pattern and it's worked so far.

What happened at the camp feels too heavy to joke about, and every step that takes us further away is a relief. Riley hasn't brought up the dreaded question, "Are you okay?" but he knows something is off. After a few attempts to form words and say something to him, I muster the courage to do the unspeakable.

I open up to a man.

"I'm not used to people helping me or doing the right thing," I admit. "I don't really like people, and I made this decision to, um, stay away. At least keep them at a distance."

Riley takes a deep breath, and his eyes shift to me while he faces forward. I'm sure he thinks any sudden movements will scare off my sudden admission of having feelings.

"Did someone…" He drifts off, pausing before he asks the question. "Have you been hurt?"

"Who hasn't?" I know I'm deflecting, making a snarky comment, and avoiding the answer I want to say.

"So out of some abundance of caution, you decided to be a loner."

He's not mocking me, but there's a jovial tone. I need that, the sarcasm laced in our conversation so it's not so serious I grab the baby and run off alone.

"Well, I am a cautious person. Always carry tampons and a fire extinguisher." I smile and take a few breaths before I continue. "It was always just my mother and me, our little family of two. Everyone else lived a few towns over. She died before all of this." I circle my hand in the air, looking around at the expanse of dead trees.

"I'm sorry you lost her."

"Thank you. She was my best friend. My dad didn't stick around because they were young and he was a piece of shit, but she was amazing. Too good of a mom. I mean if she was a little less great, losing her wouldn't have been worse than the apocalypse. But damn it was the worst thing to happen to me."

Riley nods. I expect a laugh or maybe a smile, but he takes what I say to heart even if the words are filled with jabs at the serious context.

"She had cancer and was bedridden for a long time." I picture my mother with her silk scarf tied around her head and her hands gently resting on a book. She looked peaceful even when I knew her body was riddled with pain. "When she was alive, she took care of the entire family even though they lived a few hours away. They needed money, and she found wiggle room in her bank account. Someone was sick, she made the drive to bring them soup. But when she became ill, all those people in her life got real busy."

I kick at the dirt, anger filling my chest. We walk another minute, Riley taking in what I've said.

"I wish I could tell you that wasn't common," he admits. "But in the hospital, sometimes family and friends couldn't be bothered. No matter how wonderful a person is, they might find themselves without support when things go south. I'm sorry you went through that feeling so alone."

"Oh, I didn't just feel it," I admit. "I was alone. The last year of her life, she didn't have a single visitor, and you know what, that taught me something. People only care about themselves. They won't do anything… out of, um… they won't." I catch myself before I go on. "Except you know. What you did. It was out of the norm for me."

"I can tell," he says.

My face flushes. He came through for me back in the clearing which is against every principle I have taught myself. Brian, and other men, only want sex. Women want to win some disillusioned competition. Everyone wants money, power, and resources. No one wants to help others because it's the right thing to do.

Except that's just what Riley did.

"Right, so that's why I was so confused about why you helped me and also maybe why I'm a little, um, you know."

"Flippant about the fabric of life."

"Yeah, that."

"Well, when it comes to you, I will do the right thing," Riley says. "Sometimes it's hard to know what that is. Especially now. But, I promise you I will."

I should tell him thank you or say something.

Anything.

I'm afraid if I do speak, I'll burst into tears so I slap my hands on my thighs and walk ahead. Thankfully, he lets me have a few feet of distance for the next hour.

Stopping later to rest, I sit down on an uncomfortable rock and stare at the baby. She's been good for a kid, not that I have a lot of experience. I suppose you only notice the ones throwing fits or acting like a shithead.

She traces the scars that run down Riley's face, not afraid, only curious, poking at its jagged lines with innocent eyes. He doesn't stop her, rummaging through his pack for sustenance.

It's almost sweet.

Riley's careful to let her finish the inspection before he tosses me some type of protein bar. He opens another one, holding it up to the kid and pointing it at her. She takes it in her tiny hands and bumps it against her mouth, taking a soggy bite.

"Showing her the battle wounds?" I ask.

Riley points to her thigh. "She has a few of her own." The sight of a large red circle and several deep scrapes on her leg makes me wince. "I think someone threw her. She's favoring her wrist on that side too."

"Threw her?"

He nods. "There are a lot of drops out here. Faces of hills that are almost vertical. If she fell, they would have gone after her."

There are a million wild scenarios for why a toddler would get thrown in the woods, and thanks to the apocalypse, they all make sense.

"Safe to say we won't be finding a parent, then? So what…"

I struggle to finish my question. What do we do with her? What's the plan? What are your plans for keeping me and this baby alive?

He finishes eating, lying back on a rock, and stretching his legs. He's been carrying her this entire time, and I wonder if he's sore. You get used to walking, especially with weight on your back, but he's toting a heavy bag and a human.

"Where are we going?" I ask. I need a direct answer to a direct question, and all I ever heard him tell Landon was *North*.

"North." Riley points in a direction I assume is North, but despite attending four Girl Scouts meetings when I was eight, I have no idea where I am most of the time.

"Could you be more specific?"

"I heard they don't like the cold," he adds.

"Not with the why. With the where."

"For now, just north. Toward snow."

"Great." I slap my hands on my thighs. "I can't wait to be wet and cold."

Riley shrugs, takes a bite of the bar, and talks while he chews. "Don't strip naked in the middle of the night and you'll stay warm."

"I was withdrawing from Tiza-taboo-boo or whatever it was."

"Tizanidine," he corrects me. "Just keep your clothes on and you'll be alright."

"Well, I usually try to. It's not my fault some psycho tried to rip them off and rape me."

The words slice through the air like a knife, and I feel how they cut me, opening a wound that's barely had a chance to close. Riley's face pinches in anger, and I imagine mine looks the same. The memory of him throwing punches in the middle of the night, the steady thump of his fists on Landon's skull, it all returns with a fury. My skin gets hot, and I pull at the neck of my shirt.

He lifts the girl by the back of her dress and moves her between us. She plays in the dirt with one hand, eating the rest of her bar with the other. A big smile on her face tells me toddler age is too young to read a room.

Riley's eyes lower to the ground, staring at the circles the little girl makes with a stick. "I killed him," he whispers.

I don't know how to respond, but when someone makes an admission that serious out loud, something should be said.

"Have you ever killed anyone before?"

He nods, his eyes never leaving the child.

"If it was in self-defense or saving someone else, well, then you did what you had to do."

He's clenching his jaw, visibly upset about what happened with Landon, but I'm not sure what percentage of that anger is because he tried to rape me or because my presence forced his hand to take someone's life. If I'd never shown up, the murder would never have happened. They'd still be walking together North, maybe without a kid in tow.

That fact scares me. This baby could have been left in the woods, and there's not a chance she would have survived. My mom believed everything happened for a reason, but I was more realistic. I thought my point was proven on Halloween. How could an epidemic of bloats be a reason for something?

When I look at this little girl though, I doubt myself. If Riley and Landon didn't stop for me, no one would have found her. She would have died with them too far away to ever know.

I want to carry some hope of survivors up north, to believe there lies a refuge that could take us in and make things like they were. Maybe that would stop my desire to leave this terrible world.

The truth is that there's likely nothing and no one. We're some of the few left, and most other survivors are killers, cannibals, or rapists. This isn't a world worth living for, but then there's this little kid who's so innocent and this guy who's willing to kill for me.

I groan to myself, knowing I have a soft spot for kids and this scarred hottie.

Puppies too, but everyone likes puppies.

"You help people," I say, pointing to the kid. "And thank you for, the um, Landon thing. For taking care of that."

I cannot fathom how to thank someone for murder, but I groan, knowing that wasn't it. "Should we call her something?" I ask, desperate to change the subject.

"Probably," he says, rubbing his forehead.

"Oh, wait! I know."

I scoot over and peek in the back of her dress. Finding the tag along the collar, I look for the name written neatly on the fabric.

"Lana," I say. She giggles while Riley shoots me a curious look.

"I work with a lot of moms. They all put their kid's names in the clothes for daycare. Well, I used to work with them. You know… before."

One of his eyebrows lifts. "Smart."

I sit back, grazing my arm with my fingertips, and trace the bandage with my finger.

"You'll need some more pills in a few hours."

He's reading my mind.

"How far is it? This mysterious place up North," I ask.

"I don't know."

"Do you know where it is?"

Lana stands up, her food half in her belly and half on her face. She drops some dirt from her clenched fist, and it sprays inside my mouth. I sputter a few times, Riley doing the same and telling her, "No." She frowns and moves further away to throw dirt.

"Not too far," I tell her. She doesn't respond and keeps clapping every time she empties her fist of dirt.

"Can she understand you?"

"No clue," I admit. "I'm barking orders like she's a dog. Seems to be working."

Riley leans back, his face tilting toward the sky. His Adam's apple bobs with a hard swallow.

"So, North," I press. "Do you know how far north? What's this place you're taking your girls to."

My cheeks flame red with the words, but I can't put them back in my mouth. He doesn't move his head, staring at the swaying trees above us.

"Canada."

I exhale, relieved that he doesn't acknowledge my embarrassment.

"It will take us longer to hike there not knowing their patterns," he says.

"Longer than your typical hike. You've done this before?" I joke.

"I've hiked the Appalachian Trail with my sister. So, I have an idea of the time it takes to go for long stretches."

Touché.

"Where the hell are we anyway?" I mutter under my breath.

"We're south of Louisville," he answers.

I'm sure he's aware that cross-country travel on foot isn't anyone's preference, but the task feels impossible.

"Oh, hell. That's what, a month to get there?"

"Longer."

I hold back my whine and try to think of another rebuttal. Longer than a month in winter. I'm glad he's not a rapist, but this man is insane.

"I think we're less than a day's walk from the river," he continues.

I nod, refusing to ask more questions that I'll hate the answers to.

"The river that we cross to get to Indiana."

"I know," I bite out.

I did not know, but I stare at Lana, hoping he doesn't see my face. My expressions leave nothing to the imagination, and right now it's pure confusion. I can't picture where we are or the path to Canada. The idea of walking there is akin to imagining the expanse of the universe. My brain does not compute.

"Are you in it for the whole way?" Riley asks.

I know what he's asking. Will I take an opportunity to off myself or try to make it with him to the freezing lands? My mind also can't comprehend getting colder. It's already unbearable at night without a fire.

Lana stumbles over, waving her dirty hands in our direction. She squats down in front of us with a giggle.

"I have a soft spot for kids," I say.

"So, that's a yes. You're coming."

"Well, I can't just leave her…"

"With me. The scarred murderer."

Lana laughs at that moment, a needed break in the tension. She collapses into his lap and reaches up to pull his hair, already her favorite pastime. He winces when she almost yanks it from the roots.

I know he's on the verge of being offended, and I'm careful with my words, wanting to make peace without promises.

"I like this kid, and you're not too bad either," I say. "So as long as a bloat isn't charging me, I don't see a reason to take off just yet. Do you think you can get your girls to moose country?"

Why do I keep saying, "Your girls"? It's mortifying.

Riley stands, picking up Lana from the back of her dress and plopping her on his hip. The man carries her like a football, but that's the least of our problems.

"Actually, there are more bison and polar bears than there are moose. I know how important animal safety is to you." Normally I can't stand the, *um actually*, guy, the type of man who corrects everything you say. With Riley, there's something in his tone that makes the comment endearing. He's attempting a joke, giving my sarcasm right back to me.

I like it.

"Great, Riley. More things that can kill us. Better than a death by bloats."

"Depends on who you ask."

I picture myself chased by a wild animal before it catches me, ripping me to shreds. Dread washes over me considering a death by bloats, the wild, or another Landon.

"I guess so."

My voice shakes a little, and Riley notices. "Don't worry," he says. "We'll be okay."

I can't decide what's scarier. Is it all the ways to get killed out here,

or the realization that for the first time, I'm considering what it might
be like to live?

CHAPTER
THIRTEEN

A damn kid.

I don't know how I get myself into these messes or why I care.

That's a lie. I know why I'm lugging around an oversized football. It's because Maisie would haunt me forever if I didn't help this little girl.

I'm not a religious or superstitious man, but I think there are forces at play beyond our comprehension. If there's a chance my sister could haunt me, she'd make sure to avoid the light.

She was my favorite person in the world, but when she thought she was right, she'd burn down the house with you inside until you saw things her way.

I do see things her way when it comes to Lana, though. No fire needed. This little girl would be dead within a day without me and Caitlyn.

Well, Caitlyn would be, too, just like she wanted. Except I'm not sure that's what she's after anymore. I let her walk ahead a little, looking her over, watching the subtle sway of her hips.

Her hair isn't braided anymore after losing the full use of her arm, and it's long and thick, flowing in waves down her back. She's thin, like all of us on the brink of starvation, but curvy in the right spots.

Landon's actions were disgusting, but I understand the appeal. Even her wit I find endearing, but if I let her know that, she may never give me a break, mocking me at every turn. A man can only take so much.

She moves with purpose, ready to get somewhere even though she doesn't know where we're going. I do, but I can't give directions because we have to avoid the roads. I'll keep us close enough to the highways for a path, but far enough out to stay safe.

I can see the ranch in my mind. Thousands of acres and right in the center, a little white house. A basement full of canned food, and my uncle, rocking on the porch when he isn't in his panic room. Hopefully, he doesn't have to hide, the bloats staying away from the ice and snow.

I've memorized the way after countless summers on that land. One time we walked for a few hours when the car broke down. I was ten and thought I wouldn't make it, my fingers nearly frozen from the cold. Look at us now, walking maybe a thousand miles, the winter creeping up on us every day, growing worse with every step.

We'll make it.

We have no choice.

It gets the coldest in January with icicles clinging to every tree branch and the snow falling day and night. Wouldn't that be our luck?

But if the theory is right, and bloats hate the cold, it's the best time to try and get there. I'm not sure we'd survive any longer in the States.

"Do you want me to take her?" Caitlyn asks.

I grunt, knowing she can barely manage that pack. If we're going to do this, we can't bother with niceties. She needs to be honest with how tired she is, or if she's feeling sick or feverish. Things can change in an instant.

"Was that a no?"

"You're ridiculous if you think you can manage another twenty pounds."

"I used to weigh another twenty pounds," she bites back. "So, yeah, I think I could hold her. Geez. Fine. Are you hungry yet? You sure sound like it."

I imagine Caitlyn with another twenty pounds, healthy and fed, without her bones sticking out or clothes hanging off her body. She's beautiful now, but it bothers me how sickly she is even without the wound in her arm. I shake my head, trying to free myself of the image. I remember calling her my girl earlier and scold myself for letting it slip.

Anyone with a pulse would be attracted to her, but I'm not anyone. I'm an angry murderer with half my face missing, and I resist the urge to touch my cheek and run my fingers over the jagged scars. They aren't going anywhere, but I still startle myself when I catch my reflection. Anyone who knows me wouldn't recognize me.

"Yeah," I say. "Grab some bars from my bag."

"Oh, thank god. I thought you were going to make us eat dry Ramen."

I'm tired of Ramen, but I don't say that. Adding soups or other canned food helps bulk it up and mask the texture I've grown to hate, but I'd do anything for a steak or a damn cheeseburger. I think about the cattle on the farm in Canada, how you could spot them lined up on the horizon, and my mouth waters.

Caitlyn's hand brushes against my neck reaching for the zipper on the pack. The feel of her skin sends a jolt of fire through my veins, and I tense, not wanting her to notice.

"What flavor do you want?"

"Don't care."

"Well, okay grumpy pants. Are you grumpy because you're carrying a sleeping toddler and refuse to let anyone else help?"

I glare at her, and she points the bar at my face, half of her mouth turned up in a smile.

"Might I make a suggestion?"

"You aren't going to carry her. Your arm—"

"I'm aware my arm almost got sliced off, but I have an idea that the moms I knew taught me. They would always baby-wear their kids and it let them be hands-free. It's like a crossbody purse."

What the fuck is she talking about?

My arms aren't tired, but they're cramping staying in the same spot for hours. I don't want to risk waking Lana by constantly moving her position, so I nod in agreement.

Caitlyn shoves the bars in her pocket and puts her bag down. Digging through it, she pulls out a thinner blanket, one that she needs to sleep with so she won't freeze at night.

"Don't tear that up. You need it."

"Bossy and grumpy," she mumbles, laying the blanket on the ground and folding it in long horizontal lines. I don't bother arguing back. She's not tearing it apart and that's all I care about. She pulls out another blanket and fluffs it up next to her feet.

"Okay, give me Lana for a minute."

I hand her over, and she puts her down. Lana curls her legs up, and I see her injury. It's darker and bruises are forming. Before I can worry myself with how bad it could get, Caitlyn wraps the blanket she folded around my waist, her chest so close to mine we're almost touching.

All the air leaves my body, and my heart thuds wildly in my chest, so loud I'm sure she can hear. I turn my head to the side, not wanting her to look at my disgusting scar.

She crosses the blanket's ends at my middle and pulls one side around my shoulder, yanking it tight. Every brush of her skin, her breath grazing my cheek, and the skimming of her fingertips along my neck sends a lightning bolt of need straight to my dick. I force myself to think of something else, not wanting my body to react to her proximity.

It's fucking impossible.

I try to back up, but she pulls at the blanket until I'm back against her, my pulse so fast that I'm lightheaded.

"I'm almost done. Trust me you'll like this."

Oh, I already do.

I know I'm staring at her, my face still turned to the side, and she tilts her head, tying the blanket in a knot with a smile on her face. She pauses, and I swear she can read my mind.

"There," she says, but she doesn't look away. Her chest is against mine, my dick twitching in my pants from her touch. If this was months ago and I hadn't committed murder in front of her, I'd grab her by the back of the neck and pull her lips to mine.

Instead, I force my hands to stay at my side and avert my eyes to Lana. The moment passes, and Caitlyn steps back, picking up the baby who remains curled up and fast asleep. My heart rate slows, and I relax as we wedge her into a pocket of the wrap, her arms and legs disappearing into the fabric.

"There," Caitlyn says. I hear the hitch in her voice and notice the flush in her cheeks. She rubs the back of her neck, looking over Lana who rests comfortably in a sling. Opening her mouth to speak, she takes a step back, stopping herself before saying anything. Our eyes meet, and for once she doesn't jab me with dark humor or a sarcastic comment.

"What?" I ask.

She shakes her head. "Nothing."

In another life, I'd ask her to dinner. Not bullshit coffee or inviting her to meet up somewhere with a group of friends. She deserves more than that.

I'd ask her on a real date, just her and me, because she's someone I would want to spend time with. Even when she's giving me shit, I enjoy her company. If things were normal, she might say yes to a man who isn't injured or hasn't murdered someone with his bare hands.

Except we aren't in another reality. This is our life, or what's left of it. Maybe she'll rethink exiting permanently, but there's no dating, only surviving. There are scars and death, fear and monsters. It's a woman willing to die rather than live in this hell with me, and I can't blame her.

There's no chance of anything normal.

There's no Riley and Caitlyn.

CHAPTER FOURTEEN

CAITLYN

Riley isn't much of a talker. He's more of a grunter, eye-roller, and baby carrier. Under normal circumstances, I can accept that. A few months ago, I might have dated that, taken that back to my apartment, and gotten naked with that. The thought makes my cheeks flush.

The idea of sex with Riley invades my mind, and for some unknown reason, I know he'd be good.

He'd be great.

That rugged exterior, his height, that damn scar which should be scary but instead turns me on — and now I'm getting a little wet thinking about it.

I need to shift my focus.

"How did you end up with Landon?"

He doesn't trip. I don't think the man is capable of a misstep, but his pace changes when he turns to look at me. Lana's eyes haven't opened for twenty minutes, and he's shifted the carrier to his hip per my suggestion.

When I took the thin blanket and wrapped it around his body, securing the kid to his strong torso, my little crush on him soared into hyperdrive. It never felt that way with Brian which makes me sad. I don't think he cared much as long as he was getting some sex.

Standing so close to Riley, my arms wrapped around him and our faces only inches from each other, it activated some sort of sexual launch sequence. When I'm honest with myself, the attraction was there before, but it's easier to keep in check from a distance.

He felt warm and sturdy, making me want to wrap myself into him. Not to mention the laws of nature must not apply to him because the man smells good. We are on limited resources for bathing, and he takes the time each day to wash up and put on deodorant while I undoubtedly smell like roadkill.

And to make matters worse, this big strong guy with a scar that could terrify anyone is wearing a baby purse. It's so fucking attractive I could spit.

"Why would you care about a dead man?" he asks.

"I don't," I say. "I asked how you ended up traveling with him."

"Why would you care about me?"

He's testing me, trying to put me off so I don't push any further. The joke's on him because all I do is push. I'll push him off a building if I must, so asking some invasive questions doesn't phase me at all.

"Well, we're on this grand voyage together. Seeking out our new world and there's a lot of time to kill on the way to Canada. Which by the way I did the math in my head, and it's going to take fucking forever to get there, so we should talk and get to know each other."

"Language," he chastises.

"She's asleep," I whisper-yell at him.

He takes a deep breath, his chest rising and falling before he answers. The baby doesn't stir, and I make big eyes at him, nudging his arm and urging him to speak. The contact sends another spark through my limbs that shoots right to my lady bits. This attraction is his fault. Who wears deodorant after an apocalypse?

"My sister and I were together. We went into a grocery store looking for food, and he was there."

The sun hangs low in the sky, casting shadows over Riley. There's something more than twilight that makes his face darken when he says those words. It's regret perhaps, or maybe even anger. He mentioned his sister, and I haven't asked too many questions, but there is no time like the present.

"What was her name?"

"Maisie," he growls.

Definitely anger.

"And she's…"

There's no sister around, so I gather something bad happened. Something bad always happens these days. We're probably walking straight into something bad.

Riley adjusts Lana on his hip, and I notice how his movements are gentle. He softens when he focuses on her.

"She died there. Landon lived."

"Ah," I say. There are no other words I can think to offer. *I'm sorry* or *that's terrible* doesn't quite make sense. We've all lost people, important people, and I know better than most how useless words don't make a difference.

"You know I want to ask how," I sputter out, regretting it immediately.

"Of course you do, Caitlyn. Does it fucking matter?"

I swallow the lump in my throat, my eyes welling a bit when I answer. "No. Death is death. I'm sorry for asking, but you know… it's just." I trail off, unable to justify my actions.

It's human, the desire to understand death. The idea of ceasing to exist, leaving this world, and evaporating as a person is unfathomable. We see it, and we understand someone's essence is gone, never to come back, but we need to make sense of why it happened. Then we negotiate in our minds why that would never happen to us. Even when we're outnumbered by bloats and the world is over, we think if we know the mistake someone else made, we can avoid it. Our story is different and we can survive because we asked invasive and rude questions.

I'm such a cliche.

If I tripped and fell off a cliff right now, I might be a little grateful. This place sucks, and I just pissed off my crush who also might be the last man on the planet.

"Were you and Landon friends at all? Did you think he was, um, you know—"

"A rapist? No, Caitlyn, but I don't think much of people these days. The only person who isn't an asshole is Lana."

"That's true."

His jaw hangs open, shocked I didn't argue the insult directed at me, but he shuts it and shakes his head. I am a jerk. I just asked how his sister died, making me another entry into the log of selfish assholes still roaming the earth.

"I didn't mean you—"

"It's okay," I cut him off. "So, how long ago was all that again? The grocery store."

Riley groans but keeps talking. "A few weeks ago. Landon was with three other people. When bloats showed up, he was nowhere to be found. Ran off. I can't say I blame him, but he acted like this one woman, can't remember her name..." Riley scrunches his brow and rubs his forehead. "Fuck, what was her name?"

"Language," I remind him.

He doesn't laugh, but I hope he wants to. I've felt it bubbling beneath the surface when I catch him off guard, and soon, if we don't die first, I'll get him to laugh.

"He acted like they were an item. She wore a ring, and I think they were engaged."

"You think?" I shriek out in shock. If I didn't have an injured arm, I'd give him a swat. "Did you ask him? Did you ask anybody?"

"No."

Typical. Men never get the important details. If I had been in that grocery store, I would have had hours of stories to entertain him with.

"Well, engaged or not, he was a piece of garbage," I huff. "Running off and leaving his partner especially."

"No, shit," Riley agrees.

"Did you get hurt? Is that where?" I point at his cheek and pull my hand back, realizing all too late that I'm getting every rude question out in this one exchange. There was a time when I had social skills, but without an office and a need for a paycheck, they seem to have left my psyche.

"I don't want to talk about that," Riley answers. His voice slices through the forest, changing the atmosphere around us. I swear it gets colder, and he picks up his pace, making every effort to escape the topic.

He's not getting away that easily. The talking distracts my exhaustion, even if I'm huffing in between my words. I hope we make some kind of camp soon, but I don't think we've gotten far enough yet.

"I was in a grocery store, too, you know," I remind him, my words breathless from my lips. He's still wearing a surly expression and it's not just the scar. "Seems to be a hot spot for bloats to look for us. Not that I know what happened in your grocery store. Could have been a comet or a band of burglars."

"Sarcasm is the lowest form of comedy," Riley says, annoyance dripping from every word.

"Who said I was being sarcastic? I'm putting forth a comparison of our situations with the information I have, which isn't a lot."

Riley's longer legs glide through the forest, but I match his pace.

"We didn't have much of a choice though. It's not like anyone could stick around long enough to grow food, and how else would I find tampons?"

Riley sighs, skipping up a few rocks, Lana bouncing gently in her sling. "It was too risky to keep breaking into people's houses," he says. "Too many gun owners around here."

The breath I was holding releases, leaving my lungs slowly and steadily. He only needed a change of topic, not total silence.

"I bet that's not an issue anymore."

"It's possible," Riley agrees. "First few weeks, you couldn't put your foot on a sidewalk without someone pointing a gun out of their window."

I groan from the familiar memories. Brian and me, creeping around houses, listening for the better part of an hour before deciding if we should go inside. Even then, most of the food was gone, already raided by other survivors or eaten up before the owners left. There was always the unpleasant discovery of black goo smeared across the floor which sent me screaming for the hills.

"What happened in your grocery store?" Riley asks.

He doesn't know what happened to Brian, or that there ever was a

Brian. All he found was a half-dead woman in the woods bleeding from her arm and uterus.

"Do you want just the grocery store, or from the beginning? We have loads of time. Canada is light years away."

He huffs and there's a chance of an eye roll. "Canada might be a few months."

"I can make a story stretch."

"Then just the grocery store."

I can't tell a long story short, and I'm babbling on for the better part of an hour before he asks who Brian is.

"You said you wanted just the grocery store story."

"It would be good to have some context. Was he your boyfriend?"

That question takes some thought. The truth of it is, I don't know. We could qualify for an apocalypse common-law marriage if you wanted to label our relationship. He was a boyfriend of convenience at best. Riley might think I'm depressed over Brian's loss and that's why I don't have the will to live through this nightmare.

"We dated a few times. Almost three times. Then the world ended and all we had was each other but we weren't, you know, together – together."

"Almost three times?"

"Apocalypse happened on the third date."

"Ah, I see."

"We did have sex," I add although I'm not sure why. "A lot of sex."

There is a definite misstep from Riley, but we are trekking uphill with nothing but jagged rocks to hoist ourselves upward, so it may have been a coincidence. Lana remains asleep, unbothered by the jostling and mention of coitus.

Riley reaches his hand out for me to grab, trusting the wrap will keep Lana in place. I hesitate, but I inspected the contraption myself three times so I allow him to help me. I may not make it up otherwise.

"It's not that I didn't, uh…" I grunt, using all my core strength to move my body up this damn hill. "It's not that I didn't care for him, but if the world was normal, we would have never been together. I am sad that he's dead, though. "

Riley grunts, practically lifting me over a dip in the earth.

"Because you can't have sex anymore?"

I stumble into him, my bad arm slamming into his side. He reaches out, holding me in place for a moment too long. I bite my lip, trying my best to ignore the sting of my injury.

"I can still have sex," I hiss through the pain.

We stand like that for a moment too long, his arm wrapped around me, and I panic. "With myself, you know."

Riley smirks, releasing me and tilting his head to look over my arm. His thumb traces around the bandage, touching the exposed skin with the back of his hand. My cheeks flame, and all I can do is stare at his scar which I now find impossibly sexy. I imagine he got it saving people, risking his life and face for the greater good.

I can still have sex with myself.

What the fuck am I saying?

"Are you good to keep going?" I squeak.

He must notice how my breaths are quicker, my chest rising and falling as if I'm sprinting in a marathon.

"I'm great, Caitlyn." His voice catches, just a little, but enough to show he's thinking about what I said.

"After you," I offer.

He turns around, leading the way without a mention of what I said. I can't blame him because I'm spewing humiliating garbage and any normal person would feel second-hand mortification.

I scurry after him, hoping that's the end of our Brian talk. He's a bloat now, and there's nothing more to say unless I want to sound like more of an idiot. There are maybe a dozen humans left in the world, and I'd prefer not to be the dumbest.

Sweat beads on my forehead and pours down my back. We carry on up the last part of what must be Kentucky's Mount Everest when my footing slips and Riley grabs me by the side of my pants, hoisting me sideways toward a thick ledge where we can sit.

I don't scream, but a sharp squeak escapes, and Lana yawns. He sits beside me, and I rub her back to hush her back to sleep, both of us a little short of breath.

"Do you think we're far enough out from them?" I ask.

Riley shakes his head. "Maybe, but we need to get a few more miles to be sure. And we need to get to the top of this hill. Can you do it?"

I nod. "I can."

"Do you want to? Will you?"

I look over the ledge seeing nothing but branches and rocks below. "I don't want to, but I will. I'm not going to jump."

He rests his head on the rock wall behind us, and we look out at the forest that cascades around and below. It's beautiful, a singular moment of magnificence on this grotesque earth. The only things that are ugly now are what man left behind.

Dilapidated gas stations and crumbling buildings, spray-painted highways with chipped cement. In a few short months, the lack of care is evident, and it's ugly.

"I'm sorry he didn't make it," he says. "Losing people makes it hard to want to stick around."

"We weren't in love," I admit. "I just didn't want him to be alone."

"Is that why you're with me?"

"I know you don't need me. You would probably like to be rid of me after all my talking."

"You know that's not true," Riley sighs. "Answer the question."

I fidget on the rock and force myself to tell him the truth. "I'm struggling with why I'm alive, but I'm not here with you to do you a favor. You and me, it seems right. At least for right now."

"And Bobby?" Riley asks. "He's a bloat now?"

"Brian," I correct him. "Yes."

"It's a good thing you didn't love him."

"I can have love for someone and not be in love with them," I correct him.

A few silent moments pass, and my muscles begin to ache from the uphill climb. No matter how many months I spent roaming around, I avoided anything up the side of a mountain. The exertion of walking was enough cardio.

"Your tattoo," Riley says. "What's that about?"

I touch the back of my neck, wondering when he saw me with my shirt off to notice the phrase there. "My mother's favorite saying."

Running my fingers over the raised skin, I close my eyes and think of her before exhaling and looking up at the sky.

"It's not fair," I say. "Her, Brian, everyone else."

"Survivor's guilt is a real thing," Riley adds.

"You know I cared for Brian, but I could never fall in love with him. He was always just there. I guess I didn't try to love him. Something in me just couldn't. My mother would always say—" I sputter a laugh, realizing how true her words were considering my time with Brian. "It's not love, Caitlyn. It's lack of options."

Riley gets up, and I groan, knowing that a nap is out of reach.

"Lack of options," he says, his voice low.

Fuck.

"No – no. I didn't mean it like that. Just with Brian, I wouldn't have gone out with him—"

There's something in his eyes that gives away the hurt behind them. Fuck my stupid mouth and words I don't mean.

"Riley, that's not what I meant. I—"

"I'll keep that in mind," he cuts me off. He bounds up the hillside, and I pretend it doesn't hurt my feelings when he doesn't offer to help me this time.

CHAPTER
FIFTEEN

CAITLYN

I thought I was getting through that rough exterior, maybe becoming friends. A trauma bond is still better than walking in silence for hours, which is what we've been doing for the better part of a day after an awkward night.

Silence gave me a lot of time to think about how, yet again, my mouth got away from me. Riley might be scary-looking, but that doesn't mean he's void of feelings, and I've prodded into a deep insecurity. I want to be kinder, softer sometimes, but it doesn't come naturally, especially when we're trekking through a wasteland.

"Why are we stopping?" My words are breathy, with little life left in them. I'm at the end of my energy, and I lean against a tree, letting it take the weight of the pack for a moment.

"Because we're here."

I drop my bag and stumble forward, the remnants of a city peeking out through the thinner branches of the cliff's edge.

"That city looks deserted. Here where?"

Riley lays Lana down and wraps a thin blanket around her toes that peek out. I'm grateful she's sleeping. She's been out for hours after spending the morning playing drums on Riley's shoulders. I offered to take her several times, but he called me a one-armed fool and kept going. It was the most he'd said to me since, "Go to sleep, Caitlyn," last night. It appears that the silent treatment is over, at least for the moment.

"Louisville, Kentucky," he answers.

What's left of the city crumbles in the distance. Broken windows fill the walls of leaning buildings, a gap in a freeway stretches through the sky, steel bars bent and jutting out into the air. All of this happened in months, but the soot-stained cement and burned cars left on the road-ways tell me this was more than bloats. This place went to war.

My eyes trail over the scene, and I see them in the distance, their bloated bodies swaying through the streets, marching to an unsteady rhythm. I back up from the edge of the cliffside, knowing they can't see me but fearing them all the same.

Riley turns back, looking me up and down, his shoulders slumped in defeat.

"That's a problem, isn't it?"

He trails his gaze over Lana, who sleeps on a patch of grass. We're hidden where we are, still behind a thick treeline. Skyscrapers tower overhead but there's enough foliage here to keep us covered.

"Stay put for a minute," Riley says.

I sit cross-legged next to Lana and stare at the bloats, wondering if Brian is down there. I'm not heartbroken over his loss, but there's an ache inside me over what happened. Anger too because he couldn't follow directions and let me die instead.

Looking down at Lana, her small chest moving up and down with sleepy breaths, I tell myself that if Brian couldn't identify a tampon, he couldn't protect a baby. It's good that I'm here, for however long I'm needed. She didn't ask to be born in this nightmare and then get thrown out in the woods. I want to give her a fair shot. If she never experienced life before, this world may not seem so terrible.

She turns to her side, and I gasp at the sight of her leg. The red mark from before is a dark bruise of purple and black. She's not bleed-ing, but it's caked with blood. Trying not to disturb her, I move her leg to the side to get a better look and notice it's hot to the touch. My hand wraps around her other leg which feels almost chilly in comparison.

Her forehead feels hot too, and it's misted with sweat. Trying not to panic, I get up to find Riley and see him already walking toward us.

"I told you to stay put."

"Has there been some dynamic shift where you are now the president of team Rilyn? You lead – I follow, and take your shit along the way."

"I'm the only way. The only one left. You don't have a lot of options."

My stomach sinks when he throws my words back at me. It bothered him, and that upsets me more than I care to admit.

"I am sorry for what I said before. It was shitty, and it wasn't about you."

He pushes past me, and I grab his forearm to stop him. It would be easy to shake himself free, but he stops and looks down at where my hand grips his skin. "There's something wrong with Lana."

His eyes meet mine, and I see the worry there. "We'll handle it."

He knows.

"What is it? You're the nurse. Is her leg broken?"

"No, I don't think so."

"Oh, thank goodness."

"It's worse than that."

"Fucking hell, Riley," I whine.

I resist the urge to slap him and instead, give a forceful shove to his chest. He barely moves, unbothered by my childish response, but his eyes are uneasy. They look over the sleeping baby with worry.

"I think it's an infection. We need to get antibiotics." Turning back to me, he focuses on my wound. "Wouldn't hurt to get some for your arm, too."

"You don't want me dead?"

"You know I don't. Have you been paying attention?"

It's a fair question to my stupid one. I rest a palm on his chest, thinking I should push him again, but the desire isn't there. My heart sinks, our failure hitting me like a truck. We can't keep a baby alive for a week.

"I don't think I can fight with you, anymore" I admit. "I don't want to."

"We were fighting?"

If there's a moment for him to smile, it's this one, but he refuses. It makes him impossible to read as he covers my hand with his, his heartbeat steady under my palm. "I don't want you to feel forced to wander with me. I can take care of Lana. I can get you somewhere safer. Somewhere closer than Canada."

I'm still, quiet in thought even though I know my answer.

"Caitlyn?"

"Are you going to give me more silent treatment?" I ask.

His eyebrows knit together, and he wants to argue but doesn't. "No, of course not. I couldn't get space to think is all."

He's not wrong. When I say something horrible again, which is bound to happen, I don't want him wandering off in response. I'd rather have him by my side, silently stewing in his anger.

"For now, I want to stay with you, with or without Lana." It takes everything in me not to add a joke or some witty remark, but I let the words hang there because they are true. I like being with Riley more than the idea of death, with or without access to tampons.

I can feel his eyes roaming over me, and I hold my breath, curious what he'll say.

"Okay, then." He nods, stepping back to move closer to the cliffside, looking out at our next stop.

Running my hands down the front of my pants, I collect myself and roll my shoulders back before marching over to his side.

Woods surround us on three sides with a giant city full of bloats out in front. I'm not a fan of becoming black goo, but the only place that would have medicine is full of monsters. I know what we have to do, and if it weren't for the adorable child curled up in the grass at our feet, I wouldn't do it.

"I'll go down there," I offer. "There's got to be a pharmacy somewhere in that mess."

"No way," he scoffs.

I peek over the edge even though my body doesn't want to move. Adrenaline surges when I see them, and I get dizzy looking over the side, the drop hundreds of feet to a rocky floor.

"If we both die, she doesn't stand a chance," I remind him.

"You aren't going alone."

"Listen here, Rambo—"

He grabs my good arm and pulls me toward him. We're chest to chest, his eyes searing into mine, and I can't make words. My voice leaves me, and no matter how much I want to continue this debate, I physically can't. He's not angry, but stern, and something about his hold makes me obey and stay silent.

This close, I can see every curve of his scar, the torn flesh that didn't heal quite right, the muscles that pull underneath. It must have been unbearably painful.

He notices how I stare, and a part of me hates myself for it. I'm making it worse somehow by focusing my attention on something that hurts him still.

"Caitlyn." His voice is calm but rumbles from him. He's not willing to banter or have a discussion. "If you're turned into a bloat down there, you will come right back to us. Right back to that little girl. You can't go alone."

"I thought those were just rumors. Are you sure?"

He nods his head, his hand still firmly holding me close. "I've seen it. The mind is confused at first but the stronger ones fight the change. You'll remember where we are. You'll come back. You could alert others we exist."

He thinks I'm strong, and given that I'm still alive, that's not completely out of the question.

I don't want to be strong. For weeks I've wanted to be dead, but that's the last thing on my mind. Lana is the first, and she needs medicine.

I'm not someone who wanted kids, not like the other women my age. By thirty, a proverbial clock inside me was supposed to tick so loudly that I'd go husband hunting or freeze my eggs, but that never happened. Even when my mother made jokes about dying before she got a grandchild I'd tell her, "That sucks for you," but I'd never offer one up.

Lana isn't fulfilling some deep-seated desire to be a mother, but she was that for someone. Her mother might be dead like mine, but she wanted her and loved her. I can't let her die or that woman will haunt me and make this existence even worse.

"What do you suggest? Take a baby down there?"

One eyebrow raises, the other kept low from burned skin that creeps up his cheek in thick ropes. I've never noticed that before, or I wasn't this close to look at him, to truly see him.

"We go down together."

I rip myself away and attempt to place my hands on my hips. It makes my arm throb, but I ignore the pain.

"We find a pharmacy somewhere else," I argue. "Something less surrounded by death."

"They've all been raided. She'll need something for under the age of two. That's not everywhere. Trust me when I tell you I made an intentional decision to come to a large city pharmacy."

I do trust him, but I don't tell him and give away all my power.

"Riley, I have no survival skills when it comes down to it."

"You have more than you realize. We can do this."

Lana sleeps a few feet away, blissfully unaware of the danger so close. Tears threaten to escape, so I nod and turn around, not wanting him to see.

This entire time, my coldness and indifference were intentional. The apocalypse didn't take my heart because I already lost everything that mattered before the world fell apart. What a fool I am to think I was truly numb, that I could stop caring so easily. One little kid begging for a pacifier, and I'm mush. One scarred man who saves me from a rapist, and I'm finding a will to live.

"When?" I choke out.

His footsteps come slowly while I try to collect myself, each step closer until I feel his hands on my shoulders. I lean back, allowing him to hug me from behind. The embrace pulls at my heart releasing tears that escape down my cheeks.

"We head out before dawn. They're sluggish before the sun is up."

"Riley, if I do turn…"

"I won't let that happen."

But it might, and I need him to know what to do just in case.

"I don't want to go out like that."

His arms curl around my shoulders and tighten, holding me close against his chest. "I know, and I won't let it happen. If I have to…"

"Then you have to. I can't turn into one," I repeat.

He doesn't have to say it, and I'll do the same for him.

It's not murder.

It's mercy.

CHAPTER
SIXTEEN

Riley

"Hey."

She whispers the word, her voice soft and timid, so low it's difficult to make out.

"Good, you're asleep."

I'm not, but with my curiosity piqued, I remain still, Lana curled up between us. I hold my breath, ready for what she wants to say.

"I'm trusting you, which is… probably stupid."

She's not wrong. People are garbage, and she doesn't know me. Fuck, Landon was with me so if she had a choice, I'm sure she'd be gone. I can't blame her.

She has limited options, after all.

I hate how that comment eats at me. My anger about it says more about me than her, and deep down I know why. She's someone I'm starting to care for, not just someone I need to take care of.

"I don't know why I'm here. Not just here, on the ground with a stranger and a baby, but here on this planet. Part of me wonders if I'm dead and this is purgatory. I'd probably deserve it. I'm not the best person."

She groans to herself, rolling over, her mouth at my neck. Lana gets pressed closer between us, her skin so feverish that worry slithers into my mind. Sometimes, knowing what's possible is worse. Everything I've learned from medicine keeps alerting me to every danger that lies ahead. Threats that lead to a death worse than bloats, and there's a high probability Caitlyn and I may need to make a choice. Something akin to, would you rather be hit by a bus or die slowly of cancer?

It's the bus.

Every time.

"And you know… I'm sorry that my words made you think I don't appreciate what you've done for me, or that I don't want to be here with you. I… like talking with you. If I had options of who to face a bunch of apocalyptic monsters with, I'd pick you."

She rocks herself a little, clucking her tongue and sighing.

"I'm sorry about asking about the scar. You seem pretty offended when I bring it up."

That's an understatement. I can't let her go on anymore, apologizing for something we should leave in the past.

"Let's forget about all that," I sigh.

She backs away, and I miss the feel of her, the curve of her body near mine, her warmth.

"You aren't asleep," she deadpans.

"You couldn't tell?"

"Well, Brian snored, and I never let guys sleep over."

I turn to face her, struggling to keep from smiling. That's been happening a lot lately, and at some point, I know I'll smile. I might even laugh. It feels wrong but I can't help it around this woman. "Wow, Caitlyn."

"Don't you judge me."

Her words are louder than she intends, her face freezing when Lana squirms between us.

"Don't worry. She'll have difficulty waking up."

Her face falls, every movement of her pleading eyes apparent in the bright moonlight. She can feel something is wrong with the kid. She might not be motherly, but it's something you simply know.

"That's why I'm worried," she sighs.

She rolls onto her back, staring up at the sky. The stars shine so brightly without the city lights dimming them. There's no smog with the streets free of cars and every factory abandoned. All the oil and gas and muck ceased for eternity.

I look her over, wondering if I would be some guy she rushed away before I got too sleepy. Would I make the cut and stay the night? "It's true," I tell her.

"What is?"

"What your mother said."

She opens her mouth to interject and argue, but I stop her. "So many people never venture from their small towns, their inner circles. They settle down, get married, and some of them have a great life. But others, they don't find love. They just find the best of what's available."

Caitlyn shuts her eyes, swallowing the lump in her throat. "I think she meant it as a warning to go out and meet people. Even before she died, making friends wasn't easy. I can be a bit off-putting if you haven't noticed."

I don't answer, not needing a back-and-forth spat between us.

"You know her dying before all of this, it was a blessing, but I miss her. I miss—" She stops short, her hand covering her mouth, wanting to stop herself from admitting something. "I miss being loved like that. No one's ever loved me like my mom did. That sounds weird or wrong. I'm not saying it right."

My hand itches to reach out to her, pull her close, and comfort her. "I know what you mean."

I want to tell her we should sleep. There aren't many hours before a long journey, but I'm painfully aware this could be our last night alive. Spending it talking with her feels right, no matter what tomorrow brings.

"Being loved is wonderful, but losing that hurts too much," I admit. "It hurts so much you want to die."

"Right," she lets out, the word quick and short. "And you know what? I should have died. I'm not a wife or mother, and I'm no one's best friend. I'm a good time, you know. That bonus body at the bar or the person in the office that you can talk to but never really know. The bridesmaid you ask because you want even numbers. Someone who gets invited places, but no one's waiting for me to show up. No one would have noticed if I survived or not."

"I noticed," I say. "I care if you live."

"You could die."

"Only if it's to save you."

"You're so noble." She tries to laugh but her voice cracks. "You run right into the fire."

I try not to flinch at her metaphor. She doesn't know, and it's not something I want to burden her with yet.

My hand finds hers, and we interlace our fingers. That barricade she's made around her heart is slowly cracking open.

"I'm glad you're alive, Caitlyn. You matter. You're someone worth loving. Just because you were alone for a while, doesn't mean that's what you deserve forever."

There's silence, and I let it be, waiting until she's ready to speak again. One of the best things you can do for a friend is to allow them to sit with things, and let your words sink in long enough to help.

Are we friends?

We're more than acquaintances. The way I feel drawn to know her, the need I carry to break down this wall she's created for herself, I worry I'll want so much more. More than she can offer now, or ever.

"Do I remind you of her?" she asks.

"Who?"

"Your sister? Is that why you want me around?"

A half smile appears, unable to stop myself. "No. Not in the slightest."

"Should I be offended?"

Her brow furrows with curious worry. Does she care what I think of her?

"Not at all, you just… couldn't be more different. She was quiet and overly polite to others. She gave me a hard time. And she was very…" I trail off, realizing I haven't thought about Maisie in almost an entire day. That's a first. Regret typically eats away at my heart, day by day it forces me to remember how I couldn't save her. It's been less than a month, and Maisie is already slipping away.

"What was your favorite memory of her?"

No one asks about the dead or cares enough to know them, but her question is genuine. She wants to know about my sister, something about me that isn't angry or scarred. I touch my face, knowing at some point, I'll have to tell her about that, too.

"She was a nurse, too," I say. "A good one."

Caitlyn bites her lip to remain silent. Every damn thought in that women's head spews from her mouth, and she's struggling to keep her words to herself. I love that about her. She's no bullshit, just her thoughts.

"Maisie Lou Who everyone would call her, and she worked with kids. She would put her hair up in this big circle. Her hair was um—" I lower my hand to Caitlyn's waist and she nods. The touch isn't necessary, but I crave it and won't miss an opportunity. "—really long and thick and it made a huge circle on top of her head."

"A bun," Caitlyn says before she places her hand over her mouth.

"Yeah, okay. A bun. One day this kid puts a construction paper butterfly right in her hair, and then her friend had a ladybug and somehow they stuck it in there, too."

I picture Maisie wearing blue scrubs with dark circles under her eyes, a giveaway she had volunteered for another long shift. In that memory, she's still beautiful, sweeping her blonde strands out of her face, and I think about her smiling while a child places more artwork in her hair.

"It became a tradition. She always had their crafts pinned in her bun like she was wearing a terrarium. She would even let them tape them to her hair."

My mouth feels lopsided from my injury, but for the first time since it happened, I think I'm truly smiling through the disfigurement. This is a memory of pure happiness, and it's catching, allowing me to feel a moment of joy.

Caitlyn's face lights up from my description. I hope telling her this keeps a piece of Maisie alive somehow. She, like Caitlyn's mother, is worth remembering. We should talk about them, and keep them with us through our memories.

"She wore her hair like that for years. Every morning she walked into the hospital with this bright blonde hair she spent way too much money on, and by the end of her shift it was covered in crayon-drawn birds and flowers."

"She sounds beautiful," Caitlyn murmurs.

I nod in agreement. "She's the reason I became a nurse. I didn't have a lot of… direction, but she knew I could learn just about anything."

The moment of joy passes, flashes of Maisie turn from her bright smile in the hospital hallways to the moment I lost her. The image of her eyes, full of fear, pleading for me to listen floods my mind. I can't escape it. I'll never forget it.

"And I let her die."

I place my hand on my scar, clawing into it with jagged fingernails, wanting to rip it off my face.

Caitlyn reaches out, her fingertips gliding across my arm. "I'm sure it wasn't your fault."

"You know I never lost a patient." My voice is so low I wonder if I said the words out loud. "Not one that was a trauma. We had those that were terminal, but when it came to an emergency, I never lost a single one in the hospital, and now… Every time I turn around there's death."

I roll over to my back, place my hands on my stomach, and let out a slow breath, every molecule of oxygen leaving my body. I hold it until I can't take the discomfort and allow myself to breathe again.

"No one dies tomorrow, Caitlyn."

She's silent, worried she's broken something inside of me with all her questions. Maybe she has.

Her hand lifts, curious but maybe too scared to reach for that horrible scar. She chooses instead to run her fingers through my hair. Tingles cover my scalp from the touch before she pulls it back to her side, and curls into the fetal position.

"Caitlyn," I repeat.

"I heard you, I just—"

"No one dies tomorrow. Do you understand?"

The warmth of her hand finds my shoulder, and I grab for it, my hold too tight, but I can't stop myself. One of us is trembling, and I'm not sure which with our fingers intertwined like this.

"Yes," she agrees. "We all survive another day."

It's a promise she has no business making, and if there is a god somewhere up there in the starlight, I thank him for her and those words, and I beg him to make them true.

CHAPTER
SEVENTEEN

Caitlyn

It's far too early when Riley pulls at my good arm, lifting me into a seated position. My eyes blink several times before the world comes into focus. He's packed everything, already wearing Lana on his side. I frown, knowing what the day brings.

"You could have woken me up."

"I couldn't sleep."

The admission reminds me of the night before and my promise, the one Riley was so intent on me making.

When I get back from peeing and trying to clean myself up a bit, there's one pack left on the ground meant for me to carry. I stretch my good arm over my head, feeling the bones pop before strapping it to my back. Riley is already twenty steps ahead, making his way down the side of the hill. The man must have an internal GPS pointing him in the right direction.

The sound of crunching leaves and the morning wind fills my ears as I race up to him. The air from my lips fogs between us, and I shiver from the cold. It must have dropped thirty degrees in the night, and it's only going to get colder.

"What's the plan?" I reach over to pull back the blanket covering Lana's head and her skin scorches mine. "Oh, shit she's burning up."

Riley nods, his lips in a thin line as he walks faster. The trees remain thick, with no clear pathway to walk through, and I keep my eyes cast down, hoping not to trip over rocks or a root. When I glance forward, there are towering buildings in my line of sight. They weren't as prevalent yesterday in the darkness, but our destination looms ahead, a brick forming in my stomach with their proximity.

We get closer, still walking in silence except for my teeth that refuse to stop chattering. My weak arm throbs and aches, and I quicken my pace, hoping to get my blood flowing. Riley matches my speed, and as the city comes into full view, he moves his arm across my stomach, stopping me in place.

"No further."

"Are we camping already?"

He doesn't answer me, setting Lana down before he moves through the trees, looking over the empty skyscrapers and barren streets. There's a drop-off on our left, the city wrapping around our small patch of green.

This state is filled with hills but they don't roll down gently. Cliffs with ninety-degree cuts in the earth line every path, edges where you fall to your death if you step wrong. That might have been tempting at one point, but I'm careful as I inch forward, crouching down and squinting my eyes to look at what used to be a bustling metropolis.

"They're over there." He takes my chin and moves my line of site. "By the river."

Riley leans forward, hooking one arm around a tree as he peers out of the ledge. I resist the urge to grab his shirt and pull him back toward me, but I keep still, my eyes scanning over the bloats below. They made their way through the floors of these buildings, climbing over cars, and busting down doors. Now they're stuck in a repetitive march by the river, circling the city for fresh meat.

"Oh, I guess… that's good. Is that good?"

"We have to cross the river to get north."

Not good.

"Fucking hell," I grumble.

Riley steps back, his hands on his hips as he looks at the landscape. We have a good angle up here, and at least any walking will be going down. I'm done with mountain climbing.

"I saw a pharmacy on the south side of town. There was a power surge overnight and things flickered for a few minutes. That red looked out of place, and I could make out the letters."

"Did you sleep at all?" I grumble.

He shrugs, and I can't read his face.

"How far south? A little south or still smack in the middle of downtown?"

"The middle."

I stare at my feet knowing despite the height of these skyscrapers, the city isn't that big. We'll only be a few blocks from that horde of bloats. "And we have to do this now? There's no waiting?"

"It's a necessity." There's no emotion in his voice, but the assuredness is unmistakable.

"Would you bet your life on it?"

I smile, waiting for him to catch my joke. When he does, he shakes his head and moves back toward me, the faintest hint of a smile hidden on his lips.

"I'd say that I would, Caitlyn."

He ushers me back into the tree line, and I force myself to move, inching back from the death and dread below.

"Bloats are the first threat. They are the most likely to kill us." He's so monotone, but he's right so I don't make any quips and let him continue on his tirade of ways to die. "Next will be exposure. The elements and our ailments from them. We need a hospital-level pharmacy, and that's downtown. They'll have more supplies that are likely intact. Bloats wouldn't get through a locked door or barred windows unless a person was on the other side. People would be less likely to raid any place downtown due to the high number of infected."

"So smart people would stay away."

"We don't have a choice, Caitlyn."

His words are almost pleading. I've nearly died multiple times at this point. Why not roll the dice if he's so sure?

"Okay," I sigh. "Let's get going."

I adjust the pack on my arm and glance back out at the city, daring to look at the group of bloats once more. From up here, they resemble a shuddering grey fog that moves in jerky waves next to the water.

"So who is carrying, Lana?" I ask, turning to leave. "I'm not completely useless, you know."

His hand grips my shoulder and the electricity of his touch stops me in my tracks. I don't turn around, fearful of what he'll see in my face. He steps closer, his chest at my back and fingers squeezing into my skin.

"I wouldn't suggest this if I thought there was another way," he says. "Lana's getting worse."

He's right, and I didn't want to say the words out loud. The way she's sleeping all the time, how her skin feels like it's on fire. She's sick, and without meds, she won't get better.

"I am a little bit like your sister you know." My words hang in the air between us, and I think Riley is holding his breath. It's the last thing he expects me to say. "Being a kid person doesn't always mean you're a nurse or a parent. I'm a kid person, like Maisie was. They're kind of my kryptonite."

I step forward, letting his touch fall away. It almost hurts losing the sensation, and that's when I accept I'm in a lot of trouble with Riley. This isn't just a little crush on a scarred savior. Even if a million men magically re-populated the planet, I'd want to wander around with this cranky one.

We walk in silence. The ominous presence of bloats in the distance suffocates us both. They can't hear or see us, but knowing where they are and getting closer to them puts us both on high alert. In the quiet, the fall of a leaf or crack of a stick makes my heart rattle in my chest. Adrenaline surges me forward, my legs moving on their own. The pain from my arm disappears, replaced by the unease swimming around in my veins.

I care if I live or die.

I tell myself it's because of Lana, a helpless child who needs medicine, but I'm not sure anymore. Becoming a bloat was never a box I wanted to check on my apocalypse bingo card, but if it came down to it, and I had to decide to end it before they turned me, I worry now that I won't. It's hard enough fighting the natural instinct to live when you don't care, but wanting to survive, and deciding to try and live… that adds a new complication to the mix.

"We can't talk," Riley whispers. "Too close to them."

"We haven't been talking for an hour."

He jerks his head in my direction, his eyes narrowed at mine.

"I was just pointing out—"

His palm covers my lips, warm against the freezing air, and he steps closer, his mouth touching the shell of my ear.

"While we're down there, do your best to resist snapping back at everything I say." His other hand cups my shoulder, and I do my best not to sink into his warmth. "You know I just want to keep us safe."

Except I don't know anything at this moment. He's so close, and I'm fighting the need to lean against his chest and nuzzle my face into his neck. He releases my mouth and stares, the hint of the rising sun slicing through the buildings and blinding us at our sides.

"No one dies today, Caitlyn."

I nod, once again agreeing to something I have no control over, and he backs away.

"Wait!" I whisper. "What about Lana? She doesn't know to be quiet."

He adjusts her, the cloth that carries her spreading out against her small frame, and his face sinks. "I don't know if I could wake her up if I tried."

Panic surges through me, and dammit, my eyes begin to burn. I didn't shed a tear over Brian, but I'd cry buckets over Lana. Kids are innocent. They didn't ask to be here, and not just in the middle of the big-bloat apocalypse. They didn't ask to be a part of the world, no matter how good or bad it turned out for them.

"What is that supposed to mean?"

"I think the fever is making her sleep. Her body needs rest to fight the infection. It's not too serious if we get her the right kind of antibiotics."

"And what happens when it's too serious?"

The look he gives me, the way the light in his eyes dull, it sends my heart to my feet.

He turns before I can ask more questions, not that I would know which ones to ask, but I understand we have to hurry. My hand reaches for his pack, careful to stay close and out of sight.

We are at the edge of the city, steps from leaving the safety of the trees and walking straight into danger. It could be argued that the entire world is dangerous, but this mission is borderline suicidal.

I glance up at the buildings overhead and they seem to sway, debris swinging from their broken windows. I'm hit with the smell of burnt plastic, molded wood, and something I can't place at first.

Blood.

It's metallic and sour, filling my nostrils until I can taste it.

We step further into what's left of the civilized world, cement under our feet with weeds sprawling through the cracks. I'm holding my breath, exposed and vulnerable as we walk. One hand grips the back of Riley's shirt, clenched in a fist so tight it shakes from the strain.

Our footsteps are silent and our breaths shallow, every second ticking by slower than the last. Riley points down an alley, and I see them, bloats in lines maybe ten blocks ahead as we pick up our pace, jogging further into the trenches of downtown.

Their sounds get louder. It's not only the occasional somber moan while they communicate, but the slosh of their feet sliding against pavement. It makes me want to vomit which would get us all killed, so I swallow it down and keep moving.

My body shakes with nerves and every emotion slams into me at once, uncontrollable and terrible. Dread and fear, excitement and energy, and the strong desire to sprint the other way all make me tremble down to my bones.

We stop at a street corner with three buildings and a courtyard on one side. My heart pounds inside my chest when I see the lettering on the store up ahead. We've made it to the pharmacy, but the sprint forward is across a block filled with a small playground and some benches. There's not much cover, and I curse the person who felt this greenspace was necessary.

Riley's palm wraps around my wrist, holding me tight to his side. My shivering lessens but doesn't cease, and I'm sure he's questioning having me along. He's calm and steady, and when his eyes meet mine it takes all my focus not to break down into a hysterical sob.

It is insane I've survived this long. I'm not some apocalyptic warrior, bounding off buildings and sprinting through streets of bloats. In every movie, I'd be the girl with a limited backstory and some annoying character flaw, killed in the first fifteen minutes without a tear from the audience.

I'm not built for this, and I'm terrified.

His cheek is on mine, lips against my ear. The roped edges of his scars glide against my skin, and I don't shy away, but lean into them, seeking comfort in his assuredness.

"No one dies today," he whispers.

"You're breaking the rule," I whisper back.

I don't see it, but I feel his cheek lift in a smile. Signs of life from Riley come more frequently now, and I don't want them to go away. I don't want him to die.

Over his shoulder, I look up at the sign. Half-broken red glass and dead bulbs. It's so exposed, out in the open where anyone or anything can see us.

"Is there another way inside?" My voice trembles with every word. I crane my neck to see the pileup of cars on the street next to the pharmacy, and my heart sinks. "We could walk—"

"We have to go, now," Riley insists. His hand grips my bicep, leading me forward. My heart beats so loud I swear I hear it between us, but I take a step, and then another. He looks from left to right around one side of an abandoned building.

"Are you ready?" he asks.

I open my mouth to speak, but something catches my eye. It gleams from the incoming sunlight, a prism of colors that floats in the air just above our heads. Riley notices too, his hand loosening as he turns and looks past me, his eyes focused but confused.

They float around us, between us, circles of clear light coming from out of nowhere. I point, my arm outstretching toward the anomaly.

"Are those bubbles?" I whisper. The soapy circle pops, splashing across our faces. That's when I see him, the person above us. He's leaning over a balcony a few floors up, his silent warning silently crashing across our cheeks.

"We can't go into the courtyard," I mouth to Riley, who nods in defeat.

CHAPTER
EIGHTEEN

Caitlyn

"Fuck," Riley mutters, his grip on me tightening.

We're both staring upward, bubbles popping on our foreheads and tickling our skin. The man waves his hands from side to side, frantically motioning for us to stop. He points at something we can't see from this angle. A threat I presume. That or he's a cannibal and this is all an elaborate trick.

"He looks alright," Riley whispers. "We should probably listen."

His hold on me doesn't ease my fear, and my pulse skyrockets, every breath getting harder to take. It's a miracle I haven't passed out during our escapade.

"Did Landon look alright?" I bite out.

I hear Riley grumble, but he doesn't disagree.

"If he wanted us gone, he has a kill shot."

I sigh in agreement. "Right. If he wanted to kill us, he could just throw a rock and bloats would come running." We stare upward, possibilities ticking through our minds. This amount of talking puts us at risk, but decisions must be made.

The building casts a shadow from the morning light, and Riley pulls us into its cover. "We don't have a choice here."

His other palm slides across the back of my neck as he turns me around, leading us to the broken glass doors on the side of the building. The roundabout that once spun to let everyone inside is covered in jagged shards, but the wall it shares has a gaping hole we can step through. He's pushing me along like a child, and we enter a lobby just as someone swings open a side door.

Bubble man exits, a rifle strapped to his chest, and Riley throws me behind him using his body as a shield. My legs lock up, and I bury my face in his back. If the men are communicating, it's silently. Footsteps grow closer, and when I dare to look around Riley's body, my jaw hangs open.

It's Dumbledore.

I bet he'll have some riddle to allow us safe passage into his secret lair.

My internal shock aside, this man is nearly eighty years old. I guarantee he has grandkids, or maybe great-grandkids. Not the typical survivor of an apocalypse. He must have traded his wand for a machine gun.

"Let's go." Riley grabs my good arm, almost lifting me. We're ushered through a steel door, some back entrance to this office building.

I check Lana's forehead once we're through, feeling her pulse through her blazing skin. It's slow and even, but her fever persists. Chains and steel bars lock into place behind us, sealing the door. We're trapped inside the wizard's castle, and old or young, that could be a problem.

These people could be cannibals, and when Riley releases me, I pull Lana from her wrap and hold her against my chest. She's limp, almost lifeless, her skin burning against mine. Backing up, cold cement hits my back, and I tremble against it, powerless to do anything or go anywhere.

"Caitlyn, we need to go," Riley tells me. He's holding a hand out, sensing I've crossed some line of paranoia, ready to lash out at anyone who approaches. "Now."

"We don't know these wizards," I hiss.

Riley's head rears back. "What?"

"They're coming," the man holding the gun says. The door has a sliver of a window he's peering through before he rolls over a metal cabinet, securing it in place with a large chain.

The inarticulate groaning starts, a continuous sound that invades my ears and activates my flight mode. Before I have a chance to think more about cannibalism and wizards, I'm bounding up the stairs two at a time with Lana against my chest.

The men fly up after me, and we swing around each floor, my lungs burning and legs aching. My weak arm throbs, but I don't loosen my hold on Lana.

"We can slow down," the man calls from below, but I don't listen. Riley is at my heels, and I feel his hand pull at the back of my pants, not stopping me, but slowing me, saving me from myself.

He's at my back when we swing around the sign for the fifteenth floor, his lips at my ear.

"It's okay, Caitlyn."

I'm still going, moving up the steps, panic tight in my chest.

"Twenty-four," a man's voice rings up the center of the stairwell. "Stop at twenty-four."

My head tells me to calm down, but my body won't stop. It's the opposite of everything I've felt these past few months. Dying never sent me into such a spiral before. Now I'm panicked at the thought of death, and it's sending me into a full sprint up twenty flights of stairs.

"Caitlyn, we're safe," Riley pleads. He's holding me back now, forcing me to slow, and I taste blood in my mouth from my bursting lungs. The sign on the landing reads twenty-two, and Riley's arm wraps around my middle, holding me in place. His other hand reaches around, propping Lana up and relieving me of most of her weight. We're all flush against each other, my breaths coming so fast I see stars while my body sways with dizziness.

"Breathe with me," he pleads.

I do, inhaling so deeply it reaches the bottom of my lungs. His chest expands against mine, and I let out the first full breath since we stepped into this city.

"You're okay."

It's a statement, not a question. My fingers tingle, and I worry I won't be able to hold onto Lana much longer. I look down at her chubby face, misted in sweat and pink. A few more breaths, and my vision returns with some of my common sense.

"I'm sorry," I mutter.

Riley doesn't respond but releases me, turning me to face him so he can take Lana and place her back in the wrap. Footsteps grow closer, and I fight the urge to continue running, knowing it's the bubble wizard who let us inside. I look over the center of the stairwell, watching him make his way up to us.

"I'm Riley, and this is Caitlyn," Riley bellows down to him.

"Jim," the man calls back. "You okay, sweetheart?"

His twang strikes me as endearing. It's familiar and comforting. We bounced around during my childhood, moving every few years, but most of my time was spent in Tennessee. I would guess that's where Wizard Jim is from.

As he gets closer, I remind myself this man is not a threat. The chances of him being a cannibal are low, especially because his shirt has some biblical reference printed on the front.

People have used the bible for their own evil devices before, but combined with him looking like someone's grandpa, I'd score him a two out of ten on the eating me to survive scale. He gets a few points in case his grandkids are going hungry.

"Thank you, Jim," Riley says. "I didn't see them. We couldn't."

Jim gets to our landing and leans against the black bars of the stairwell. He pulls a handkerchief from his pocket and dabs his forehead.

"They're getting smarter. Lookouts go first, usually smaller ones to see anyone coming. Those big crowds of 'em only activate if they get the right whines from the herd."

"And did they?" Riley asks. "Get activated?"

He's thinking what I am. Even with bars and chains against the door of this building, if a mass of bloats thinks people are inside, they won't stop until they get to us. They'll climb the side of the skyscraper, tearing off their limbs in the process if they must.

I remember sitting by the tree back at the grocery store, a piece of glass buried inside my arm and bleeding out. Out of sight and mind may be true, but more and more, I think dumb luck kept them at bay.

Our luck may have run out.

"Nah," Jim answers. He straightens himself to pass us and continues up the steps. "Lookout came over because of a sound but there are still animals wandering these parts. Feral and mean. But…" He stops, turns to us, and shrugs. "Well, we'll know for sure when we get to Missy. Few more floors to go."

I'm not sure why the lookout of choice is a geriatric man, but he's making it up the stairs with ease, and we follow. Now that the adrenaline is seeping from my veins, my body aches with every step, my arm screaming in pain from the exertion.

Riley notices, looking over me with concern, but he doesn't say anything. We don't want to appear weak to these people. They may have saved us thinking we can help them in some way.

Jim reaches the landing of the twenty-fourth floor and slams his hand against the steel in three purposeful strokes. A few seconds pass before we hear the clang of metal, something releasing on the other side.

When the door opens we're greeted by another man holding a rifle and wearing a smile. If I had to guess I'd say he's older than Jim, and I try not to let my face show my shock.

"How goes it, Alan?" Jim asks stepping through.

"Missy says it's clear, and that you shouldn't turn off your radio." Alan waves us inside, his eyes flicking to Lana when we pass.

"Well, if they got in, I didn't want them hearing y'all up here now did I?"

Jim pulls out a radio at his side and fiddles with the buttons, a sharp static sound escaping before he secures it back to his belt. I see the bubble gun strapped to his waist and almost giggle. It's so out of place considering the rifle he's holding. Alan notices and taps on the one attached to his belt loop.

"It's quiet you see. When you get close to 'em, you need a way to get someone's attention."

"And a radio makes too much noise," Jim adds.

"Give me your gear," Alan tells Jim. "You've been down on four all morning. I'll take over the lookout."

Jim nods and hands him a few things before Alan tips his ballcap to us and slides around, making his way down from where we came.

Riley and Jim share thanks while I stare agape at the two of them. Following on shaky legs, I resist the urge to slap myself. This can't be real, and if it is, we have more people I have to be wary of. Albeit geriatrics but it's grandpas with guns.

The floor opens to an industry-grade kitchen, and I salivate looking at all the canned goods stacked on the counter. When I spot the tower of Ramen, I do my best not to groan. There's a wall of what I would guess is baby formula, except there's something different about the label. It's not pastels and cursive writing, but more medical. I can make out the vanilla flavor on the bottom right. There's a medical kit attached to the wall, and I rush over only to find some gauze and a defibrillator.

"Your little girl sick?" Jim asks. We haven't been subtle with the way we check on Lana and carry her. Add that to the fact she's flushed and almost unconscious, and anyone could guess she's in trouble.

Another woman enters the kitchen. She's my mother's generation, maybe a little older, but the scowl she makes ages her another few decades.

"Jim," she greets him. There isn't an ounce of kindness in her voice. I imagine she wants to use his full name and berate him like a child even though he's her senior.

"Missy, these folks have a sick kid."

I don't correct him. That won't help us or Lana, and Riley doesn't budge an inch, standing steady with a very sick little girl strapped against his chest.

"We were trying to get to a pharmacy," I explain. "She's got a fever. An infection."

Missy raises her palm to me, stepping forward and slamming a towel that was over her shoulder on a table nearby. Its snapping sound makes me stand at attention, and I clamp my mouth shut as Riley steps between us.

"You two can turn right back around then," she hisses. "The pharmacy is across the street."

"Now, Missy," Jim objects, but his voice is weak, any resolve lost from the presence of their ominous leader.

A few other people trickle in, all Jim's age and all armed.

"You turn around, now." She waves her hand at one of the men, directing him to escort us in the other direction. "I'll radio Alan to let you out."

CHAPTER
NINETEEN

Caitlyn

"We didn't ask to come up here," I explain. Hands on my hips, I narrow my gaze at this woman. She can't be that tough with the name Missy.

Riley turns, his eyes glaring at me to stop talking. This isn't the time for me to argue the point, but they're acting like we raided the castle. A few men behind Missy ready their rifles, and I reach for Lana, but Riley presses her against his chest, keeping his body between me and Missy.

I crane my neck around him. "We haven't even caught our breath from all those stairs and you want to throw us back down."

"You can walk if you don't want to be thrown," Missy threatens.

"Enough, enough," Jim says. He looks tired, weary of whatever game they're playing up here. "They had lookouts rounding the corner. These two would've walked right into a hundred of them."

Missy glares at him. Her wordless expression tells us all she does not give a fuck if we dive right into an ocean of bloats. We aren't her problem.

"Look at the baby," Jim pleads. He steps over, pulling down the wrap that covers Lana's head. "When was the last time any of you saw your grandchildren?"

"When I watched mine die," Missy counters. She waves a hand at the men behind her to come over. "Take them downstairs."

I scan the room, realizing we are the youngest ones here next to Lana, and by a lot. Missy is the only one under the age of seventy-five.

There's something else I notice.

Several residents that have wandered in to see the show are what my mother would call, butt-ass naked. As nude as the day they were born. It is a sight and I feel my jaw hit the floor. This is a serious moment, could be life or death, but I'm staring at some great-grandfather's balls that are almost to his knees.

"Now wait one damn minute," Jim argues. His voice gets louder with every word and by the widening eyes of the crowd, I'm guessing Jim hasn't raised his voice to anyone, let alone Missy. "What is going on with you all?"

"Exactly," I say. "Aren't you cold?"

I notice a couple of women to the side that have a pretty nice body for it to be their final years. That gives me hope. It seems the trick is to not have very large boobs because those things will plummet to the floor, nipples down, swinging by thin and wrinkled skin.

Luckily, I have the tiniest breasts ever seen.

Everyone grows quiet, and I realize I'm pointing at a grey crotch when Riley pushes my arm back down to my side.

"I'm sorry," I sputter. "I'm used to clothes. You all look great. Amazing."

A few chuckles come over the crowd, and Jim turns around and shakes his head.

"Put something on, everyone," he says.

"Hey, you don't have to," I say. "This is your house and you know. Go for it. Be yourself."

"You're rambling," Riley whispers.

"I know I can't stop," I rush out. "There is a lot of skin and other things."

"Like I was saying," Jim raises his voice again, and I do my best to pull myself together. "Look at the kid. She's sick. Even if the lookouts have left, she isn't in any shape to keep going with her parents like this."

I try to keep my face passive at his use of the word parents and the fact that my eyes have just seen about nine old penises. I have never seen that many dicks at once. Even in porn.

Riley reaches for me, his palm open, and I take it, playing the part of the worried mother. His large hand clamps over mine, each finger holding me tightly, and I squeeze back.

We're twenty-four floors in the air with a dozen elder vigilantes. If they called me a fairy I'd try to fly. If I need to be a nudist, hey, I can strip.

Missy seethes in silence for what feels like minutes and then snaps her fingers at a man behind her.

"Smith," she barks. He moves his gun to his back, and she whispers something to him before he goes up to Riley and reaches for Lana.

He is clothed, thank goodness.

We both step back, unsure of what he's doing. We can't make a run for it down twenty-something flights of stairs when they have guns, but we aren't going to simply hand over our pseudo-child.

"I'm a doctor," Smith says.

"I'm a nurse," Riley smarts back. "She has an infection, and we're nearing sepsis."

"See," Jim bellows out. "The kids dying. What's wrong with all of you? Put your damn guns down."

No one moves, and we're in a stand-off.

"Oh, for fucks sake," I groan. "You can look at her and see for yourself, then. But keep guns and, um, any peni away from my kid."

Riley's hand squeezes hard, and I'm shocked those words came out seamlessly, but it looks like they believed the lie. It's more of a fib. Everything is finders keepers, and we found this baby.

"And we should take a look at you," Smith adds, his eyes narrow in at the bandage on my arm. Somewhere in the rush through the city or up this building, my wound opened. Blood seeps through the white, a few globs making their way down to my elbow.

"No," Missy argues. "Just the kid."

Smith eases Lana from us, and the moment she's in his arms, he shoots Missy a look. His lips form a thin line as he walks over to her, his shoulders lifting to his ears. It doesn't take a long examination to see Lana's got a horrible fever and she's limp.

"Now what is going on here," a frail voice comes from behind the armed Dumbledore army. "You just... move over you." There are two voices, ladies and surprise surprise, they are older than Christmas but at least they're wearing dresses.

"Oh, my goodness a baby!" one squeals.

Missy pulls at one of them to push them back, but four others come behind her, oooing and ahhing at the sight of Lana. They stand around Smith, their hands flying to their mouths and worry filling their eyes. Some are naked, but I give up.

Riley and I stand near the doorway, ready to be kicked out at any moment. There is still an argument brewing between the men and Missy. A few times I hear Jim raise his voice, the group visibly disturbed by his anger.

Smith goes to turn on the sink and curses at himself when nothing comes out before he gets some water from a cooler and wets a rag. Old habits die hard.

He cleans her up a bit, examining her leg and the rest of her while Riley and I wait.

"What's wrong with her?" one of the old women asks, her nipples swaying as she walks. I cannot look away. It's mesmerizing.

Smith mumbles something to them, and I strain to hear but can't.

What's best for Lana is for us to wait, but as time passes I grow edgy, my arm throbbing and aching. Riley eyes my wound, and when Jim comes over, he asks if we can dare to use any of their medical supplies.

"Do you have any gauze? Anything?"

"I'll ask, but..." Jim trails off. Missy and Smith walk over, stopping at Jim's side. One of the clothed women holds Lana, rocking her back and forth.

"Let's sit," Smith says before Missy can open her mouth.

I don't like her, but she hasn't tied me up to a spit to roast me and serve me to her nudist colony, so I'll tolerate her while we're here. Smith motions to a cafeteria-style table that's folded down by the window. I take the time to look around before we take a seat examining everything while we walk.

There's a calendar that hasn't moved since October, some health company's logo displayed as the top image. This place has four refrigerators, which I'm guessing don't work and haven't for some time. A balcony outside has open coolers to collect rain.

There are a few walkers in the corner and an abandoned electric scooter. All the posters on the wall are people who are much older with white hair.

We're in an assisted living facility. Maybe it wasn't that before, but it is now. This could have been a rehab center or medical office space. They could have sold supplies here, perhaps.

Smith waits until we all take a seat, and based on the look on his face, he doesn't have good news.

"We have antibiotics here, but Missy is reluctant to use them on strangers."

I avoid looking in her direction. She doesn't sit, instead pacing near the table, refusing to give Lana a second glance. Part of me understands her motives. This brave new world is full of assholes, and she's trying to keep her people alive, but this is a baby. Even my dark heart bleeds for a kid.

"What kind?" Riley asks.

"Everything from Amoxycillan to Vancomycin."

"This is some sort of home… medical center or something for senior citizens?" I ask out loud. It's been half an hour of me keeping my thoughts to myself. They had to spill out eventually.

"We were an adult living center," Jim offers. "The workers left, but the supplies are still here. We've managed, and I think we can make it."

"So why do you have that sorry look on your face?" Riley asks. I hold back a laugh, curious if I'm rubbing off on him.

"Because Missy won't allow you to use the antibiotics without replacing them. We can administer your daughter, um—"

"Lana," we both say in unison.

"We can give Lana a few day's worth of treatment, but you have to return with more antibiotics or Missy won't allow any more."

"And she rules this place?" I ask. "She's god here?" She can hear me. I know this, and I hope she chokes on my words.

"She's kept us alive," Smith says. "And I don't disagree that we can't diminish our supply without being paid back in some way."

"I disagree," Jim huffs.

Smith places a hand on his shoulder. "And your vote was taken."

One of the women stomps forward. "Was our vote taken?" We turn to the crowd of ladies that has grown by a few. They are in awe of Lana, giving her attention and love.

"Have I steered any of you wrong before?" Missy bites out. "You love that baby so much, well, without antibiotics at some point, there won't be anyone to care for her."

"Is that formula?" I point to the stacks of cans, and Smith turns to look.

"It's a nutritional supplement, but yes, you could call it formula," he answers.

I remember where I've seen cans like that before. My mother ate that with oats when she got sick. That much, and a shelf life of a few decades, they could survive here until Lana is twenty.

"Take the baby to the living area," Missy orders.

She's worried I'll try to steal something, but she's way off base. Riley's hand touches my thigh, squeezing slightly. We're both thinking the same thing.

"I'll just run over to the pharmacy, grab some bottles that end in 'cin, hope for the best," I say, scooting my chair back and standing. It makes a loud scratch on the slick floor.

"Just like that?" Smith raises an eyebrow.

I shrug. "And if we don't make it back?" I ask. "What then? What do you do with her."

One of the ladies is already digging around in a dead refrigerator, no doubt trying to grab some medicine for Lana.

"Maggie, wait a minute, let me help," Smith says, standing and walking over to her.

"You don't replace the antibiotics, we'll stop the treatments," Missy orders.

"We can't—" Jim interjects, but she grabs her gun and points it at us. "We won't continue, and she'll die."

I don't buy it for a second, but I won't risk it either. Riley rises, grabs me by the elbow, and heads for the door, Jim scurrying after us.

"A little dramatic, Missy," I mutter under my breath. Riley shushes me as we make it to the exit.

"I wish things could be different," Jim mutters as we walk toward the exit.

Except they are already different. With or without more antibiotics from a pharmacy, they will help her. I know it, and so does Riley. We're going, but if we die the second we leave this building, Lana will live.

"I'll take you down," Jim says.

We both nod, and I ache to say goodbye to Lana, but she's too out of it to notice. That and I don't want to do anything to risk the arrangement just made. Her life depends on it.

"Hey, Smith," I yell out as we pass through the door. "Tell the vag-coven thanks." His jaw hangs open as the door shuts.

We start down the stairs, and I take the lead. Death waits for no one.

"She's a confusing young thing," Jim tells Riley. "Beautiful, but odd."

"You have no idea," Riley agrees.

CHAPTER
TWENTY

"You'll have to forgive Missy," Jim tells us. "We're all just doing the best we can." He's walking with us back down the abandoned stairwell, a backpack slung over his shoulder this time. It's musty, the air thick with dust, and my legs burn from the effort. "And don't worry. Smith has this under control. He's a vet. "

"A vet?" Riley barks.

"You know some say becoming a vet is harder than a doctor," I add. "Animals can't tell you what's wrong."

Judging by the look Riley shoots me, that was not the thing to say. I skip down a few more steps to get some distance between us.

"We have a drone," Jim says. "Wherever you manage to get to, I'll land it there as soon as I can. Load its basket with the medicine. The sooner we get it over, the safer that baby will be."

This we all agree on, and as we descend the last few floors in silence, my stomach ties in a knot. The metal door to the lobby might as well be a doorway to hell.

"Is there anything else we need to know about them? Things you've observed from above?" Riley asks.

Jim removes his ballcap and scratches his head, his face contorting with thoughts of the bloats surrounding us.

"They can't see that far. They're slow as a snail unless they have a target."

"Oh, we know," I groan. I cross my arms and lean against the chains, hearing them clink behind my back.

"I've watched about a million die, but the numbers don't look any lower. Makes me wonder if some are hiding somewhere."

I've never seen a dead bloat, and I wonder what that looks like. I imagine a river of black sludge, and the knot in my stomach tightens.

"It's hard to say if there's something else that could help you. We always have someone on watch on the fourth floor, but not today if you all are going over there."

"Because any attention will be drawn to us so why bother," I chime in. Both men fix their eyes on me, and I sigh. "I'm just being honest."

"I'll be where I can best fly the drone," Jim says. His smile doesn't reach his eyes, and I can't seem to return the gesture.

"Thank you for all you've done, Jim." Riley places a hand on his shoulder, some act of forgiveness for the sins of his neighbors. Something about the embrace is a goodbye and not just for now. It's forever.

I think about the looks on the women's faces, full of joy at the sight of Lana. What a childhood, growing up adored by a dozen grandparents. On the road with us, she doesn't stand a chance. That's all we can give her. A chance.

"They move in packs," Jim continues. "Lookouts take the lead and alert them with some high-pitched wailing noise. No clue what the language is. We've spent this whole time analyzing the sounds and nothing. Eventually, they combust, that ooze leaking everywhere. You might see some dark stains on the pavement, but so many have exploded, who knows."

I hold back the vomit in the back of my throat.

"I'm sorry, they explode?" I ask. "They eventually become a goo grenade?"

Jim nods. "Not quite that lethal. More like a goo overflow, and then they kind of collapse. The ones that are most distended are the first to go. They look like a walking balloon."

I rub my palm against my stomach and suck in a few deep breaths. "That's just super."

"It is," Riley adds. "Their numbers must be dwindling. That's great news."

Riley starts unlatching the chains across the door, but he focuses on me. I'm sure he's finding me to be quite the liability, but it's too late. Lana isn't his patient, but he's taken responsibility. Even if I'm not much help, he could throw me in the way of a pack of bloats. I might roll and take them out like bowling pins, some of them popping along the way.

"Watch out for the halflings. They're smart, and they don't turn people, they take them, never to be seen again. If I had to bet, they're the ones calling the shots."

Riley pauses, his hand against the door, and I cock my head to the side. Judging by his blank expression, this is new information for both of us.

"We don't know what you're talking about," I say. "Halflings?"

"Oh, good. Something I can help you with."

Jim perks up, stepping forward to help Riley with the cabinet blocking the door. "There are some that never change completely. They look very human compared to the others. We've seen a few speak their language and English. I witnessed one on the street convince a woman to talk to her and then they walked together to the apartment building a few blocks from ours."

I think of the woman at the grocery store, half-changed, still recognizable as a person. She didn't speak to me, but what could I offer her? It was Brian and me alone in the store, and she thought we were dead on arrival. Was she their leader?

"What happened then?" I ask.

Jim sets down the last chain, the door now free to walk through. "I don't know. We never saw her again."

It doesn't need to be said what happened to her. I wonder if halflings ever pop like the others. Will there always be a threat and the only hope is some snow-covered cabin in Canada? Damn, I'm tired of being cold.

"I need a weapon," I murmur under my breath, wondering what I would do if I had no chance at escape. Would I be able to slice a critical artery or jump from a building? These are questions I should have asked Smith the vet. There are the pills Riley carries, but those would take too long in a pinch.

"I brought what I could get out of Missy's sight," Jim says. He puts his backpack on the floor, pulling out a few things. One gun, which Riley snags before it registers with me what he's holding. A sheathed knife that I assume gutted animals at one point, but I am technically an animal, so I take the heavy metal, fastening it into the back of my pants. He gives Riley a radio and a firm pat on the arm, sending him off in some wordless goodbye. "There's some food still in that pharmacy. I've seen it with binoculars."

I smirk at Riley and place my hands on my hips. "Great. A last supper. Maybe they have Ramen."

He rolls his eyes before giving Jim a half hug. "Thank you, Jim. Will you be on the other side of the radio?"

"Yes. You're a nurse you said?"

Riley nods.

"Okay, so you won't need Smith. You know what to get."

"Yes. As long as I can get to it."

The two men separate, Riley turning and placing his hand on the door handle. He pushes down, his shoulder pressing into the steel and every cell in my body awakens, ready to run or fight.

"Thanks. We appreciate it," I say to Jim.

Following Riley, a gust of cold air hits my skin as we step into the empty room, the steel door creaking shut behind us, and the dull noise of closing locks begins.

We could run. Leave her behind with our weapons and maybe our lives, but I know that's not possible for either of us. Riley has some sacred duty to help people, and I'm a sucker. If I'm going to die in this apocalypse, I'm not going to do it an asshole. Maybe I don't think there's a lot of good left in this world, but Riley is changing my mind. He's changing me.

I almost break out into laughter at the thought of being one of the last few good people alive. I'm not the nicest person if you ask around.

Too literal for everyone's good. It's not like I gave to charity or volunteered, and I'm the definition of a lapsed Catholic. My mother would say I'm "figuring it all out," but that's a nice way to say I'm selfish.

Sure I don't want others to die alone or in pain, but I had no greater purpose in life. There was no desire to save them unless thrust upon me. Things feel different in this empty lobby with Riley.

I feel responsible.

The knife hangs heavy on my back, and I imagine myself poking a rounded bloat, its contents popping like a balloon. I gag at the thought.

"Are you ready?" Riley asks.

"No."

He takes my hand, pulling me along, our footsteps echoing and sounding impossibly loud. We step through the opening of glass, shards crunching under our feet.

Our backs remain flush against the building wall as we edge closer to the street, shuffling ourselves closer to the grassy open area.

When we get to the corner, I look up, hoping there will be some hidden message in bubbles overhead.

There's nothing.

My hand grows sweaty against Riley's, nerves taking over. He holds the gun in his free hand, and I assume it's ready to go. I've never shot a gun, and I wonder if he has.

We can't radio Jim out in the open and draw their attention to us, but at this angle, we are at a severe disadvantage. I remind myself not to scream if I see a bloat. That is the last fucking thing we need right now.

Riley pulls my hand to his chest, his grip on me so tight, it throbs in his hold. He's about to take off, and I peel myself from the wall, readying myself to sprint.

Before he starts, he lifts our clasped hands to his mouth, his lips meeting my skin with a soft kiss. My head spins in a daze from the kindness. It's unlike him, and maybe that's because we are about to die. A kiss goodbye of sorts.

I would have preferred it on the mouth, with his tongue gently massaging mine, his hands running underneath my shirt and—

Riley takes off. My fantasy interrupted by the yank of my arm.

My mind goes blank as we sprint through the open block, exposed to any bloat in sight.

CHAPTER
TWENTY-ONE

I don't dare look around, fearful of what I might see. There's still a small chance I'll scream if a bloat comes into view, so this is better for everyone. We reach the pharmacy door, and by some insane miracle, it's perfectly intact. Riley pulls at the handle, and I wince, ready for some blaring chime to ring out.

There's no sound, thanks to lack of electricity, and I help him get it open, the weight of it unusually heavy without a motor to help. Stepping through, he yanks me behind a checkout counter, and we fall onto a pile of cigarettes, change, and dollar bills left from the behind register.

At one time, money ruled my life. Will I have enough for rent? Should I have splurged on sushi with coworkers when my electric bill doubled this month? The credit card debt felt like a weight on my back, a nagging reminder creeping up my neck whenever I swiped. Would the damn thing decline, leaving me embarrassed? Standing at checkout with a cart of groceries caused unbelievable stress.

We're lying on hundreds of dollars, rolls of change that have burst and left shiny pools of quarters and pennies, and neither of us cares. It's worthless paper, trinkets from a past life.

On top of Riley, my heavy breaths against his chest, I try to relax. My fingers curl into the fabric of his shirt as I remain still, focusing on staying silent and waiting to hear their noise.

Minutes pass with both of us ready for our inevitable end. It's not smart, Riley splayed out on his back while I lay on top of him, his arms wrapped around my body. If a bloat army burst through the doors, we wouldn't be in a position to fight.

But I can't move.

His arms tighten around me, and I sink, my eyes closing for a moment, allowing myself to rest against his chest. This isn't something I could do with Brian. He wasn't a person to hold. That may be because any indication of physical contact signaled to him we should have sex. A woman can't relax when every touch leads to her pants off, even if it is nice most of the time.

Most of the time.

"We're okay," Riley whispers. I don't move, not wanting this moment of peace to end. I'm not okay. I'm terrified that everything I thought I knew about myself is shifting. There's this man I'm beginning to care for and a baby that needs us both. If my mother is somewhere watching, she's certainly laughing. She always got a kick out of my best-laid plans bursting into flames.

"Are you ready?" he asks.

"Yep. Yep," I lie.

Moving both hands to his sides, I lift myself, his grip loosening around my middle. Coins clink and slip beneath my palms while his fingertips trail down my body. His touch feels too perfect, sending small sparks across my skin. Resisting eye contact with him, I stand, brushing off the legs of my pants and kicking a few boxes of menthol lights to the side.

"Have you ever smoked?" I ask, desperate to refocus my crazed mind.

"Those things will kill you. Might be a good time to start." He pauses, waiting a moment before standing. I laugh and bounce on my toes a few times from nerves.

"Let's go," I say as he rises. The awkward moment has passed, but now the real fun begins.

"Pharmacy is in the back."

He steps past me and hits the lock on the door, moving back so fast I don't register what occurred. "We need to stay away from the glass. Not out of the woods yet."

I almost chuckle at his actions. "You think that tiny lock would stop them?"

He shrugs. "Slow them down, maybe. This way."

Without thinking, I reach out my hand. He glances down, and I try to yank it back, realizing how ridiculous I'm being, but then his palm is against mine, warm and strong, leading me to the dusty pharmacy sign that hangs in the store's corner.

We tip-toe through the aisles, weary of what could jump out and surprise us. Most everything has been ransacked, and every step we take is over garbage and empty boxes. Riley stops, and I follow suit, my body pressed against his back knowing this has been too easy. My heart pounds inside my chest, every one of my senses on high alert.

"Should we grab those?"

Riley points to a pink box. It's in pristine condition with women stretching in fancy yoga poses on the front. Tampons. A find of epic proportions. There's a few behind it as well, and I make a sound of delight into his shirt.

He rips open a box and dumps it into his bag. I'm smiling so big my cheeks hurt when Riley looks back at me with a lopsided grin. I'm getting used to that sight. He squeezes my hand which sends a bolt of lightning through my body.

When we reach the pharmacy, the high from moments earlier dissipates. This was too easy, and we've reached our first obstacle, and it's a big one.

Being downtown, I should have known there would be something between us and a room of narcotics, but I had hoped that the bloat army hit so fast they wouldn't have time to lock up.

No such luck.

I can see the medicine lined in pretty rows behind a thick pane of glass. Everything we need is within arms reach, but it may as well be in the clouds. I place one palm on the window and rest my forehead against the cold barrier, my breath fogging up the glass and blurring what's inside.

"Fuck," I grumble.

Riley releases my hand and walks around the corner of an aisle. The drive-through is visible from where we are, all barred up with lines of black steel.

"Fuck," he says noticing we're blocked on both sides. There's a consultation window, also blocked by two-inch-thick glass.

"They must have been closed for the night," I grumble. "Some places do all this extra protection because of what they carry I guess. Can we break through it?"

Riley shakes his head, rubbing the stubble of his chin in thought. He must shave somewhat regularly, and I can't blame him. I bet where his scar is located, it makes a beard look and feel a bit odd. Maybe we should scrub the mission, grab some razors with our tampons, and get out of town.

No, Caitlyn, I right myself of the negative thoughts. *We are getting her medicine back there.*

"Okay, so what's easier to break through?" I ask. "The glass or the wall."

"Exactly what I was thinking."

I pace in front of the pharmacy, inspecting it as best I can with my very limited construction knowledge. "But you do think we can get through."

Riley pulls out his gun, staring at the chamber. My chest tightens knowing what he's thinking and part of me, the suicidal part, agrees it might be the only way.

"That looks like it's going to be loud."

He nods, shifting his eyes from the glass to me.

"If you get a few shots in the same spot, we can break the glass open enough to get through, can't we?"

He nods, again.

"You think there's an ax in here?"

I sprint around the store before he answers, ducking when I get close to a window. Riley's feet shuffle along somewhere close, and I find an automobile section, finding what looks like a wheel club. It's heavy with a large hook at the end, enough to give me some leverage if I grab onto the glass and pull. When I reach Riley, he's holding an aluminum bat.

We both take a deep breath and make our way back to the fortress of a pharmacy. Riley pulls out his radio, turning the dials until the static clears.

"Jim, you there?"

"Yes, sir. Glad you two made it. Coast is mostly clear."

Mostly?

"That's good because we have an issue."

There's silence on the other side, Jim waiting to hear what might kill us next. He seems nice, a rarity these days. I grab at the radio, but Riley won't release it from his hand. Hitting the side button, I speak to Jim while Riley watches.

"Hey, if we don't make it, we need you to make sure Lana is okay. Steal all the antibiotics if you have to. Lana seems like a sweet kid in the few days we've been with her."

"You're not her parents?"

"No," Riley admits. "But she deserves a chance. We're risking our lives for her, and I know it's a big ask for you to do the same."

I smile at him and lean into his chest. His arm wraps around me, and I swallow the lump in my throat. We haven't known each other long either, but I think to myself how we deserve a chance, too.

"I wouldn't worry too much, kids. The women have barricaded around her. She's safe."

I exhale in relief. He sounds honest, and those women looked caring.

"What are you planning to do?" Jim asks.

Riley pulls the radio back to his lips.

"Pharmacy is secured with tempered glass. I'm not sure how many layers, but I'll have to get some rounds through before it breaks."

I can hear the clicking of the radio, Jim is starting to speak but is apparently at a loss for words. He's likely going through the scenario himself, thinking about options and running out of all ideas except the one we've proposed. The one that will surely kill us.

"We can make it to the roof, at least," I whisper against Riley's chest.

"Jim, do you have the drone on the roof?"

"I – I will in sixty seconds. I promise. I didn't want to… make noise while you were in there."

That ship has sailed.

Right into the Bermuda Triangle.

"Hey, Riley. There's a lookout about twenty blocks west. That's not at your doorstep, but once they signal, you'll have about five minutes."

"That's enough time to get to the roof," I say aloud.

Riley clicks the radio on once more. "When you hear the shots, get moving on the drone. We'll work fast."

"Okay, and one more thing."

We wait, ready for some monologue about how we can do it, and this isn't the end.

"I'll die trying to save that kid," Jim promises. "You can count on me for that much."

As much of a relief as those words are, I know what he's saying without telling us.

We are dead.

<h1 style="text-align:center">CHAPTER
TWENTY-TWO</h1>

Halloween wasn't my favorite holiday, but I'm about twenty-plus years removed from trick-or-treating age. I don't have kids, and I lived in a high-rise apartment. All those things added up to an anti-climatic All Hallow's Eve.

For some reason, costume parties were all the rage, but I avoided them by volunteering at the hospital most nights. Maisie loved this because I was the only male nurse who would do whatever she wanted for her kids' Halloween events. I had no choice. She was my sister, and no matter how old we were, she threatened to tell Mom.

There were a few times people would offer to take my shift under the guise of being a friend. In truth, it was a few nurses taking bets on who could get me out first, and from what I understood, the pool had gotten high. If they wanted to win, inviting me to a Rocky Horror Picture Show wasn't the way to get me on a date.

I politely declined, as always. It's not that my co-workers weren't smart or beautiful, but they were similar to all the other women I came across. It would be a waste of my time and theirs.

Working in a hospital, you have a truer sense of making every moment count. I watched people leave this earth far too soon, and that was before the apocalypse. My adult life has been filled with the knowledge that we aren't promised tomorrow, so when someone who wasn't my type asked me to go out, I refused for both our sakes. Why waste someone's time with me when they could be finding the person meant for them?

It's math and science, and nothing more. That's medicine and that's companionship. You need chemistry between each other, an attraction to the person, and a desire to spend every moment by their side. Once you find them, there are a finite number of years before times up.

That number is markedly shorter after the world went to shit.

This past October, Maisie dressed up as Elsa, a crowd favorite for about a decade running. I would wear whatever she'd picked out as soon as the sun went down without complaint. Trick-or-treating started at dusk twice a week, but in a place where kids can't leave the bed, we bring the candy to them. I expected to dress as whatever Disney character would make little girls light up when I entered the room, and that was fine with me. Rumor was Maisie wanted me as either Kristoff or his reindeer Sven.

I was rooting for Sven.

When four in the afternoon hit, I texted Maisie that I was taking a nap in an on-call room. I'd been up since three in the morning, and if I didn't get some rest, I wouldn't make it to dozens of rooms with a smile on my face.

She sent back a thumbs up, and I fell asleep as soon as my head hit the flat pillow. Hours later, when the chaos made its way into our hospital, turning nurses and doctors into something I couldn't imagine in my worst nightmares, Maisie was the first thing on my mind.

It started with screams, which isn't uncommon for a hospital, but these felt different. Visceral and panicked, the cries that echoed down the hallway sent a chill down my spine.

Sickness and pain can change a person, making them look inhuman, but when I opened the door to the outside world, I knew this was something new. A plague or medical warfare, and for the first time in my career, I didn't know how to help.

A woman in her hospital gown, one that I hadn't seen out of bed for weeks held a man in place with her bony and bruised arm. His feet hovered over the ground while she lifted him, something inside her flowing into him, changing him. They vibrated together while patients, nurses, and doctors cried out in shock at what they saw.

"Maisie!" I screamed, knowing I had to get to her.

Someone sprinted to the stairwell on my left, and I joined them. We flew down the floors, hearing the mayhem right outside the cement walls.

I needed to get to my little sister.

You learn about illness in medicine, but most people don't see the horror in real life. Smallpox, Yellow Fever, and The Black Death were all things the world remembered from history. Whatever I witnessed in that hallway was a rapid manifestation of something new, and I had to get to Maisie before it found her.

She wouldn't want to leave her kids, but I couldn't let what happened to that man kill her. I wouldn't.

They were evacuating the floor when I reached her, beds scattered around the hallway and my sister checking rooms in a ripped and bloodied Elsa dress. If it wasn't for the explosion coming from the surgical wing, I don't think I would have gotten her out of there. She would never have left.

It rocked the building and knocked her into a cement wall. Her limp and unconscious body was easy to carry, and once I found a hallway not spewing with the infected, we escaped.

Several families followed in my direction down the back hallways of the hospital. There weren't any children who didn't have a guardian by their side twenty-four hours a day, especially on a trick-or-treat night. That may not have saved them, but it gave the kids a chance.

When we scattered into the street, I took for the hills, knowing easy prey was first to go. Some followed and others didn't, but it was too late to go back for anyone. My only regret is not grabbing medicine on my way out. There wasn't time, and it wouldn't have saved Maisie, but I would do anything for it today.

Caitlyn doesn't know about pharmaceuticals. From what I understand, she had a corporate job that couldn't be further from the medical field. I think she understands the basics. Infections cause fever. Fever is a bad sign. Antibiotics fight infection.

She doesn't know what to look for in there. Mixing agents, what has to be refrigerated, and things that could make a treatment useless are in my memory. She shouldn't be here, but there's no way she would let me come alone. Missy wouldn't be keen on letting one of us stay behind either, so we're stuck.

I may not like Missy, but I understand her and the decisions she makes.

A rogue leader, one that volunteered themself into a position of power because they had the confidence to do so, despite not having the knowledge or skill. Someone who leads innocent people to slaughter under the wrong circumstances. It's been in our history for generations. Ever since someone stood up and said, "I'm in charge," and everyone else breathed a sigh of relief that they didn't have to make the decisions. Missy's been lucky in her command, but I see the cracks in her system.

They have lookouts on the same floor day after day. Over time, bloats will notice. Their food supply isn't secured, and during the commotion of us entering their kitchen unannounced, one man stole two cans. I'd bet several of the weapons don't have enough ammo, likely stolen from offices or apartments in the building.

I grab the radio one more time and tell Jim all of this. He needs to know and make sure Missy turns that place into a stronghold.

I hope that's what we find up north. Societies need enough population to keep an eye on a perimeter. Food supplies have to be kept up and projected to maintain a population.

They're Rapunzel in a tower, completely dependent on what they have to last, waiting out the enemy.

They can if these monsters keep dying, but not without a few changes. When I'm done, Caitlyn is standing against an aisle of vitamins, her eyes welling with tears.

"Not a chance of surviving is there?" she asks. "For us?"

I swallow the lump in my throat and look her over. She's dirty and thin, and somehow still, too beautiful for words. I'm drawn to her, and the need to protect her surges through my veins.

I take a wide step forward and grab her by the waist before she can pull away. "Listen to me." Her hands reach my shoulders, the touch exhilarating, and I fight the urge to kiss her.

"No one dies today," I promise before I release her and aim the gun.

CHAPTER
TWENTY-THREE

CAITLYN

I cover my ears and close my eyes, waiting for the blast that will seal our fate. This was bound to happen, some massive fuck up sending them to us. We both knew it but showed up here anyway.

It didn't have to be this way. Riley is the type to prevail on his own, but then he finds some blood-soaked idiot in the woods. Despite his outward appearance, he's too nice to outlive the apocalypse. If he never stopped for me, they would be halfway to Canada, Riley none the wiser that his partner is a piece of shit.

I bite my lip and try to calculate how fast someone can walk a mile, and how many miles there are to Canada. Maybe he'd be a tenth of the way there, but the point is, he wouldn't be in a dilapidated pharmacy about to shoot out plexiglass to get antibiotics for a kid.

The gun remains steady in his hands, his aim square in the center of the window. I want to ask him if he's ever shot a gun, but he looks the part so I keep my mouth shut. He doesn't bother to ask if I'm ready. Neither of us is, but all we can do is keep going.

"Kneel behind that shelf," he says jerking his head to the side. "In case the bullets bounce back."

"That can happen?!"

I can feel him rolling his eyes, but he doesn't move. "Honestly, I don't know. Can you get out of the way, though?"

I step to the side, my hands still over my ears, and the moment I crouch down—

Bang.

The sound vibrates the walls, and I peek my head around the corner. A small snowflake spreads across the glass, a pinprick hole in its center. I squint, focusing on the spot to see if it made it through.

Bang.

The second blast startles me, and I land on my knees, my hands slapping on the slick floor. When I look back up, I see the second blast landed less than an inch from the first.

Damn, he's a good shot.

Bang.

The spiderweb of cracks grows wide, reaching the wall's top and sides before he shoots again.

Bang.

"Caitlyn!" he yells, raising his boot to kick before he rears back with the bat and swings.

I grab my tool and hook it into the glass, using one foot as leverage against the wall below. With all my body weight, I lean back, the hole growing and spreading. It's working. Our efforts make a hole big enough for us to crawl through. The relief is short-lived when the radio crackles to life.

"They're coming!" Jim warns.

We don't respond, but the words send Riley into a frenzy. He throws his bat through, and grabs me, my feet lifting from the ground as my tool clangs to the floor.

I go feet first through the opening, barely finding my footing before Riley is at my side, both of us face to face with neat rows of white bottles with tiny black writing on the labels.

I'm clueless about what any of it means, but Riley moves with purpose, his eyes scrolling through the short aisles, bolting down one that catches his interest.

"Find the exit to the roof," he yells back at me. "It's in here."

"How do you know?"

"Because it wasn't out there."

Passing Riley, who's shoving something from a shelf inside his bag, I move along the perimeter. I'm a rat in a cage, but there has to be an exit.

A steel door comes into view, warning labels plastered over the front. I sprint toward it and push the lever, but nothing budges. My body flies into a panic when I push again.

Locked.

"Riley we have a problem!"

"I need another minute. I'm coming."

The radio buzzes again, Jim's voice giving us more bad news. "They're at your heels. Get moving."

My hands slide over the metal, looking for something to help us escape. There are a dozen warnings, paths of egress, and then…

"I have to pull the fire alarm to get out!" I yell.

"Do it," Riley orders. "I'm almost done."

"Will it sound?"

"Do you think it matters, Caitlyn? Get us out of here."

It feels wrong to draw so much attention to ourselves, signaling with sirens where we are located even though they know. In less than a minute, this place will fill with bloats, but I still have to force myself to wrap my fingers around the red lever that reads, *fire,* and pull.

"Pull it, Caitlyn!"

"I will! Dammit, Riley. This sucks. This sucks. This sucks."

"Now!"

I wipe my hands down the front of my pants, hype myself up, and yank.

The sound roars to life, loud and angry, still alive by some battery that must last decades after the world ends. Riley jogs toward me, bat in hand as the door clicks open.

"What do you think that's going to do?"

We push through, and he uses the bat to wedge against the handle, locking it as best we can from the other side.

"Don't lecture me about how this won't hold them off," he says before grabbing my hand and yanking me up the metal stairs. I bite my tongue because, dammit, he's right. I'm dying to crack a joke about that pathetic attempt at a barricade, but mostly, I'm just dying. We both are. There is no getting out of this.

The alarm still sounds through the stairwell walls, its ringing alerting every bloat and human of our location. The door to the roof opens without a struggle, and we step out into the sunlight. Riley points to the edge. "There."

The drone sits at the ready, and Riley sprints to it like he's sliding into home base. He finds the hooks to secure our precious cargo, Jim's voice blaring through the radio. I'm too far away to hear his warnings as I creep to the edge, daring to look over the side.

Hundreds of them pour through the streets. It could be thousands. I was never very good at math. They run with purpose, their swollen bodies fluttering and spitting dark oil in their wake. I hold back my vomit. Why does the end of the world have to be so disgusting?

This is the moment.

I have to decide.

They are coming, and one way or another, they will find us and turn us.

"It's ready," Riley screams into the radio and steps back from the drone.

"I've got it from here. See how to get out of there," Jim orders.

I laugh, turning to Riley with my best, *what the fuck*, expression. "Is he serious?"

The drone comes to life, its propellers spinning in place and lifting from the concrete. We're three stories up on this side, the pharmacy roof overhanging a side street for deliveries. Jim is in our line of sight only a story above. He's directing the drone with skill, careful not to let the thing we're dying for crash.

It flies away from us, and I wave. What else is there to do?

"Did you leave the gun behind?" I ask.

He doesn't look at me, shaking his head, disappointed with my question. "We aren't shooting ourselves."

I groan in response, stomping my foot like a child. It's not that I would have the courage to do it, but it's a solid choice considering the alternatives. He could at least be a gentleman and shoot me.

The bloats are at the front of the pharmacy, glass crashing as they make their way inside.

He steps over to my side, and I sigh, watching him look around the roof and up at the buildings all around. I grab his arm and pull him to face me. He's calculating something in his head, his forehead scrunched and eyes darting around, looking everywhere but my face. I've accepted our fate, but he thinks there's a chance to survive.

He's wrong.

"Where did you get the scar?"

"Now's not the time, Caitlyn."

"I'm dying to know," I say. "Literally."

That sends his focus to me, his eyes finding mine before he steps closer. More glass shatters from the floor below, and I flinch. His hands lift to cup my face, gentle when they touch my cheeks, but he doesn't speak. The groaning from the bloats below grows louder, and I want to close my eyes and avoid seeing what's about to happen once they get to the roof.

Except I can't stop staring back at Riley.

If this is the end, I want to be looking at him when it happens, even if he refuses to tell me about that damn scar. I cannot believe I'm going to die without finding out. The nerve of this man.

"Lana will make it, right?" I ask. "You found enough of what we needed?"

He nods, still declining to say anything. I can't bear the silence, desperate for distraction from our incoming death riot.

I imagine every bloat below us, climbing over each other, beating down the doors and walls to get to the rooftop humans.

His thumbs graze my cheeks, and I place a hand over his scar. He doesn't jerk away or pull it down, and the ten seconds we stand there embracing each other, embracing death, feel like a century.

This isn't a terrible way to go, saving someone's life with a man who saved mine. There are and have been far worse fates. I think of my mother, sick in that bed for so long, and in so much pain.

"Promise me you'll live a little, Caitlyn," she had begged. "Do some wild things. Sunbathe naked. Go parachuting. It goes by fast, my love."

"She was right," I whisper between us.

Riley squints, not knowing the thoughts spinning around in my head.

I wrap my arms around his neck, my hands cupping the back of his head, and bring his lips to mine. He kisses me back with lips full of passion and need. It's thrilling and full of promise, both of us knowing if we were anywhere else, it would lead to so much more.

He pulls me against him, and I take that moment to do what I must. He doesn't stop me when I step off the roof, letting us both fall over the side.

CHAPTER
TWENTY-FOUR

RILEY

I could stop her.

I'm stronger and don't have a death wish.

If I tried, I could pull us back, hold onto her, and swing her back to the rooftop.

No. I won't do that.

I lose myself in that kiss, letting it take me, convincing my worried mind that there's no better way to go. Our chances of surviving are next to nothing even if giving up feels wrong. Kissing her is everything right in the world, even if it's a ploy to get me to fall to my death.

Our lips don't separate right away once we're airborne. I hold her tighter against me, hoping somehow I'll break her fall. It's instinctual, the need to protect her, but it doesn't work.

We hit, and the force pulls us apart, teeth banging together before her head slams into my collarbone as we slide.

We're sliding.

I open my eyes, seeing the blue fabric move away from us as we glide down. My hand reaches out, the other securely around her waist, and I grasp for something to hold onto. Nothing catches, the vinyl fabric slipping from my grip before we skid faster until the canopy below us runs out.

My back slams into metal just before Caitlyn falls on top of me. All the air leaves my lungs, my vision darkens while I look at the grey clouds above. I can't speak, the shock of the fall knocking the wind from my lungs. Caitlyn's fists grasp at my clothes, her body slipping from me, but I have a grip on what I hope is her good arm, and there's nothing in this pit of hell that will make me let her go.

She takes a shuddered breath, trying to sit up, her head moving from side to side. I want to speak, to tell her we're okay, but I still can't get a word out. Air finally enters my lungs, and I gasp for it, letting it burn and bring me back to life.

"Riley," she shrieks. She's crawling around looking for an escape. I can hear the clang of metal echoing through my skull.

"Riley, get the fuck up!" Her fists grab at my shirt, and she yanks, pulling me to a seated position.

I cough a few times, and the movement sends spasms of discomfort through my insides. It's a dull pain deep in my chest, and I know adrenaline is the only thing keeping me from passing out.

Caitlyn grabs me by the chin and turns my head to the side. The shock of what I'm seeing takes over, and I forget every broken bone and open wound.

We're next to the pharmacy atop a semi-truck in the delivery bay. The awning above hangs lopsided from our fall and partially blocks us from view. Through the window, hundreds of bloats crowd the pharmacy. Black smudges spread across the glass only a few feet away.

"We have to go," I get out. "Now."

"No shit," she retorts.

The impact from the fall hasn't left her worse off, although she wasn't in the best shape to start with. I've broken some ribs, my body protecting Caitlyn from the impact, but there's no blood where we're sitting. We'll survive. At least for the next thirty seconds.

My bag, which has our only gun, is still wrapped around my right arm, and the radio is attached to my hip. All good things considering we are in a horrible predicament.

Caitlyn's eyes are manic, and I move us away from the glass, looking around to spot any bloats outside the pharmacy. From what I can tell, they're all on the other side of the glass and barreling toward the fire alarm. We hang our legs over the side of the semi facing away from them.

"Are we jumping?" she hisses. "Again?"

I don't answer, sliding us both over the side where we hit the concrete in a jumble of limbs. She rises and grabs her arm, her face pain-stricken from the impact. It stabs at my heart, but there isn't time to comfort her.

I open the cab of the truck, and when I lift her, my ribs crack and scream but I ignore it and get her inside. Small moans of pain leave her lips. I hate that I've hurt her, even if there wasn't any other choice. Running to the other side, I hear their animalistic noises grow louder. They're on the roof, and there are only moments before they look over the side.

The keys are in the ignition. The driver must have been here the second chaos broke loose downtown.

Before I start the engine, her hand reaches out to stop me. She shakes her head, her nails digging into my skin.

"I need you to trust me," I say.

"You told me you wouldn't let me turn into one of them."

"I won't," I promise. "I would have shot you first."

She believes the lie and releases her grip. Sitting back in the seat, her chest rises and falls with a shaky breath. "Oh, that's good," she sighs. "Wait, so do you have the gun?"

The radio at my side comes alive, Jim's voice timid through the speaker. "Hey, kiddos. I don't know if you're there anymore."

Neither of us moves, listening intently as he speaks.

"We got the medicine. More than we need. Little Lana's going to be fine. I promise you that. I'll make sure she's taken care of."

The radio goes silent, and I wrap my fingers around the key.

"I mean it, Riley. Don't let me turn into one of them. I can die, but I can't…" Her voice trails off, her bottom lip quivers as she speaks.

"I don't know how many times I have to tell you."

"I know, I know," she groans. "No one dies today."

You can't die. That can't happen.

I don't say the words aloud, and when the engine booms to life, the sloshing and groaning of the bloats goes silent.

They know where we are.

CHAPTER
TWENTY-FIVE

Caitlyn

There he goes, making more promises he can't possibly keep. The truck starts up without trouble, the engine so loud I cringe. Not that it makes a difference. We're a few feet away from a bloat mosh pit. They'd find us in seconds, anyway.

Riley doesn't waste any time, his hand flying to the gearshift as the truck jerks forward. The pharmacy windows shatter beside us, bloats tearing themselves apart as they pour through the shattered glass.

My hands grip the edge of the seat, and I ignore the throbbing in my arm. I know without looking that all my stitches have torn, and if we survive, another round of pain lies ahead.

"What exactly is the plan?" I shout over the engine. The groaning and wheezing noises chase after us followed by banging against the truck. It reverberates through the metal, and I scream. We burst out of the alley and almost jackknife, skidding sideways into the street. I slam into the door of the cab which shuts me up. Agony hits me in a wave, the last of whatever was holding my arm together breaking free. Riley reaches over, grabs me around my hip, and slides me next to him.

"Hold on!"

"To what?"

Without thinking, I grab onto his thigh, feeling him flex when he presses the gas pedal to the floor.

The radio comes back to life, Jim's breathy voice on the other side. "Is that you?"

Fiddling at Riley's side with my bum arm, I unclip the radio and bring it to my lips.

"Who the fuck else—" I take a breath and remember Jim is a nice person. "Yes, it's us, Jim."

"They'll catch up. You can't outrun them."

"What am I supposed to say to that, Jim?"

There are a few clicks, but I've left Jim speechless.

I had no idea semi-trucks could go this fast. We're flying down the street, clipping cars as Riley weaves through large obstacles. He changes gears again, and I brace myself, holding onto his thigh for dear life. It doesn't help that Jim is right. We're not in a sports car, and bloats could be coming from all angles of the city for all we know.

A swollen body slides down the front windshield and bounces off the hood, its black blood making it too slick for it to get closer to us. The thing hits the pavement and pops, dark matter flying up and splattering back on the windshield. Vomit rises in my throat.

"Oh my god, that's disgusting," I croak.

"There could be a dozen crawling over the truck," Riley hisses under his breath.

"I do not want to become zombie roadkill, Riley."

When I dare to look at the side mirror, I see the mass of them close behind. They move in unison, a fleet of monsters with one singular mission.

"Riley!" I scream and almost crawl into his lap. "Tell me what to do."

We drive over something that makes me catch air in the seat. I drop the radio and almost fall under the dashboard. The metal from the back moans and cracks as we fly down the road, every wheel hitting what feels like a giant speed bump. Jim's saying something, but I can't make it out.

"Trust me," Riley says.

I want to scream at him to stop telling me that, but I need to stop distracting the driver of our getaway vehicle. The truck slopes down, and I'm barely back into my seat before I'm flung forward, and pressed against the dash. We're driving downward, the water coming into view.

I lunge forward and grab the radio, clicking it back on. "Jim, you need to listen," I yell. "I may not be Lana's mom, but you need to get all those penises in pants. Do you hear me? That's a kid, and you need to make sure the nudist show is over in your little orgy party."

"Yes, ma'am," Jim agrees.

We hit the uneven ground, and the radio slips from my grasp, but I know Jim got the message. It needed to be said.

"Riley!" I shriek. He snakes one arm around my waist, pulling me back against him. "The river, Riley. Do you see the river?"

He doesn't answer, his foot firmly pressed on the gas without letting up. I pat his thigh rapidly. "River! Lots of water!" I point. The look of determination on his face tells me he knows exactly what he's doing, and I squirm against him, unsure how I should prepare myself.

"It's going to be cold," he warns.

"No fucking shit!" My fingernails dig into his leg, my arms stiff, bracing for the impact.

He lets go of the wheel, holding me with both arms. "We can do this."

"I'd rather drown than be a bloat," I say.

"Inspirational," he quips back.

"This is no time for jokes!"

I deserve the look he gives me with that comment.

The truck slams through a chicken wire gate, slipping down the last bit of grass that ends with a drop into the water. We skid, all eighteen wheels losing traction as the truck's load slides to the side, taking us with it, flipping us in a one-eighty, and putting us in reverse.

Riley holds me tighter. "Hold on for the drop."

Pulling me into his lap, I cling to his chest before the truck tumbles over the cement perimeter of the grass, the last stop before we drop into the Ohio River.

"I've never been in a car accident," I scream out.

We catch air, freefalling backward for a moment before the truck's load hits the water. The cab jerks up toward the sky, giving us a full view of the bloats sprinting toward us. I'm screaming like a hysterical maniac.

"This technically wasn't an accident," Riley admits. He's right. He drove us into the river on purpose.

Our descent backward into the river pauses long enough for us to witness the magnitude of bloats running towards the truck. We're only granted a few seconds of panic before we start sinking, and fast. We tilt further back, both of us still looking through the cab window. I choose to focus upward at the hazy sky, the last light before the sun leaves sending us into darkness.

How fitting.

We bob a few times, the radio still screaming at us from somewhere inside the truck.

Enough, Jim.

Lower and lower, we fall back into the water. The thought has me gasping for breath already.

"Once we're under, we'll roll down the windows," Riley orders. "They crank which is good."

The sound of rushing water gets louder, encapsulating us into the river. "How deep is it?" I ask.

"It won't be bad here."

"That's not a fucking answer!"

Water trickles in on the sides of the windows, the cab sinking slowly below the surface. I slam my hands against the glass, the urge to escape taking over my senses.

I'm still in Riley's lap as he keeps his arms around me, my palms slipping from the cold glass.

"Look at me," he orders.

His eyes bore into mine. It's enough to distract me from the rising water surging outside the windows, inch by terrifying inch. It's getting darker, his face shadowed from the depths of the river.

"Caitlyn, you will swim up with me. Do you understand? If I have to pull you to the surface with every goddamn stroke, you are getting to the other side of this fucking river."

A slam startles me, and I turn my body as best I can to find one bloat who has landed on the windshield. Seconds later, it explodes into a mass of black sludge. The glass shudders a few more times, bloats jumping in after us. None of them do more than bob around before they pop. They're like giant, partially deflated beachballs. Each one is taken by the current the second they hit the truck until I can't make them out anymore. And as the seconds tick by, I can't see much of anything.

It's the darkness I didn't expect. Fear rises in my throat, making it hard to breathe what little oxygen we have left. The deeper we fall, the less light makes it into the cab. I move my hands over Riley's body, feeling him, making sure I'll know where he is when there's nothing but blackness.

"Caitlyn, calm down. I'm going to get the windows open."

"No!" I scream when he slips from my grasp.

His hand reaches behind my neck, his lips finding mine to kiss me once more. It's hard and fast, and everything inside me kisses him back. His fingertips reach under my shirt, and the knife still strapped to my back releases just as his lips leave mine. In the last bit of light left, I watch him wedge the blade between the doorframe and the glass.

There are a few loud grunts as he struggles to get the window cranked down before rushing water slaps against the seats. The river sprays everywhere, hitting me on the chest and sending a shock through my system.

A cold unlike anything I've ever experienced seeps beneath my skin. I feel it in my bones, and it wraps around my heart. My lungs freeze more with every breath. All I can do is wait and hope the truck will hit the bottom of the river before I turn into an ice cube.

"Let it fill the cab before we swim out."

Riley is yelling over the sound, and I want to answer, but I'm too cold. My teeth chatter and my hands go numb in an instant. Icy water covers my thighs, sending numb pinpricks up throughout my body.

His cool hands run over my limbs, finding my hair and turning me to face him. Hot breath glides across my face as the water rises to my waist and creeps up my chest. It's getting difficult to find my breath with the temperature turning my body into stone.

"You can do this, Caitlyn."

I nod. It's all I can manage to do. As the water ascends to my collarbones, he kisses me again.

His lips bring me back to life. Water rushes up my shoulders, and I whimper into his hot mouth. I know kissing him in a warm bed without the threat of death might be better, but the few seconds our mouths are one feel like pure bliss. This is what I was missing with Brian and all those dating app losers before.

Yearning for someone.

Melting into them with every touch.

He pulls away, his thumb tracing my lips.

"Deep breath in. Three—"

I open my mouth and tilt my chin up.

"Two—"

Air rushes into my lungs, and I inhale until I think they will burst.

"One."

My lips shut, air filling my cheeks as Riley pushes me out of the window and into the river.

CHAPTER
TWENTY-SIX

Riley

Maisie was a great swimmer.

Our neighborhood had a pool, and as soon as our parents trusted her enough in the water, we spent every summer there. She joined the local swim team, and I remember watching her put all that hair under a swim cap, using the end of my comb to push the last few strands inside.

I thought of myself as a decent swimmer until Maisie was about ten. She found her stride, and it was fast. No one could keep up, and I did my best to get half the laps she did when we raced. My room had a few medals from random sports, but our dad built shelves for Maisie's awards. An entire wall of her bedroom sparkled with gold coins and statues. Girls and women standing on podiums in swimsuits.

Swimming got harder for me when high school came around. I had it in my head to bulk up like the other muscle heads in my class. I wasn't exactly buoyant before, and although I could swim for hours, my speed vanished. Maisie would mock me. She called me a swim team dropout and meathead, singing a tune from the movie Grease with her teasing lyrics.

I may have lost my skills over the years, but staying afloat is all that matters. It's something I'm grateful for today, because not another being on this earth sinks quite like a bloat. They can't swim to save what's left of their miserable lives.

At least I hope so.

When we were scavenging homes, Maisie and I got lucky in some upscale neighborhood. It was a gated community, and most of the people fled, probably lifted off in their private jets to safety. We were met with threats and rifles pointed at our heads everywhere else, but Graynote Gardens was a ghost town.

We found non-perishable food, a wine cellar that wasn't difficult to break into, and some Vicodin in a medicine cabinet. Maisie had sprained her ankle not long before, and the discovery felt like a blessing. If I had known how things would end, I would have convinced Maisie to stay there. Planted vegetables in one of their covered gardens and used telescopes to see bloats coming so we could hide.

I would have done so many things differently.

After a few days in the abandoned community, Maisie checked out the pool house. We split up to look further out and find more food. Her screams one afternoon made me regret that decision.

I found her standing at the pool's edge, backing away until she hit the fence, her hand over her mouth and trembling. She couldn't tell me what was happening, but taking a few steps closer, I understood what frightened her.

Black water overflowed the pool's cement rim, lapping in waves from the wind. In the pool's center, dead bloats bobbed face down. I stepped closer, and she grabbed my arm, but I brushed her away.

Two. No, three of them floated in the dark liquid, the pool stained from their decaying bodies. I'd never seen a dead one until that day.

"What happened?"

"Please," Maisie begged. "We have to go. We have to get out of here."

"They're dead, but you go inside. I need to check this out."

"They could have heard me scream."

"Go inside. They just passed through here. We have a few more days. These must have been left behind."

She turned to run but fell to the ground, grabbing at her ankle with a pained expression on her face.

"Take that medicine," I scolded her.

She nodded, lifted herself, and wobbled back to the house.

I never figured out what killed them, and since that day, I haven't seen any of them dead. We were too busy running from them to look back, and considering how they explode, well, you don't have a lot of bodies.

Except for the ones that drown before they get too large and pop. Something about the water reacting to their skin I think. It's not conducive to swimming. They can't even put their arms down by their sides. Like the meatheads from high school, they sink.

That's what I tell myself as I push Caitlyn out of the truck window into waters so cold, that I can't feel her slip from my grasp. They can't touch her long enough to turn her. It doesn't take long, a few seconds maybe, but in the water, we can slip away.

When I get through the window, my shoulder bumps into Caitlyn. She's not fighting to swim to the surface, and I don't know if she's scared or trying to die. It's possible she can't swim. I didn't ask her before I plunged us into the Ohio River.

The headlights of the truck beam through the darkness, shadows of drowning bloats making them flicker. I wrap an arm around Caitlyn and swim up, but we don't make it far before the current catches us. Its pull forces us to swim diagonally to the surface, making it a longer journey to the precious air. This is a complication I hadn't considered, but it's too late. We swim or die.

Caitlyn's trying, her arms flailing around her, legs kicking in all directions, mostly hitting me. I pull her against me, and her movements slow as mine speed up. My arm burns as I reach, stroke after stroke to get us higher. I can't feel my feet but I know I'm kicking. It's getting dark outside, hiding the surface of the water, but I know it's close.

The current yanks us harder, flipping us around, but I don't let her go. She'll be bruised from my hold on her, but she'll make it to the surface.

She stills, her body going limp while I continue. We're close. I know it, and just when my heart beats so fast I think it might explode, icy wind hits the back of my palm.

We rise into frigid air, my lungs burning as I gulp in a breath. Caitlyn's head hangs, her hair covering her face in thick chunks. I lean back, pulling her atop my front, swimming backstroke to get us to land.

"Breathe, Caitlyn!" I scream at her. I don't recognize my voice. It's strained and pleading. "Breathe, dammit!"

She's lifeless, heavy on my chest, the river fighting me while we glide on its surface. The rushing water in my ears drowns out my cries, and I swim faster, harder. "No one dies today. Do you hear me?"

I'm angry but not at her. I'm yelling at everything I've lost. My sister, our parents, friends, and all the patients in the hospital. So many have died, but sometimes living feels worse. What's left is pain and loss until it's our turn. Caitlyn may be right. This isn't living. It's barely existing in hell.

Surviving doesn't change the misery of our existence, but knowing that, feeling it in this moment when my muscles burn and I'm scared she's gone, I can't bring myself to give up.

Seeing her in the woods brought something inside me to life. I'm still someone who helps people, and even though she may not want it, Caitlyn needs my help.

My heel catches on the river bottom, a patch of dirt within sight. In seconds, I find my footing and drag us to the shore. The wind bites through me, colder than before, freezing the clothes against my skin.

"No one dies today," I mumble to myself. I hoist her to a flat surface. My numb fingers struggle to find a pulse, but there's nothing. "No one dies today. No one dies today. No one dies today." I'm a robot, repeating the phrase to myself over and over, as if I'm casting a spell over her.

Finding the right spot over her chest, I palm her heart and place my other hand on top before I pump. My movements are hard and fast, and I count.

Except my counting is in rhythm with the words I can't stop repeating.

"No. One. Dies. Today. No. One. Dies. Today."

After thirty chest compressions, I check for a pulse again, still repeating the mantra that's turned into a prayer.

Please, Caitlyn. I can't be responsible for another death.

I pump her chest again, forcing her heart to work and send blood through her veins. "You can't die," I scream at her. "Come back. Come back to me."

I check for a pulse once more, and this time, there's a heartbeat. Slow and faint, but it's there. I turn her to the side, and the most amazing sound comes from her lips.

Vomit.

She coughs and spews river water into my lap, and I feel my scarred skin pull when I smile. It doesn't stop me even though the nerves send pinpricks of pain through my face. This is worth the pain of a smile.

"Get it out, castaway." I pat her on the back, careful not to hit too hard but to use enough force to clear her lungs.

"I.. I c-can't."

"Don't talk," I tell her.

She rolls, her face almost hitting the dirt before I lift her on top of me. Her torso and limbs drape over my legs while I pull her into my warmth, my hand pounding her back, begging all the water to escape. She takes in a few uneven breaths before the stiffness in her muscles subsides and she relaxes.

I let us remain like that for minutes. Time ticks by, and I can't tell how much because I'm so damn grateful she's alive. The wind picks up around us as the night sky grows darker. We're wet and cold and need to get out of the open.

"Caitlyn, I'm going to pick you up."

She tries to shake her head, but I overpower her stubborn protests, lifting her in my arms and heading for some cover. The skyscrapers of downtown are further away, the current taking us farther than I could have imagined. I scan the water for any sign of bloats but there's nothing.

"They can't swim, but that doesn't mean there aren't some of them close. Stay quiet."

We're far from the city, but nowhere near the suburbs. There are parking lots of eighteen-wheelers and enormous box-like buildings. This is a shipyard or factory area. I can't decide if that's good or not, so I walk toward a parking lot, hoping to find cover between the trucks while I decide.

"You could have said that." Her voice is weak and scratchy, but it sounds so good to hear her speak.

I was close to losing her in the river.

Too close.

"I told you to be quiet."

She squirms in my hold, but I tighten my arms around her legs and back, the pain in my side returning from the loss of adrenaline. It doesn't make a difference. I could have a knife in my gut and I wouldn't let her go. Pain doesn't stop me. It's always there, hovering beneath the surface and waiting to surge forward. A few cracked ribs won't slow me down.

"You could have said—" She lets out a few rough coughs, wincing and wheezing until she gains her composure. "You could have said, hey, Caitlyn. I'm gonna drive into this here river because bloats can't swim."

My feet hit the pavement, and I move between two trucks, their dark shadows providing cover in the flat lot.

"I wasn't sure they couldn't swim."

She's shivering, her body convulsing from the cold. "But you drove us into a river?"

"It was an educated hunch."

She smacks me on the chest, but it's barely a tap. Her open wound glistens with blood in the moonlight, and I wince at the sight. She needs antibiotics. Especially after wading around in that river.

"What if I couldn't swim?" she asks.

"You can swim?"

I'm not entirely joking, but she laughs, coughing a few times from the effort.

"Set me down. I can walk."

She can't very well, but I need to free my hands and check these truck doors. Setting her down slowly, I wait to make sure she's good on her feet.

"Thank you," she says, taking a few unsteady steps.

"Sit down. Wait for me here."

She waves me off and keeps walking, crossing her arms at her chest and quivering.

"Stop it, Caitlyn. We need to find a place to hunker down for the night, and I don't need someone seeing our tracks if we aren't alone out here."

She squares her shoulders, and I know her well enough to ready myself for a rebuttal. It's surely some quip to remind me she's smarter or doesn't care if she dies, but the words don't come. Taking a step back, she leans against a truck tire and sighs.

My shoes are water-logged, and I take them off, dumping the debris behind the tire before I shoot off, checking every handle as fast as my legs will run. I don't want to leave her alone and freezing for a second longer than I have to.

I'm two rows ahead and maybe twenty trucks checked before a handle opens, the metal squeaking when the door slams into my shoulder.

Finally.

When I get back to Caitlyn, I don't ask her or give her a warning that I'm carrying her to the truck. I hand her my boots and she doesn't argue when I lift her. Her body is cold to the touch and the wound on her arm gapes open but doesn't bleed more than a trickle. Even with that small stroke of luck, she's in bad shape, and I need to get her warm.

Once we're safely inside the cab, I pull down the shades for the windows and lock the door.

"Another eighteen-wheeler," she quips. "How f-f-fun."

Climbing in the back, I unfold the bed from behind the seats, ripping down the blankets secured to the sides.

"Get undressed," I tell her.

I rip my shirt off over my head and toss it in the driver's seat before I start on my pants buckle.

"Caitlyn, now. Take your clothes off."

CHAPTER
TWENTY-SEVEN

Caitlyn

"Have you lost your mind?"

My teeth chatter so hard, I don't think my words make sense, and my lungs burn with every breath. I know I drowned in that river but somehow, I'm here arguing with Riley once again. That's twice this guy has brought me back from the dead.

We were swimming, or I was attempting to swim, flailing around without any real direction through the dark and dirty water, when what little air left in my lungs ran out too quickly. I panicked, my shoes and heavy clothes dragging me down. Riley wrapped his arm around me and swam, giving me a fraction of reprieve until there was nothing.

His face was the last thing I saw before the world went quiet. I felt safe enough to give in, being held by someone who saved me, someone who cared if I made it to the surface.

That's the last thing I remember before I awoke, facefirst in the mud with what felt like gallons of river water leaving my lungs and Riley pounding on my back.

And now he wants me naked.

His arms reach between the two front seats, fingertips grabbing at the edge of my shirt. I push him away, but my arms are heavy and fumble around, making any refusal useless against his will.

He makes a lopsided frown, and leans forward, both hands clutching the wet fabric until my top moves over my head and down my limbs. He flings it to the floorboards and takes me by the waist of my pants.

"Stop it! Stop it!" Panic surges through me, prickling my skin and turning my stomach sour. Memories of Landon hovering over me flood my mind. His blurry face smiles down at me while he reaches inside my clothes. His satisfaction about what he was going to do, what he could take from me, written all over his face.

"No," I repeat. "Don't!"

I reach for the door. It's too heavy, and I fling my body into it, my wounded arm feeling the effects. I cry out in a wail before I'm yanked back and fall into the seat.

Riley looms over me, securing the door before he whips around, pulling me into his arms. Tears escape, warm floods against my frozen cheeks.

"No. No. No. Stop," I beg.

"Shhh," Riley whispers into my ear. "You're borderline hypothermic. Do you hear me? Do you understand?"

His slick skin makes it impossible to get away, and although I think I'm putting up a valiant effort, I'm barely squirming in his grasp. Every movement takes all the energy I have left, and I worry I'll pass out at any moment.

"I wouldn't hurt you, Caitlyn. You have to know that by now."

It's true, but I can't let go of the fear. It's choking me from the inside out, telling me to run.

"Caitlyn, I should have explained first. I'm sorry. You're okay, but you're freezing. We need body heat. You have to let me warm you."

The cold combined with memories of Landon has my body trembling uncontrollably. The shaking won't stop, but knowing he's right doesn't change my body's reaction.

"We'll wrap ourselves in the blankets," he continues. "I won't ever hurt you. Are you listening?"

He wouldn't hurt me.

I try to nod, but I'm unsure if he can tell. "I—" The word barely catches in my throat. Tears stream down my chin, dripping on my legs.

"I've saved you too many times to let you get hurt."

Riley's face is full of worry, the scarred lines taut next to wide eyes.

I catch my breath, focusing on every inhale and exhale, forcing myself to see reason. My hands ball into fists and run up and down my thighs. His palms touch my wet cheeks, and he feels me nodding.

"I… I know," I finally get out.

He adjusts us, fitting me into his lap. My bare back rests against his hot skin and the sensation is a shock to my system. I'm colder than I realize, and he feels so good, so warm.

"Caitlyn," he whispers in my ear. "You're okay. We're okay."

I wait in silence until my soaring heartbeat returns to normal, and when I take my first calm breath, he loosens his grip.

"I don't know why—"

"I know why," Riley interrupts. "With what happened to you, it makes sense."

His hands cup my shoulders and move down my arms, careful not to touch my wound. He trails his fingers around it, measuring it somehow, noticing how it refuses to heal.

"You need to get warm. Skin-to-skin, it's the best way."

I swallow hard, not because I'm afraid anymore, but because I'm nervous. Skittish about a man I'm attracted to curled up with me in a confined space.

When was the last time I bathed? The river is not a bath.

With trembling fingers, I reach for the waistband of my pants and pull them down, lifting while Riley helps me slide them past my hips. The heavy fabric makes a puddle on the floorboard, and in nothing but a thin bra and panties, I climb into the back.

There's some rustling and a thump as Riley removes the rest of his wet clothes. Curtains for the windows pull shut, covering the moonlight and making the cab pitch black. He climbs behind the seats, his presence thickening the space, the cot too small for us both to comfortably fit.

"I'm going to move you on top of me."

I nod, my hands gripping onto the blanket, the cold sinking into my bones.

"Caitlyn?"

"Yes. Okay."

His hands, so warm I almost moan from their touch, slide against my skin and lift me until I'm sitting back in his lap. He lays back, and I go with him, adjusting the blanket so it doesn't get stuck.

"There's another one in the ceiling." He reaches up and so do I until we both find the corner of a second blanket and yank it down.

"Is it better if I'm on my stomach?" I ask. He's stretching out the fabric, a difficult task in the backseat of a semi-truck.

"Yeah, I think so. Roll… uh, this way."

It's awkward, and I'm fumbling around, painfully aware I'm rubbing all over his damp boxer briefs. My wet bra scratches at my clammy skin, and I pull at the bottom, attempting to adjust it while I shift and turn. Water droplets trickle out and Riley reaches for the back, releasing the clasp.

"What are you doing?"

"Did you… want it off. I thought that's what you were doing."

The straps fall from my shoulders, and I move them over my wound before freeing my arms and tossing my bra to the ground. My tits are officially nipple down on Riley's chest.

"You are surprisingly good at that?" I tell him.

"At what?"

I rest my head against his chest, a shiver running through me as he whips the blanket up to spread it over us. He tucks the sides into the cushions below him, making a sleeping bag with both of us cocooned inside.

"At unhooking a bra," I murmur into his skin.

"It's a metal clasp. Why would that be hard?"

"Ask ninety-nine percent of men," I retort. "Lord help them if they come across a sports bra. That's like a labyrinth."

I chuckle into his skin. Despite living off of Halloween candy and noodles, Riley is a wall of muscle. His chest is wide enough to suffice as my pillow, not that I've had a pillow in months. Something about his bruteness mixed with the fact that he's a nurse makes him more desirable. He could kill a man with his bare hands, but also heal him. It's an intoxicating mixture and I'm resting on it, topless.

"This is why women survive longer than men. They can't even unhook a bra."

"I see you're feeling better," Riley muses. "Your wit is back."

It's true. I'm warmer and the numbness in my toes and fingers is gone. If only the aching in my arm didn't rear its ugly head at the same time.

"First try, too. And one-handed. You must have had some practice." I say.

"I work in the medical field, Caitlyn."

"Worked."

I didn't mean it as a cruel reminder of where we are and what we've lost, but the statement saddens us both. A heavy sigh comes from Riley, and it lifts me, his chest expanding against mine.

That motion makes me painfully aware of how we'll sleep tonight. Half-naked, holding each other, and wet.

It's enough to make a girl want to live.

"You know I've almost died five times," I turn my head and Riley moves an arm over my back. The weight of his limb rests heavy against me, comforting me, its glorious heat radiating into my body. "And that's not including the night of the haunted house where we all almost died. That's five times I should have found myself six feet under."

"I count three," Riley says.

"Three?" I think back, curious about where he got the third. There was the morning he found me almost bled out and the river. "Are you counting when we fell off the building?"

"When you pushed us off the building. Yes."

"Semantics."

His hand sprawls across my back, and I love the feel of it pressing into my spine. I don't know what we'll find when we get out of this truck, or how much time either of us has left, but tonight, I almost feel safe.

"So is it six then?"

"I guess so." I sigh heavily, wondering why my mind is so alert. It could be that a half-naked man in a tiny bed has activated my womanhood, and I'm wide awake and ready to play.

"What were the others?" he asks.

"Well… I fell into a quarry running from a group of cannibals."

Riley chuckles, his fingers rubbing circles into my back. "Did you know they were cannibals or is that a theory."

"A strong theory."

"How deep was it?"

"The quarry or the theory?"

He's silent, waiting for me to respond, but I know he's smiling. I feel it somehow, the subtle tells that he's reacting, letting me know he's enjoying this moment.

I am too.

"I fell for a while, but it was full of water. I seem to have this issue with bodies of water. I almost drown once a week."

"I'd think you'd be a better swimmer given all the practice."

If the sheets weren't taut against us, I'd smack him.

"I had shoes on. No one can swim with shoes on."

"Ahem."

Oh, he's smiling. No doubt about it.

"Okay, fine. In the quarry I didn't have shoes on so it was easier to swim out to a more shallow place. None of the cannibals jumped in after us. Your turn?"

Another long sigh from Riley, his chest rising and falling, taking me with it. It's like riding a small human wave.

"I've had a few close calls, not all with you."

"What about—"

I stop myself, realizing I'm close to crossing a line.

"My scar?" he asks, his voice barely over a whisper.

I'm silent, worried whatever words I say next will be the wrong ones.

"That was a close call for me. It was the only time… the only time I wanted."

He pauses, unable to say the words.

"The only time you wanted to die."

"Yeah," he says.

"Do you still want to sometimes? Or, am I just that crazy?"

"I did for a long time, but not anymore."

Me neither.

I want to say the words but I can't. They catch in my throat, refusing to be set free.

Instead, I say, "Seven."

"Seven?" he asks. "You remembered another near-death experience?"

"If we count before the apocalypse, then yes."

The feeling in my body is returning, the cold wearing off. Replacing it is the rush of dread from the memory of my first brush with death. I don't know why it's coming to mind this night, but it's with me after so many years of pretending it never existed.

"What happened?" he asks.

Memories fill me. Wood piles chipping away in his yard. A fence falling over in a wave, holding back a dog that barked and growled, threatening to rip the flesh from my bones. The man was so awful, inside and out. The sight of him deflating all the hopes and dreams I had as a little girl.

"I found my dad when I was fifteen," I explain. "He wasn't happy to see me, but I kept insisting he let me in, give me a few minutes to talk. I just wanted to get to know him a little. Know what it was like to have a dad."

There's a flash of his yellow teeth spitting at me to go away, but I didn't listen. Some woman from inside the house coughed on her cigarettes, screaming for him to come back inside. He was letting all the warm air out of the house. I was standing on his porch in ten-degree weather without my good coat.

"It never occurred to me he wouldn't want to meet me so I kept begging him to let me in," I continue. "He pushed me, pulled a rifle from the house, and shot into the floor of his front porch close to my feet. Told me never to come back."

"Caitlyn, I'm so sorry," Riley says. "That had to be awful. Damn. I – I don't know what to say but I'm sorry."

"Me too," I say. "My mom found me. She wasn't even mad. She was sorry too."

Riley's hand runs up my back, and I lift my chin. His lips meet mine, soft at first but I forget myself and my injuries. I'm messing up the blankets, writhing against him. My hard nipples slide across his bare skin, sending a sensation that overshadows all the aches and pains and the hurt I'm feeling inside. Dipping my tongue into his mouth, I replace the bad memories with ones that I want.

Someone who wants me.

Someone who won't throw me away.

"Caitlyn," he gasps between kisses. He's hard beneath me, and I push my hip against the length of his cock. He grunts. "You're hurt and upset. You need to rest."

He's right and I know it, but I want him. I want this.

"Caitlyn." One hand moves to my neck, hard enough to pull me away, but not too much to bruise or choke me. "I want this, but not after you've almost died and are emotional. I want this when you are well enough."

He's right. I'm sad and confused and damn him for still being so noble.

"Okay," I agree. "I'm sorry."

"Don't be sorry," he interrupts. "Let's get some sleep, okay?"

I nod.

There's a flash of regret on his face, and I revel in it. This isn't our moment, but we will have our time.

What I don't tell him, but I'm sure he knows, is that day with my father was the last time I ever tried to get close to someone.

Until now.

Until him.

Warm and curled up against Riley, I should be able to find rest, but my mind wanders.

"Caitlyn?"

"Yes," My voice is too high, nervous from the thoughts taking over my mind.

"No one dies tomorrow, either."

I laugh, closing my eyes and thinking about tomorrow. Maybe we can stay in this truck longer. Rested, warm, and naked, anything is possible.

One thing is for certain.

If we survive tomorrow, I'm kissing him again.

CHAPTER
TWENTY-EIGHT

Riley

We're further from the city than I thought. It's shocking how far the river dragged us. Standing on top of the truck with the sun barely cresting the horizon, only the tips of Louisville's skyscrapers are in my line of vision.

I turn the dial of a two-way radio I found in the cab, trying one more time for a signal, knowing it's hopeless. At least it's battery-operated and we can take it with us.

Before the sun gets too high, I crawl back in through the window, not wanting to be an obvious target. Caitlyn's still sleeping, but I was restless all night.

I kept checking on her, concerned about dry-drowning. Telling her the risks wouldn't change anything, so I chose to stay awake and wait, letting her sleep in peace.

My body sinks into the front seat, and I kick at the clothes in the floorboards. I should have hung them over the steering wheel, but we were too cold and tired to do anything except find warmth. Wringing them out, I hang them the best I can so they dry.

The moment she fell asleep, I regretted not doing more last night.

Well, parts of me regretted it. The right thing to do was to let her rest and get better so she could make decisions with a clear head.

I imagine what it's like to enjoy her mouth, let my tongue slip inside, grab her hair, and expose her neck until—

"Riley?"

Her voice is small and full of worry. I jolt forward in the seat, my cracked ribs sending sharp pains throughout my chest. Hissing through my teeth, I grab the steering wheel and grit through the anguish. Her eyes scan me for injuries, but she should be concerned with herself and that arm.

"I cracked some ribs, but it's not a big deal," I tell her. "I'm fine."

"Oh," she says, holding the blanket against her bare chest. The sides of her breasts are exposed, perfect curves of skin that I'm drawn to in the dim light. She notices me staring and lies back down, curling into herself.

I should apologize, but with the pain passing, I'm using all my focus to keep my dick from getting hard.

"How's Lana?" she asks.

That does it.

"I can't get Jim on the radio."

"You thought to grab the radio?"

"No." I shake my head. "This was in this truck. The other one's on the bottom of the river. I did get the bag with our things from the pharmacy."

"Oh. I would think Jim would answer. Do we not have the right station or something?"

"We're too far," I tell her. "Maybe ten miles."

"From the city?"

I shrug, just as shocked as she is. We had to have been flying with that current.

"What do we do? What will they do with a baby?"

"Not everyone is a cannibal, Caitlyn."

She sits up, her perfect tits shaking behind the blanket. If the bloats don't kill me, resisting her might. I remind myself I look like the Phantom of the Opera and I'm a murderer, so she may have changed her mind after a good night's sleep.

She rants on about what percentage of people she thinks are cannibals. I'm not willing to poll people, so I don't disagree.

With a huff, she finishes her point and slams her back against the cot. I'm not sure everything she said, but I crawl between the front seats and sit with her. It's half the size of a twin bed, so there isn't much space, but I'm hoping I can talk her into letting me sleep now that she's out of the danger zone.

"I put so much medication in that drone that she'll be fine. Jim made a promise, and they have a doctor."

"A vet," she corrects me.

I shrug. "They have people that want her and care. Hell, that group of grandparents will probably dote on her better than anyone else left alive."

"But how long can they survive up there like that?"

"A long time. Long enough."

Caitlyn's breathing grows ragged and she scratches at her chest. "Part of me feels like we abandoned her. At the time, it seemed like the right choice, but now…"

I rest my palms on her legs, stilling her, hoping she'll listen to what I need to say.

"We could draw bloats to her. To all of them, if we tried to go back."

She places her face in her hands, and I know she's frustrated at how right I am.

"Listen. The river took us south. Not ideal when trying to get to Canada. We'll loop around and get close enough for a signal. The truck radio is a hand-held."

"And if they say they ate her?" she asks.

I pull at her wrists, revealing her face. It's still dark in the cab of the truck, but rays of sunshine peek through the edge of the curtains.

"Then we can end it. Cease to survive on this wasteland. I'll join you. We'll jump into a large body of water, and I'll tie myself to you so we sink like a rock."

She doesn't want to smile, but it happens and I let out a sigh of relief.

"Under normal circumstances, I can swim," she reminds me.

I nod, not wanting to ruin her mood.

"Are you sure we can get a signal?" she asks. "We will be able to talk to them and check in on her?"

"I'm sure I'll try my best."

In our talk, my hands have slipped down, resting with hers and grazing her thighs. I want to pull her forward and kiss her again, but her wound catches my attention.

She sees me looking and bites her lip. "It's bad, right? Think it'll kill me?"

"No one dies today. You know my motto."

She rolls her eyes and dares to look, gagging when she does.

The cut on her arm has opened so many times, I don't know if it will ever heal right. It will take several internal stitches to keep it closed which means more pain than last time. We're lucky the bleeding stopped, but without antibiotics, it could kill her.

I have some in our bag, along with a suture practice kit which will have to level up for our purposes. We won't know if it's enough until a few days pass. She's already feverish. I felt it last night despite her shivering, but I'm not sure if she realizes it's more than the cold river affecting her health.

"I got most of what we need at the pharmacy."

"What did you forget?"

"I didn't forget anything, but lidocaine was at the bottom of the list."

"Because you hate me?"

Her words hit me like a brick even though I know she's joking. The woman must know I'm falling for her.

She's got eyes, and she's caught mine staring at her body more than once. We're flirting, but her mother's words are true. I'm all there is for now, and I don't know if that's enough.

"Because you can live without it," I sigh.

I need to sleep. I rub the back of my neck, my stomach growling and my head pounding. The sooner I stitch her the better, but I can't see straight.

Caitlyn wraps one of the blankets around her chest and crawls through the front seats. She opens a mini refrigerator that sits on the floor, and her head jerks back. Turning to face me, her expression fills with disgust as she closes its door.

"Nope. Gross."

I smile to myself, wondering what she found in there that's festered for months. She opens the glove compartment and a few protein bars and some colorful plastic tubes pour out. Music to our ears. She tosses some at me, and I inspect the package just as she starts laughing.

"Temptations cat treats," she chuckles. "Salmon flavored."

I flip the food over in my hand, noticing the smiling fish on the front. "Ingredients look decent."

"Why does everything say paste or puree after it?" she asks. "Fish paste. Vegetable paste. That's not food, Riley."

Much to her horror, I rip open the package and pour it down my throat. Swallowing is somewhat difficult, but food is food and we need calories.

"It's not that bad," I tell her. "Just do it quick."

"I'll have the bars," she argues.

"Sure, you can have all of them, but boil the frog first."

"Oh, hell there are frogs in this?"

I shake my head. "No, it's an expression. Do the worst thing first, the thing you don't want to do, and then it's over with. Save the bars as a dessert."

"I feel like you're daring me. Is this a double dog situation?"

"Only a suggestion. But listen, if you pour it out like a pixie stick at the back of your tongue, you won't even taste it."

"Are you asking me to deep-throat cat food?"

"I was simply suggesting, wait — what? No!"

She tosses a few more packs at me with a smile, and rips open the energy bar. "When the time comes, I'll swallow the spooge, okay. No sooner."

I raise my hands in surrender, content that there's something to eat and regain our strength.

"Do you think a lot of these trucks have snacks?" she asks.

"Yes," I say. My eyes are heavy, and I rub my face to keep myself awake. "Don't go out looking."

"Well, I have to pee."

I sit forward, resting my elbows on my knees, and stretching my back. If she asked me to run a marathon this morning I would probably find the will. It's getting impossible to say no to her. "Let me check around. Pee next to the truck."

She shrugs. I imagine it's not the first time she's squatted in an odd location in front of someone she doesn't know well. That's a right of passage in your twenties.

Hopping out, I stretch, making a circle around the truck. It's quiet, the sun higher in the sky and sending long shadows across the parking lot.

Too quiet.

There aren't any birds or morning animal activity. It's unusual, but not a reason to run. We can't leave yet, not until she's stitched and has medicine in her for twenty-four hours. All that walking could make her pass out or spike her fever.

I step up on the side of the cab and catch her pulling her shirt back over her bare breasts. It's still wet and she tilts her head back in frustration, pulling the fabric from her stomach and letting it slap back down. She turns, catching me looking, her gaze staring back at me for a moment too long.

She raises a finger and tsks at me, waving it back and forth as I sheepishly open the door.

"Don't wear cold and wet clothes."

She rolls her eyes. "Having me naked is more fun, I'm sure."

"You're the one that can still have sex with yourself, right?"

The moment the words are out I regret them. Not only because she looked embarrassed, which wasn't nice of me.

It's that someone else heard us.

And they're coming.

CHAPTER
TWENTY-NINE

Caitlyn

We both hear it. The sound of running feet on a rocky pavement. It's uneven and heavy, so unlike them, but that doesn't take away the fear. Riley stops, his head jerking toward the noise, but he doesn't take long to decide what to do next.

"We have to get out of here," I hiss at him.

He slides into the truck, closing the door behind him with as little noise as possible. I wince from the click, and the realization hits.

We are trapped inside this tiny metal box.

Again.

Last night that sounded great, but right now, I want out.

Climbing into the back, I position myself in the corner of the cot while he tosses our still-wet clothes onto it. When he opens the curtains, I want to scream at him, beg him to stop.

I mouth, "What the fuck?" but he stays silent, checking the front seats for any signs of our existence. The running grows louder and scattered. These are the sounds of other survivors, not bloats.

That doesn't make me feel any better, especially when I make out what they're saying.

"Here piggy, piggy, piggy. Don't you want to come play?"

Riley climbs behind the front seats.

"The curtains are open," I whisper. "You need to close them."

"That draws suspicion."

"Oh, shit. You're right."

He nods, feeling along the wall by the driver's side door. He moves his thumbs along a slit in the fabric before he draws out a divider and slides it to the other wall, clicking it into place. It cuts us off from the front seats, making our area a bit smaller, but hidden.

I open my mouth to speak, but he brings his finger to his lips and shakes his head, forcing me to clamp my mouth shut.

"Here piggy, piggy, piggy."

The voices continue, followed by the sound of something dragging on the concrete. It could be a weapon, an ax, a rifle, or any nightmare my mind dreams up. Maybe these cannibals will use a giant knife to cut us into pieces.

And these are cannibals. I'm not overreacting this time.

Our situation only gets worse when my need to pee takes over, becoming my main focus while we hide in the backseat of a stranger's eighteen-wheeler. I tap on Riley's shoulder and then to my bladder. He looks confused, his forehead creasing as best it can with his scarred face.

Once more I point to my bladder and cross my legs, bobbing a little up and down.

"Here piggy, piggy."

Both of us freeze. Our breathing halts and we wait for them to draw nearer. They're close, but not right outside the truck. A minute passes in silence before I point again, giving my best effort at backseat charades. Something in his mind clicks and he nods, lifting his finger and signaling for me to wait.

I cannot wait much longer.

Moving his hands over the pockets that line the wall, he carefully opens zippers so no sound escapes. He's not going to find a toilet in there and I'm one strong sneeze away from niagra falls.

The best case scenario is I kneel on this cot and pee in front of the guy who I want to screw. Worst case is I urinate all over myself while being murdered. If that happens, I hope my urine spoils the meat. This was easier when I didn't care for him. My period was everywhere the first day we met, and it didn't matter. Things are different now.

We're different.

Riley's focused, looking for something to help relieve me, and I begin to sweat, a reaction to my bladder bursting. This will not be attractive. I may be the last woman on the planet, but peeing in a styrofoam cup six inches from a guy, the smell of urine, and that sound, it's enough to turn off any man.

Well, not any guy. This one girl at work told me about her husband's peeing fetish, and holiday parties were never the same after that. Still, I don't think Riley fits that category.

He finds a plastic bag, the best I can ask for in this situation. I should be grateful that it zips closed, but all I can think about is how much this sucks and how only a week ago, death seemed to be the better option. This might swing me back to that way of thinking.

We silently argue, Riley motioning that he can hold the bag for me and my stubborn ass refusing help at all costs. When he concedes, averting his eyes while I position the bag with my body contorted in a way where I can pee, the voices start up again.

"We know you're out here. We have food and clean water. Come on now. Come out to play."

Their mocking tone sends a shiver down my spine and my skin prickles from their proximity. We don't hear the slamming of truck doors or the creaking of metal, and I hope nothing seems out of place with the truck so they keep walking past us. This divider wasn't up before, but I'm not sure if they would remember. Hundreds of vehicles sit in this lot, and this one has food inside. They haven't inspected them all closely.

Riley turns back to face me, and I palm his scarred cheek, turning him back to the wall so he doesn't watch my mortification. With focus and desperation, I release my bladder into the sandwich bag and try not to let out a moan of relief.

When I'm finally done, I zip up the bag and place it in a side cup holder, hoping it doesn't burst open.

Oh, hell, what if I have to poop.

"Here piggy. Come on out now."

Someone drags something against a nearby truck, and I'm nauseous at the sound of metal on metal. Riley reaches his hand back, feeling for me to see if he can turn around.

I tap him on his shoulder, and he shifts, pulling me against him and placing his hand across my mouth. Annoyance is replaced with panic as something bangs along the side of our truck, growing louder until there's a tap on the front windows.

My fingernails dig into Riley's skin as I do my best not to scream. It's still my go-to reaction, another sign that I should not have survived this long.

"Hey lookie here," a voice says.

They are right outside our door.

Riley pulls me closer, his heartbeat thudding against my ribs. I'm shaking, my body taken over by fear, and I close my eyes, not wanting to see what happens next.

"Is that a fridge?"

Footsteps walk toward our truck and the sound of someone's palms against the glass makes me jolt. I decide I'll throw my bag of pee at these cannibals if they open the door.

"Yep, but this is a Willis vehicle. They're not drinkers. Come on, Travis."

They never try to open the door, the sounds of their weapons banging across other trucks fade into the distance.

We both relax, shoulders lowering, Riley's hand leaving my mouth. They're still out there, but they don't know we're in here.

Yet.

It's a momentary reprieve, but reality hits when a distant voice yells, "Patrol the lot. They can't hide for long."

CHAPTER
THIRTY

It's a few hours of hiding in the back of the truck before we don't hear them anymore. They're still somewhere, wandering around, searching for the strangers concealed in their territory.

Looking for us.

Humans are animals – scrappy, hungry, and ruthless animals. The end of the world brings out that side. Some wander, looking for scraps and staying out of sight. Others stake out a homeland, believing they can and will protect it at all costs. That's what our friends at this plant decided. They have pissed all over the border of this parking lot, staking out their property, planning to kill anyone that trespasses.

Caitlyn may have been right about the cannibals.

There's not much we can do with them hot on our tail, and I don't know if their bloodlust will die out before they find us. They heard me, loud and clear, someone walking this lot. There are woods on one side, and if we're lucky, they'll think we've scaled the hill and run off.

There aren't too many of them, but it only takes a few to rip your entire life from your hands.

I know that better than most.

The building we're next to has a familiar red symbol on the white brick. It's a food production plant, and they've been squatting here, using up its resources. Our presence threatens their survival, or that's their belief. If they find us, we die. I feel that with everything in me, and as the hours tick by, my mind going through every scenario, I come to no other conclusion.

We have to leave tonight before they start opening doors.

"Do you think we could get the pee out of here?" Caitlyn whispers.

Her voice startles me awake again. I've been sleeping on and off, exhaustion taking over.

"What?" I mumble, clearing my throat.

"The pee baggy. It's gross."

"We haven't bathed in days, and you're worried about a little urine?"

She thinks about this, her face contorting as she sniffs her shoulder. I notice the sheen of sweat on her forehead and the flush in her cheeks. She's getting sick, and time is running out to get her cleaned up and medicated.

"We had a river bath." She offers a lop-sided smile, one that is impossible not to return. The motion sends a few pinpricks of discomfort across the damaged nerves in my cheek.

I point to her arm and she rolls her eyes. "I know," she says. "It's gross. Kind of like the pee baggy. I'm disgusting."

"You're perfect."

The words are glimmers of what she means to me, and I can't stop them from escaping. She stiffens, holding her breath for a beat before exhaling.

"We have to stitch it, and I need to get some antibiotics started," I say, refusing to shed more light on the fact that I find this woman smart, attractive, and funny. "And don't worry about the pee. That's the least of our problems."

I worked in a hospital where urine was a day-to-day occurrence. She can't possibly believe it bothers me.

The medicine is pushed into the corner of our small area, along with our dirty clothes and the cat food. When I reach for the bag, our bodies touch, impossibly close and desperate to get closer. I can't be sure, but I think she leans into me, her hot skin seeking mine. I reach for the bag with medicine but waste a few unnecessary minutes digging around before pulling out a few items.

Caitlyn groans when I set them between us.

"It's going to be painful," I admit.

Her face falls, and her fingertips move up along her arm almost touching the wound.

I have penicillin which I plan to inject directly into the exposed flesh, but with the threat of strangers somewhere right outside, I don't know if she can stay silent. I have a suture kit and take stock of the medicines from the pharmacy. She sees the needle and points, her mouth opening without words escaping.

"Are you allergic to anything?" I ask.

"Needles," she jokes.

I stretch my hand across her thigh, telling myself I want to check if she's trembling, but in truth, I want to touch her. Skin-to-skin feels right with Caitlyn.

"You have to stay silent," I remind her. "Completely quiet."

"Can't we wait?" she begs. "Until there is some soap and water."

I hold up the needle. "Nothing works better than this." Her wound will get cleaned out, but I don't want to bother her with that fact as well. She didn't pass out before, but I don't see how that's possible this time. I'll work faster once she loses consciousness.

We start, not wanting to delay the inevitable any longer. She rests her head on my shoulder, sweat beading at her temples and her teeth digging into my skin, bearing down, doing anything to avoid screaming. It's an awkward angle, but I don't ask her to move. I can take whatever she needs to give.

"You're okay," I tell her. This time there isn't a countdown I can offer. There's a lot of damage, and I need to flush the wound, give her the injection, and stitch it in layers.

Her grip on my bicep tightens, bruising my arm, but I don't care. I'll let her rip off my muscle if it helps her to get through this. It's not long after I begin that her hold loosens, her hand flopping down to the cot and her body growing heavy against mine. I let out a sigh of relief. She's out cold, and I work with purpose, every movement fast and controlled, hoping she doesn't wake up.

Without worrying about her pain, I stitch thoroughly, using up the entire suture kit. I clean the wound with antiseptic wipes and a small bottle of saline before giving her the first round of antibiotics. When I'm done, her arm is red and inflamed, but I feel better about her prognosis.

I've heard them wandering around while I worked, tapping on windows, kicking up gravel while they pace between the trucks. Caitlyn didn't scream or make noise, and they had no reason to open our door.

But it's only a matter of time.

The effort from the past few hours makes it impossible for me to stay awake any longer. We both should sleep during the day, anyway, and leave when it's dark.

Positioning her so she rests on her good arm, I slide behind her, my body spooning hers. She's limp, but I feel her back move against my chest. It's a steady in and out of breath that gives me peace of mind before I drift off.

The dreams that come aren't of my sister this time. In the darkest parts of my mind, Caitlyn is in my nightmare. She's tied up by the men looking for us. They do unspeakable things, things that make me hold her close on our tiny cot, things that wake me up every few hours with my heart pounding and my skin slick from sweat.

Every time my eyes open, I check over her, feel her body for fever, and make sure her breathing isn't labored. Light from the outside dims, and I know the time to leave isn't far off, but I try one last time to rest, curling my knees up behind hers and tightening my arm around her middle.

She curls a palm over my wrist and scoots closer to me.

"Riley," she whispers, testing to see if I'm awake.

"How's your arm?" I ask.

"Fine."

It's a lie, but I know what she means. She's not in excruciating pain and will manage.

"Riley, I…" she trails off.

I don't ask her to elaborate, sensing I won't like the question.

"We have to leave tonight," I tell her. "They'll start searching inside the vehicles."

Her head nods, and I think about kissing her. We like to do that when death looms near.

"Don't let them take me, Riley. If it comes down to it—"

"I won't."

"If they do," she argues.

"I'll kill you first," I lie. I couldn't hurt her, but it's what she needs to hear.

Someone bangs on the cab of a nearby truck, and her body jerks, but she doesn't make a sound.

"Would you like me to return the favor?" Her voice is so low I can barely make out the words. I let them sink into my gut, mulling over the question.

"Riley?"

"No," I say.

I don't tell her why I should stay alive. That's a longer story for another day. One I'm not ready to tell her.

If I'm taken by monsters or cannibals, tortured, and murdered, it's what I deserve.

It's only fair I suffer as my sister did.

CHAPTER
THIRTY-ONE

Riley

"How long can we live off of cat food?" Caitlyn whispers.

"I told you," I sigh. "They know someone's here. Before long, they will open the truck doors and we'll be trapped. Rats in a cage."

She lets out a long breath of air, her fingertips running alongside her stitched wound.

"How's the—"

"It's fine," she cuts me off. "I bet there's a signal in that building."

I shake my head, and she huffs, knowing the answer before she asks the question. That building may get us a signal to check on Lana, but it's certain death shortly after. She's worried, and I am a little, but she's safer there than with us.

"How long can Missy and her crew live off their rations?"

"Decades," I answer. It's the truth, and as long as they continue to be careful, and bloats eventually lower in number, they can make it. There has to be an end to them. Only so much of the population is left to turn. The ones left need to survive, and then eventually, someday, this will all be over.

Caitlyn frowns and brings her knees up to her chest, wedging herself in the corner of the cot. Our small area has grown almost hot with our bodies filling the tiny space.

"She's not ours," I remind her.

Caitlyn rests her head on the wall of the cab. "She was for a little while."

I'm not sure if I've won the argument, or maybe discussion, but we're done with the topic. We can't say goodbye, and I plan on keeping us alive, so there's no need.

Silence spreads between us until we hear faint footsteps heading back in our direction. They've been following a pattern, flowing between the vehicles in the same manner, which is stupid but works in our favor.

"Are we leaving now?" she asks. "Before they get too close?"

I strain to listen, hoping I don't hear them opening doors or breaking windows. There are footsteps of two or three men, and something else. It's a sliding sound, repetitive and steady, growing louder with every minute. Caitlyn hears it, too, and her brow furrows in confusion.

"What is that?" she whispers.

I place a finger over her lips, and she grabs me by my wrist, her fingernails digging into the skin. The sloshing gets louder. It overshadows their footsteps, moving ahead of them and making its way to us.

Caitlyn's gripping me harder, shaking my arm until I free her lips so she can place them by my ear.

"Bloats."

I jerk back and give her a look. "No," I mouth.

She points to her ear, her eyes frantic with the idea, and nods her head in argument.

I listen again, closing my eyes to focus. It doesn't make sense, but that's the familiar sound. They move on concrete with that steady rhythm while they scavenge for someone to turn.

She's right.

Things are worse than I thought. Worse than I could have imagined.

Inside the truck, it's pitch black, the parking lot lit by the moon, and I dare to crack open the shade between the front and back seats. I motion for Caitlyn to lie down while I keep myself close to the door, inching closer to the driver's side window just enough to peek through.

We're both taking shallow breaths, afraid to make any noise while I wait for something to come into view.

Something does.

"What is it?" she whispers. I reach back, placing my hand on her hip and squeezing, urging her to stay silent. She squirms but doesn't ask again.

These strangers have captured bloats, small ones, maybe teenagers. I make out two of them, and through the darkness, I would guess they were small in stature to begin with. They are restrained with straps that connect to a long steel pole. Each one held by two men, and not steadily. They grip it like they're playing a game of tug of war, going back a step and forward two as the bloats fight the restraints.

I can't understand why the thing isn't going mad for the humans holding it at bay, but as they step into the moonlight, I see black sludge spread over the men's faces and clothes. They've tagged themselves in some way. I've never thought of that, fearful it could spark an infection, but it's smart.

Every few paces, the bloat tries to turn around, but the pole keeps them forward. Wearing their blood is enough to calm, but not repel the things.

Shutting the curtain, I slide back into the cot. Caitlyn shakes me, her movements pleading for answers. My arm wraps around her shoulders, bringing her closer before I whisper into her ear.

"They're holding bloats… hostage maybe. They have them tied up to a pole that they kind of push forward. Dog on a leash."

She doesn't move as her mind takes in what I would think is impossible information. There's a lot of impossible lately, and we adapt. It's all we can do. Her cheek slides against my scar, and I shiver from the contact before she responds.

"They… allow that?"

I shrug. "They've covered themselves with the bloat blood. I think it's confusing them a little. Keeping them passive enough to control."

"Why? What are they going to do? Sniff us out?"

I think on this, curious why they would put themselves in such danger. Bloats don't have loyalties. If they spotted us, releasing them would mean death for everyone.

Or, would it?

Bloats are point-and-shoot animals. They will go after what they see and nothing else. If we're within eyeshot, and they somehow get loose, their carrier isn't the one that gets killed.

"It's intimidation," I say. "This is their land. Bloats are scarier than humans."

"Makes it less likely to be taken over by new cannibals," she agrees.

"They're waiting us out," I tell her. "They know someone's here, and they don't know there's some food and water inside the trucks. If they get a glimpse of movement…"

"So safe to say these people don't want to be friends. No bonfires with s'mores."

I pull her against my chest, pressing her body against mine, and sigh. This complicates things, especially if truck doors are opened. If one spots us back here, I can't fight it off. We won't stand a chance.

"After they make this pass, we leave."

"I could go for a night run," she jokes. "I'd also like to get away from the bag of pee."

Their movements grow louder, both of us freezing in place. The bloats speak to each other, their growling and groaning noises sounding almost pained. It's inhuman the way they talk, animalistic and fierce.

There are thousands of languages in the world, all manipulating sounds with our tongues and mouths. The noises they make aren't close to anything I've ever heard. It sounds wild and savage. Sounds that should not come from a person.

We hold our breath as they pass, and the last thing we hear is the labored breathing of the men pushing them along.

Caitlyn's body relaxes once they're gone, and I release her. We don't have time to waste. Rummaging through all the compartments in the back, I shove anything I think might be worth taking inside my bag. There's still no sign of anyone close by when I open the curtain, keeping a palm on Caitlyn to tell her to stay back.

There's not much up here besides the leftover cat food and a sole energy bar, which I grab. After giving the space one more look around, I motion for her to slide forward. She trembles a little when I touch the door handle, and before I can turn it, she moves her hand over mine.

"Remember your promise," she reminds me. "Kill me first."

I nod, pushing down on the lever to begin our escape. It doesn't creak, both of us moving it slowly until there is just enough space for us to slide out. I go first, each foot hitting the pavement without making a sound. Once outside, our breaths make puffs of steam in the cold air, and we hear them.

Caitlyn crouches down, looking underneath the trucks, and points to where she sees feet. When she rises, I jerk my head in the other direction, and we move, keeping close to the vehicles and hoping to stay hidden. When we make a turn through another row of trucks, Caitlyn grabs my shirt and shakes it a few times. Even with the cotton soiled and dingy, the white fabric almost glows in the moonlight.

I rip the shirt off and place it atop a truck tire before we continue. The first few aisles go without a hitch, their footsteps pushing further and further away. We can see a treeline in the distance, woods that extend from the river, and if it was possible, I would sprint to them. This slow and steady pace makes me want to crawl out of my skin.

"We're close," I dare to whisper to Caitlyn. She nods, and the sound of a truck door slamming makes her jump. We wait and the noise echoes again, the loud metal clanging closed and then voices saying words I can't make out.

I feel the urge to give her an *I told you so*. If the tables were turned, she couldn't resist saying it to me, but I hold my tongue. If we make it to those woods, we can pick at each other all we want.

My hand hooks her elbow, turning her toward our destination, and we slide through another row of trucks. A few minutes pass like this, our bodies flowing in rhythm, walking alongside the vehicles, sneaking a look and listening before bolting to the next row.

It's almost too easy.

Then I hear the yelling. One man screaming at another, this time loud enough to make out.

"They're out! Look at this."

I know he's found my shirt, and I curse myself for not putting it into my bag.

"Should we let them go? Boss said scare 'em off."

"Hell, no!"

They run through the trucks as best they can, fighting against the push of their bloats. Their pace quickens with the knowledge that we've escaped.

Caitlyn and I do the same, maintaining our route but jogging it, trying our best to stay ahead of them. There are three rows of trucks before the woods, but when I look over to move to the next one, I see them.

One man and his bloat are running toward us, the pole occasionally clanging on the sides of trucks.

"Here, piggy piggy," he calls out. I'm getting so fucking sick of that hillbilly chant.

There's a noise from the bloat and the sound of the pole crashing to the ground before I turn to Caitlyn.

"Run!"

CHAPTER
THIRTY-TWO

Caitlyn

Tip for surviving the apocalypse.

Become a world-class athlete or a cannibal. That's all I can come up with as we run from murderous bloats.

Again.

I never thought I would find myself running for my life in literal terms. That's a phrase only used for extreme exaggeration. I ran for my life to get my can to the garbage person. I ran for my life when my neighbor's Shih Tzu escaped the fence.

Most days before the world went to shit, I thought paying my bills on time and making it out of the house for work was fighting for my life.

People grow accustomed to their situations, and I'm currently in a cat-and-mouse game with two bloats and a dozen cannibals at my heels.

It's a typical Tuesday.

Riley's holding the hand of my good arm, his back muscles gleaming in the moonlight as we sprint. It's not the time to admire the man's physique, but I can't help myself.

We pass the last line of trucks, and I think we might make it. Maybe my Olympic prowess has emerged in the fight for survival these past few months. I don't have what it takes to be a cannibal, but I can live with being a track athlete.

When Riley stops, and my body crashes into his, my escape plans crumble.

"What the fuck are you doing?" I hiss at him.

He drops his bag, grabs what looks like a toy gun, and yanks me behind him. The bloats fly in our direction, swollen bodies rippling while they run.

"Cover your eyes."

"What the fuck," I scream instead of listening.

When he fires, I'm blinded, hunching down and hiding my head behind his large body.

The sharp sound of a firework screams into the night sky. It's a bit early to celebrate our freedom, but I trust he has a reasonable explanation for shooting this off.

Growling sounds from the bloats fade into the background, and he fires again. The streaks of red light up the night sky, creating a glow around the things chasing us. Once more he fires, and the curve of the light moves past the bloats that have stopped in place, their heads following the beacon.

The black orbs that used to be eyes stare up into the dark sky and away from us. They turn, making a one-eighty as the lights soar toward the men behind them.

Riley yanks me with him before I can say a word, my mind spinning with what he's done. The stampede of monsters runs in the direction of the strangers, their terrified faces lit up by the flares.

We're going to get away.

I trip over my feet, my head turned toward the carnage that I can't stop watching. Arms wrap around my waist, hoisting me against Riley's body and over his shoulder while he runs. All the while, I keep staring at the group.

They have about ten bloats in captivity, and two dozen men stand helpless. All it took was one to break free. Or, be let loose. We'll never know. The prisoners escaped, but so will we.

Gunfire sounds, bullets ricocheting off the surrounding trucks, but I know it's useless.

Do they?

Bullets don't stop these things once they have their sights on you.

One man is held into the air, his body shaking with the change, his arms vibrating while his head rolls back. The rest scatter, but the sound of their screams tells me no one makes it far.

I tilt forward as we make our way up the hill, the dirt from Riley's boots flying in the air. He doesn't slow down, and the carnage fades, hidden by the trees and brush.

"I can walk," I say, thumping him on the shoulder.

He ignores me, tree branches slapping against my body, rocks, and soil crunching under his feet.

"Riley stop. I can walk. You'll wear yourself out."

This only makes him speed up, and I bob in his arms, the moonlight growing brighter and casting shadows on the forest ground. We're still moving uphill, the path growing steeper.

"Riley!" I hiss and beat on his back a few times. "Stop!"

"No."

"I'll throw out the cat food shoved in my pockets. That's right. I'll send you to bed without supper."

There's no laughter or response, only his heavy breaths from the exertion. Seconds turn into minutes as he carries me in silence until finally, his pace slows.

The foliage begins to thin this high on the hill, casting our long shadow on the dirt and fallen leaves below. They would make a wonderful bed, and as if he can read my thoughts, he takes a few steps before setting me down and falling limp beside me.

"Riley?"

I brush my hand over his face and touch cold sweat against his hot skin. My fingertips find his scar, and I trace the lines.

An imperfect face for a seemingly perfect man.

"Are you okay?"

His breathing is labored, but he manages to answer. "Yes."

I lie beside him on the ground even though I have no right to be exhausted. "How did you know?" I ask. "The lights. That they would follow them."

"Calculated." He takes a few quick breaths and reaches for my hand. "Risk." More breathing, loud and fast. "They… don't seem… to see well at night."

"Anything else you care to share with the class, sir?"

Leaves crunch as he shakes his head, and before I can say another word, an explosion shakes the ground beneath us. We scurry to our feet, but it's a struggle to see. Riley finds a vantage point, a tree with low branches. It's unfathomable that he has any energy to climb, let alone hoist me up, but he does.

The building is on fire along with people, or bloats, there's no way to tell. They're running with their bodies lit aflame. His arm tightens around my waist before he leans against the tree trunk and what few leaves remain fall to the ground.

"Cutting their losses," Riley says. The blaze in front of a large warehouse grows and the pop pop pop of gunfire carries through the woods. Every few shots, a walking ball of fire stops in place.

"They won't be making their way up here. That's a plus," I comment. My head rests against his chest, and I listen as his heartbeat slows.

"We need to make camp. I haven't slept in, um…" His eyes close in thought or from exhaustion.

"Here's good, right?" I ask. He can't go any further tonight, but he's stubborn enough to try. "The bloats on the loose are getting taken out by the cannibals."

Instead of arguing with me about their supposed cannibalism, Riley agrees. He insists we make sure every ball of fire stops walking and doesn't make it into the woods. It won't take long, but my eyes grow heavy while we wait. I make my way to a seated position on the branch, resting my head against his calf and using it for balance. That's the last thing I remember before I drift off.

Peanut butter.

I smell it before I open my eyes.

The shelf life of peanut butter is coming to an end, and I whimper at the thought before waking up to the protein bar Riley waves in my face. It's chocolate peanut butter, a huge step up from dump soup ramen, and I'm grateful.

Riley is still shirtless. That's also a plus this morning.

"Were you cold?" I ask. He wasn't. I felt him curl against me last night, his touch warm and comforting. If my body hadn't forced me to sleep instead of having sex, I would have turned around and crawled on top of him. The reminder makes my cheeks flush, and before I take a bite of delicious peanut butter, a thought crosses my mind.

Does Riley feel the same way?

I kissed him before jumping off a building. He kissed me before drowning. Do we need to be on the brink of death to make out? Then he was a gentleman because I told him my deepest secret. Understandable but still, is it possible he's only being polite to his only friend?

Every man wants and likes to see women naked. That doesn't count for much. If he doesn't want me and I make a move, this trek to Canada will be awkward as fuck.

Or, he could appease me kind of like I did Brian.

I might be okay with that. His hotness is becoming irresistible.

"Warm enough."

"Huh?" I ask, flushing with the thoughts swirling around in my head.

Riley sits beside me, looking me over while his eyes linger on my wound. "You asked if I was cold. I was warm enough, but if we come across clothes..." His palm rests on my forehead, checking for fever I suppose. "Are you feeling okay?"

Great. He thinks I have a head injury because I was daydreaming about sex and then spiraled into questioning if he also wants sex, and now I'm staring at him without speaking.

"Much better." I hold up the half-eaten protein bar. "Thanks to peanut butter."

He looks off into the distance, eyes scanning the woods around us. I do the same, searching for any hints of blood spots that stain like oil, or the trampling marks of a bloat horde.

Nothing.

"Anyone following us?" I ask.

He shakes his head. "But I'd feel better if we got further north, just a half-day walk until nightfall, just to be sure."

"And then?"

"Further north."

My lips turn up in a smile. "And then?"

He rises, brushing off his jeans before pointing in some direction, claiming it's northeast and giving me more terrible news.

He plans to take a walk through the suburbs. We might as well walk through some lava or try bungee jumping without a rope while we're at it.

"It's worth a stop to get fresh clothes, maybe some tampons for you," he adds.

"My period was over two days ago, and we are restocked," I inform him. "Don't blame this escapade on me."

"We need supplies, Caitlyn," he argues.

I shove what's left of my protein bar into my mouth, saddened when I realize it's gone. "Ahbanndonndpff."

Riley waits for me to chew and swallow before I speak again.

"Abandoned neighborhood. Right! How do you know?"

"I don't, but—"

"People converge in places like that," I remind him. "Bad people. Cannibals."

Riley rolls his eyes, his favorite expression, and it fuels my fire.

"Maybe it's not a cannibal. I don't know for sure, but there are more bad people than good."

"I know, Caitlyn. But we need to stock up on food and find supplies where we can."

"People that rape women," I continue. "People that kill others just for fun. Like there's a surplus of humans around or something. It's insane."

Riley turns his back to me, taking a few steps toward what I guess is northeast. For all I know he could be leading us back to the river.

"Are you hearing me?" I ask.

"Yes." He doesn't give me more, and it infuriates me. I get a say after all we've been through. It's not like he's dragging me on a cot through the woods anymore. That was last week, and he needs to get with the times.

"I'm not going in there. I'll eat seeds and earthworms. The way grocery stores and houses end for me, let's just say it rarely works out."

"I know, Caitlyn."

"Do you? Ask Brian. Oh, wait. You can't. He's dead."

Riley stiffens. He knows I'm making a point. The idea of walking into another stronghold like the one we just left is asinine.

"We need to stick to the woods. Live off the earth. Do you hear me? Do you know what happens—"

"I know, Caitlyn!" He turns, taking two large strides until he's inches from my face, his lips almost touching mine. "Look at my face. Don't you think I know?"

My heart thuds inside my chest, but I'm not afraid. He's not wild with rage. He's… scared. One hand reaches around my neck as he tilts my face upward, my eyes staring into his.

"Caitlyn, I've tried staying off the path. It's getting colder, and the further north we go, it'll only be worse. Things die in winter. We need coats and good shoes. Food if we can manage, but we won't make it like this. And I know, fuck do I know, there's a risk stepping foot into a hot zone like that." His forehead rests on mine, and I hear his voice shake. "I'll keep you safe."

I kiss him.

And not because his lips were the first thing I thought about this morning, well, after the peanut butter of course. I kiss him because we should be kissing. Our paths were meant to cross. His cranky personality and my stubborn nature fit, and even in a room of a thousand men, I'd want to kiss him.

In all my terrible blind dates and online hookups, I've never liked someone. I've liked parts of them, or I liked not being alone for a night, but not them.

I want all of Riley. Scarred and angry Riley gives me butterflies in my stomach and argues with me like there's no tomorrow, which may be true in our case. He challenges me and protects me. He's fucking likable.

My feelings swarm, overwhelming my senses and instead of hashing them out, I kiss him.

And it's perfect.

The way our lips find each other in a flawless rhythm. The way he lies me down on the earth, cradling my head while his tongue searches my mouth. How he makes me let out a soft moan as his hands run up and underneath my shirt. It's blissful to kiss without interruption.

This means I have my answer. He wants me just as much as I need him. I can feel he does, the hardness of his cock throbbing into my hip.

We grow more frantic, feverish with need, and I don't want him to stop. This moment should last forever, both of us desperate for each other, for a release.

I go to kiss his neck, his hand finding my breast and playing with the nipple. My tongue licks his skin, and I moan against the ridges of his scar before I kiss him there.

He lifts his head, turning away from me.

"Don't do that," I say. Taking his face in my hand, pulling him back toward my mouth. "I like it."

"No. You can't possibly. If you knew—"

I blink a few times, waiting for more. His hand, still warm against my breast slides away, and I ache when his touch leaves me.

"Riley? If I knew what?"

CHAPTER
THIRTY-THREE

It's shock.

That's why she's kissing me. That, or she's trying to convince me not to venture out to an abandoned neighborhood that she believes is full of cannibals. Her tactic works. Leaving this spot is the last thing on my mind.

All I can think about is her perfect hot mouth. It's on mine willingly, without the threat of death at our heels. Whatever her reasons, I can't stop kissing her, pressing my body against hers, running my hands over her skin until I've touched every inch of her.

I'm ravenous.

And so is she.

Running my fingertips across her ribs, just underneath her breast, and feeling her tremble with the touch, sliding my tongue inside her mouth and tasting her. It's not enough but still too much.

Until her mouth sends a spark of pain from the ridge of my scar.

I can't help my reaction, and she can't help the question that follows.

"If I knew what, Riley?"

She's poked around this topic before, wanting to know where I got my scar, and what happened to my sister. This time feels different, because this time, I know I'll tell her.

There's something about Caitlyn, the way she's looking at me right this moment that fills me with the need to be closer to her in every way. I can't go another day without her knowing every part of me. All the things that scarred me inside and out.

If she's agreeing to head north, to try and survive this hellscape, she has a right to know the man next to her. Who he was and what he's become.

"I won't judge you," she says. "I wouldn't. You're… Well, you're the best person I've ever known."

It's a knife to the gut, stopping me in my tracks and sending me backward. She clings onto my shoulders, refusing to let me pull away from her. I pause and lower, not wanting to separate our bodies just yet. Her closeness, her touch, her kiss, it's inescapable.

Our lips find their way to each other again, slow and soft. It's a kiss of consolation.

"Maisie didn't stand a chance," I mumble, my mouth still grazing hers. "Where she was and the person she was." She opens again for me, and I take advantage, my tongue massaging hers, a moan leaving her mouth before she pulls back. I kiss along her jawline, making my way to her soft neck until my tongue glides along her collarbone.

"Do any of us?" Caitlyn asks, but I know she doesn't understand.

Her hands cup my face, and she moves me to look at her. Those eyes plead with me to unburden myself. It's as if she can feel the weight I carry with this, the way it hurts. She's the reason I don't think of Maisie morning, noon, and night. The need to protect Caitlyn replaces the hate I feel toward myself.

Reluctantly, I move to her side. If we keep kissing like this, the story will take hours. She curls her body around mine, and I hold her.

"I'd kiss you in a room of a thousand men," she says.

I huff a laugh. Even in moments of sadness and passion, if there's a thought in her head, she's saying it out loud. Although this admission, be it truth or simply kindness, is something I need to hear.

"Don't tell lies," I say jokingly. It's not that I want to call her a liar, but the words may be ungenuine, meant to lift me up when I'm feeling low.

"I'm not," she says. "I wouldn't do that."

That rings true. She's too mean and blunt to bother with dishonesty.

"Thank you for saying that, for telling me you want—"

Me.

I can't speak the words aloud, afraid I'll see something in her eyes telling me I'm wrong. I pull her tighter against me, feeling her breasts press against my bare skin, wishing we were both shirtless. Maybe then her mind would be clear, free of every burden, and solely focused on pleasure. "You know I want you, and it's not just because there's only you. You're someone I'd be…"

I don't know how to finish that sentence. Our old life might as well have been a movie we watched years ago. It's too far away to think about, and it's heartbreaking to remember it existed.

"So, now that that's out of the way." Her hand reaches up to my scar, and she doesn't need to ask again. It amazes me how I don't flinch when she traces the imperfections across my cheek, down my chin, across my neck, until she rests her hand on my chest. It's time, and I take a deep breath before I spill it all out.

"A few weeks into November, most people had an… unspoken understanding. If you went into a grocery store, you carried out what you could. They defended their houses, but I don't know. You saw more humans back then. You never knew who had a gun or was crazy. Everyone kept to themselves, got what they needed, and stayed inside as much as they could."

Caitlyn's lips touch my skin, grazing a few kisses across my chest. If she keeps doing that, I won't be able to keep talking, but it's pleasantly distracting.

"We were in some fancy-fuck organic store. A family was there, and a few couples came while we were filling up those overpriced reusable bags. I remember they were seven bucks. Seven bucks for a paper bag." I shake my head. "Anyway, Landon was there." She stiffens, and I kiss her forehead.

"Keep going," she urges.

"Everyone was learning the bloats' patterns, figuring out you have time after they leave before they come back again. Looking back, I know where we went wrong. There were more of them. Not enough had popped so one group left and another came while we were on a grocery run. Too many to keep track of them back then."

My voice trails off, letting the memories flood back. I'm squeezing Caitlyn too hard, but she lets me.

"They came through the front, everyone goes running for the back. The locked back. People started panicking – shooting. Someone hit the boiler I think. That started the fire, but what exploded… it burned me like an acid. Maisie too. I remember ripping my sunglasses off and touching my face. It felt like hamburger meat."

Looking down at my hand, I force myself to feel the other scars, ones not so noticeable that came from that day. My pulse thuds in my ears when she interlaces her fingers with mine. I push through, needing to get this out. Maybe if I tell it to someone else, it won't hurt so much. Caitlyn shouldn't carry the pain, but she wants to. It's so apparent with her eyes, her touch, the way she kisses my fingertips.

"I tried to get Maisie out. Smoke was taking over, and she couldn't walk. She was… badly burned, screaming in agony. I don't know where everyone went, but it felt like we were the only ones there. More bloats came in, walking over the ones killed from the blast, and that's when she just, forced me to… to go. She just—" I can't bring myself to say it, even though I see it. Over and over again in my mind, I see it. Every night, the memory comes back.

"She was screaming at me to go, and I could have carried her, but it would have hurt her, you see. She was… so burned. It was… it was horrible and I couldn't figure out how to… to t-touch her without…" I'm choking on the words, each one a knife to my heart. The image of her disfigured body is clear in my mind. The sound of her screams so clear I swear I'm hearing them in these woods. "When she realized I wouldn't leave her, she ran into the fire."

Caitlyn's hand squeezes mine, and I hear the sharp intake of breath. "She killed herself so I could run, and I tried to go after her, but she… She just sort of—"

"That's enough." Caitlyn places her fingertips across my lips.

"Thank you for telling me. I know that was hard. I'm so sorry. I know she was an amazing person, and that's horrible. That was an accident, Riley. Do you hear me? There was nothing, nothing you could have done."

Maybe she's right. That doesn't make it any easier. Night after night, I've thought about everything I missed, everything I could have done differently.

It was, and is, the worst thing that has ever happened to me. The apocalypse is second to losing my sister, and having her die in such a horrific way destroys me. Even when I knew in a split second that she couldn't survive her burns, and delaying the inevitable would have been torture, I couldn't leave her. I wanted to save her, pull her from that place, and keep her from danger forever.

Sometimes letting go is the kinder choice, but I couldn't do that. My lack of action forced her to run into the flames. Holding Caitlyn, I wonder if any of us would be able to walk away from someone we love, even if it's the right thing to do. If there was no way out, would I do as Caitlyn asks and pull the trigger? Or, would I make the same mistake again and force her to do it herself?

"I know that kind of killed the mood," she says. "But if you can go through all of that, and still want to get close to a grocery store, it must be important. I guess if you insist, we can walk to suburbia."

I clear my throat, swallowing the lump there. "It is."

"I want a coat so warm, I'm sweating. I should be able to climb Mt. Everest in this thing. Do you think there are any bloats on Mt. Everest?"

Her lips press against my throat, and something inside me lifts, releasing the tiniest amount of worry and guilt. She's not repulsed by what happened and how cowardly I acted. We don't have to keep rehashing it and talking about the past. There's no more to say, and her ability to recognize that endears me to her. Caitlyn knows when I'm done talking and when my threshold of emotion has hit its peak.

"We will get you a very warm coat and lots of layers," I answer. "And no, I do not think there are bloats on Mt. Everest."

"How can you know? Oh wait," she interrupts herself. "That's why we are going to Canada. Snow and blah blah blah."

"Yes. All the blahs. Bloats don't do cold."

"We hope," she retorts.

We lay there for a while longer, comforting each other. My stomach growls a few times before she insists I dive into the rations. She may want to chuckle as I eat cat food, but I'm okay with that.

I try and fail to get Jim on the radio. Her face falls after I admit defeat, but part of me thinks it's for the best. Keeping in touch could end in heartbreak. There's already so much of that going around. I hope for the best outcome, and I have confidence they can wait it out, but distance lessens worry.

Finding a high ridge, there's a clear view of neighborhoods in the distance. The rooftops look so small, and the paths between them, once filled with cars and people, appear empty. It's quiet, but my ears are open. We don't know the paths of any bloats in the area. I'll need to watch for them today, and try to sleep tonight. Another evening of hoping the fires create enough warmth and we'll head out tomorrow.

"I hope they aren't down there," Caitlyn says.

"We want to see them," I tell her. "That's a half-day walk. If we catch a group passing through, that gives us a few days to rest and relax."

"And find a decent coat and please, a hot bath."

I turn to her. "I'll keep you warm."

She flushes, and I wonder if I should tell her I meant by making a fire.

Maybe that's not all I meant.

There are other ways to get her blood to rush and fill her with heat. Once I get her to a safe place, I'll show her how.

CHAPTER
THIRTY-FOUR

CAITLYN

The sexual tension is palpable. I could reach out and touch it, or better, I could touch him. Ideally, I could fuck him. That would fix it.

Except he's completely exhausted after not sleeping the past few days. Then he goes and stays up all night looking for bloats to run through the houses below. It's terrifying how much I want to sit on his face, but alas, I will restrain myself and wait to climb him like a tree.

I've been up for hours when first light makes its way through the trees. I awake and imagine unspeakable things I could do with this man, things I've never done with anyone.

"Hey!" I pipe up.

His eyes are already fluttering open when I say, "Wakey wakey." He reaches up to stretch, and I can't help myself. My leg makes it over his torso, and those big hands of his find their way to my hips, fingertips digging into the sides and pulling me forward just enough to feel every part of him is up.

"You're straddling me," he croaks.

"You're observant." I place my hands by his sides and kiss him. It's not as long as I'd like, but we're out of gum even though I'm out of self-control.

Pulling myself away, his fingertips run along my legs until I'm free. A low groan rumbles in his chest, and I pretend the sound doesn't soak my panties. I'm being a tease, but if we've waited this long, which isn't long at all but in my head it's decades, I want it to be a little special.

I want it to be after a bath.

The sooner we make it to one of those blue squares at the bottom of this hill, the sooner someone's backyard pool becomes my giant tub. Chlorine can kill anything.

I hope.

Riley's up and moving in no time, catching up to me as I get a head start walking. As predicted, he saw bloats last night, and leaving this morning is the right idea. We need to be awake and alert in case anything else finds us walking across their manicured lawn.

It's a few hours' trek, and I keep the conversation light.

What was something you ate every week growing up?

Riley: Spaghetti, which is not to be confused with bolognese. They were not that fancy.

Me: Deer spaghetti. I notice Riley smirk and tilt his head with that admission. I'm not sure what part of me cramming down ramen soup made him think I'm a picky eater, but I'm not. And, yes, deer tastes good. Especially because our neighbor gave it to us for free. Free food is always better.

What was your pet peeve at work?

Riley: When patients complain about the food. Correction. The patient's family complained about the food. The people in need of care didn't eat much and were thankful whereas some weird aunt wondered why we didn't have real butter for the biscuits.

Caitlyn: Showers of the wedding and baby variety. Why don't I get a shower for not making terrible life decisions and everyone gives me a gift because I live alone and don't have a dual income? If the world gets it together in another hundred years and that shit comes back, someone needs to make the celebrations fair.

The topic of Maisie comes up once, and he tells me about when they were kids. Their non-fancy spaghetti was had every Wednesday. Maisie liked extra noodles and Riley wanted extra sauce.

Maisie was quite the swimmer and Riley was on the team, too. She loved picking on her brother which may be why he puts up with my ass.

When he wants to change the subject, asking me what my comfort movie is, I let him. He's opening up, and I'm not trying to jump to my death. We're making progress.

We remain silent for the last thirty minutes, keeping a close eye on the houses not too far ahead. I spend the time imagining how clean I'm going to get so he can put his face between my legs. I'm creaming by the time we get to paved roads.

In my former life, I would have spent over an hour getting ready for a date. All the washing and shaving and contouring followed by the cutest outfit and perfect perfume.

I just want a damn bath with soap. Any soap. I don't care if my skin is flaking from dryness or if I smell like an Irish spring.

Riley lifts his hand to stop me. "Wait here," he says.

Rolling my eyes, I keep following him. He hears me and turns, his hands on his hips.

"I should go first and scope out a safe place," he says.

"In case you are ambushed by cannibals, killed, and later eaten, I should come."

He rubs the spot between his eyebrows with a groan. "The cannibal thing, Caitlyn," he mumbles.

"Plus, there's no point in living without you, so I need to come. If something happens, we die together."

He freezes because what the fuck did I just say?

"I didn't mean it like that," I add. "Not like you're the only thing worth living for." I raise my hands to the sky theatrically, and remembering we should be quiet, I drop them to my sides and stare at my shoes. "I just meant, the captain should go down with the ship?"

"Are you the captain in this scenario?"

"No," I scoff. "I'm a passenger on the ship."

"I don't know what's happening."

I grab him by the wrist and march forward. "I'm going with you."

He relents, searching with his fingers to hold hands with me which makes my heart flutter. My head buzzes and I'm floating, blissfully unaware of any danger that lies ahead.

A few steps onto a paved road, and I lose all my resolve. Frozen in the middle of a street, abandoned houses only steps away, I can't seem to take a step forward. My feet shuffle backward, bumping into Riley who brings his lips to my ear.

"This way. Out of sight."

We scurry over to the side of a house that appears to have every window broken. There won't be anything in there, and when I look around, I notice they are all in the same state.

"Riley," I whisper. "We won't find anything here. Look."

He's not paying attention, gazing off in the distance at the rows of wrecked and robbed houses. "I mean there might be a coat," I say. "I bet the pool is dirty."

He gives me a quizzical look, but I only shake my head in response.

"We need to get to the gates." He points, and I get up on my tip-toes to see what he's talking about. There's a part of this community in a different tax bracket than the rest. Giant homes sprawl out over large lots behind gates that are somewhat intact. I bet those pools are huge.

"Lift me up," I order.

He shakes his head instead of doing what I ask. "Come on, let's go. This way."

Dilapidated patio furniture strewn across the lawn will give me a boost if he won't. When he sees me climbing a three-legged chair, his arms wrap around my hips until I'm lifted and the mansions beyond come into view.

That's not all I see.

"D-down. Down. Down. Down," I order, smacking him on the shoulder.

"What is it?" he asks, but I'm already slipping from his grip, sprinting toward the front door of the closest house. Locked.

"Dammit," I hiss. The broken glass of a basement window is the next best thing, and Riley is at my heels, questioning me, begging me to stop.

What I saw is not possible. It's simply not. I bounce on my toes, my heart in my throat. We have to get into this basement and hide.

"Is it bloats?" he asks. "Talk to me. What are you doing?"

I spin in a circle, looking for something to cut away the shards of glass. We have to get cover and now.

His hands pull at my waist, forcing me to look him in the eye. "What is it?" he begs.

I'm frantic, pointing at the basement window and trying to make sense of what I saw.

When the motorcycle revs in the distance, I cover my mouth so I don't scream.

CHAPTER
THIRTY-FIVE

I scouted the area, watching through the trees as we walked down. My eyesight is perfect, and still, I walked her right into danger.

The glass will make a terrible noise, but so does the motorcycle, so I take a chance. Grabbing a broken lawn chair, I use one of the legs to bust through the sharded edges surrounding the window pane.

After a minor dispute about who goes first, I slide Caitlyn through and into the basement. The bike turns onto our street, its engine rumbling over the pavement. I don't spot the driver and hope that means he doesn't see me either. He's someone unafraid of what that noise brings which makes him insane or he has a death wish. Anyone left knows to keep a low profile.

My feet hit the cement floor seconds before the whoosh of the vehicle flies by the house. Caitlyn's standing a few feet away clutching her throat, her breaths coming short and far too fast. I reach for her, pulling her against me and running my hand up and down her back. The rumble of the motorcycle drifts into nothing, and the steady ticking of a grandfather clock somewhere in this abandoned house lulls her back to calm.

Please be abandoned.

I press my cheek against her hair and whisper to her, "What did you—"

"Halflings," she interrupts.

I step back, unsure if I heard her correctly, but when our eyes meet, I know I did. She's terrified, tears welling around her irises and her jaw trembling.

"More than one?" I ask.

She nods. "I saw three."

"And they saw you?"

"No." Her eyes move rapidly from side to side. "No," she repeats. "From what I could see, one was already getting on a bike, and it looked like he was…"

She stops, the tears falling from her unfocused gaze, her mind searching a memory she doesn't quite understand.

"What? What else was happening?"

"It looked like they were talking." She covers her cheeks with her hands and steps away from me, her back hitting the cement wall. "They were talking to each other. I'm sure of it. They looked at each other. Moved their mouths like us you know. Not that damn moaning and wailing."

"And you're sure it was halflings. Not men. Some people look a little rough after a few months."

Her hands drop to her sides, and her look of disgust I've grown to like so much shoots daggers in my direction. "I know what I saw. They were halflings." She crosses her arms at her chest and pops a hip, her fear replaced with defiance.

Bloats we've seen everywhere for months which allowed us to study their movements and patterns, learn how to avoid them, and even kill them. They speak but not to each other. They're pack animals, moaning and groaning in some unified language. There is no back and forth. Halflings are rare, something we didn't know about until recently. It's possible they still have human language.

All I can do is agree with Caitlyn. There's no talking her out of what she saw.

"Okay then. Three talking halflings."

She starts pacing, kicking up dust in the dim basement. "Just okay?"

"They aren't circling us from the sound of it, and if they were talking, maybe there's a little bit of human left. Either way, it's not safe to go with the original plan of ransacking the mansions." I look around the space covered in spiderwebs and stacked boxes. That doesn't tell me much. Basements are meant to be left and forgotten. "I don't think anyone is staying here, but we need to check."

"What about all the broken windows? Anyone could just come in."

She bites her lip and rolls her eyes. "Not that a window would stop a bloat. I know. I know."

"Or a cannibal," I add.

I'm so relieved by the smile on her face that I forgo the impending argument. If I ask her to stay in the basement, she'll fight me and head up the stairs anyway. Even if she didn't mean what she said earlier, I don't want to live without her either. Before Caitlyn, surviving was the only answer. I realize now how I need something, or someone, to live for. Captain, ship, crew, or whatever. We are doing this together. Being with her, that's living.

"After you," I offer. She rolls her shoulders back and tip-toes toward the stairs. I make sure I'm in front when we reach the top and turn the door handle. A slight creak echoes through a hallway as I peer through the cracked door.

Nothing.

I reach for her hand and step forward, the last bit of daylight shining through a dirty window and blinding us. She squeezes my palm, and we take a few hesitant steps before our confidence builds. After a few minutes of finding nothing, we weave from room to room with less fear.

Every corner of the house smells stale and feels cold, its walls haunted by pictures of strangers. They portray a family of five, three kids that might be teenagers. There are a few degrees framed in a large office. Thousands were spent on education. A lot of good that did them in the end.

The only sign of struggle is in the bathroom. Someone emptied every drawer, damaging the wood before throwing the contents of the cabinets onto the floor. We step over old sunscreen, and Caitlyn scoops up some tampons, placing them on the counter with a wink. I gather someone here was looking for something particular, maybe pills, and then left in a hurry.

We come across a locked room, and I beg Caitlyn to hide inside the hall shower while I check it out.

"You're a screamer," I remind her. "Listen, if you hear a scuffle, just run in and die with me." She concedes with the offer and closes the shower curtain with a huff.

It takes a few slams with my shoulder, but the door breaks open, wood splintering at the frame. Collectibles fill countless shelves, weird figurines covered in a layer of dust. There's a king-size bed and an attached bathroom, but no bloats or dead bodies.

Returning to an anxious Caitlyn, I let her know nothing was exciting. "Maybe they thought a lock would be enough to stop someone trying to steal. But it was just the master bedroom." She shrugs stepping out of the tub.

"Judging by the bathroom, it may have," she agrees.

We don't take a deep breath for half an hour, searching under every unmade bed and digging through someone else's closets. We take corners of the remaining rooms, meeting in the middle with a silent nod to confirm that there's nothing left, not people anyway.

In the kitchen, Caitlyn hands me a package of ramen and wiggles her eyebrows. I don't laugh, but I feel the urge behind my smile. A pantry holds plenty of canned goods, and I exhale, relieved we've found some luck.

"I saw a few coats in one of those bedrooms," I tell her. We've searched through every nook and cranny, and it's getting dark. "And snow boots."

Her eyes sparkle. "That's good."

The motorcycle hasn't returned, and I don't know what to make of what Caitlyn saw. There's nothing we can do about it tonight, but after we've rummaged through this place, things are looking up.

We make our way to the living room, and she draws the curtains before sitting crisscross on the couch. "Why did you want to go to the bigger houses?" she asks.

"More rooms, more stuff," I answer. She looks down at her hands and grimaces. We're both filthy and exhausted, but I know what she's after. "I saw something in the kitchen that you'll like. Get naked."

She lets out a chuckle and stands. Calling my bluff, she pulls at the hem of her top, lifting it past her bare stomach. It takes everything in me to turn away and walk to the kitchen, but I know what I have to show her will get her squealing with delight.

Some things are worth the wait, building the anticipation until we both can't take it anymore. I'm close to pinning her against a wall and showing her that this life is worth living.

Soon.

I spot what I'm after, a 20-liter refill for this family's water cooler. I drag it to the spare bathroom, hoisting it onto the counter and kicking the garbage on the floor to the side.

"The master only has a shower," I say when I hear her step into the doorway. "Hallway bath has the tub."

"Oh my god what a find," she gasps. "I wish it could be warm, but beggars can't be choosers."

"I'll get it warm. I just need to—" My voice catches in my throat, and I swallow hard.

She's in her bra and panties and nothing else.

My jaw hangs slack while my dick springs to life. She notices, glancing at the bulge in my jeans. Gripping the edge of the counter, my fingers turn white from strain, and I force myself not to maul her.

"You know what you're doing," I say.

"With that?" she points to the water canister. "Or that?" She wags a finger at my dick. "I mean I can handle both."

As confident as she sounds, her cheeks flush. Her arms wrap around her middle as if that last quip made her painfully aware she's almost nude and we're an arm's reach from one another.

Caitlyn reaches out, but instead of touching me, she rips a towel from a hook, shaking it out a few times before wrapping it around her.

"Better?" she asks.

No, it's not fucking better, but I nod anyway.

I find another towel, one not thrown onto the floor, and wipe down the tub before pouring the water inside. "There's another one of these refills in the pantry," I tell her. "I'll get a fire going and warm up some of the water."

The blood drains from her face, and she shakes her head. "Where? The backyard? What if the halflings come back?"

She's right, but I know how much she wanted a hot bath.

"It's too risky," she continues. "I'm happy for water and that bar of soap over there. She points and I pick up a box of store-brand bar soap. "Throw that in and I'll make do. And that's enough water. Save the rest for you or you know, to drink. So we don't die of thirst."

I nod, disappointed our unwanted visitor ruined her wish. "I'll wash up after you." I rip open the box and toss the soap in the tub. "I'll see what I can put together from the kitchen."

"Okay," she nods and drops the towel before reaching around to unhook her bra.

CHAPTER
THIRTY-SIX

Caitlyn

I am a mad woman.

Mad with lust, maybe?

Desperation, definitely.

When Riley walks past me, his eyes avoiding my bare breasts when I unhook my bra, I'm a frustrated woman.

I'm so mad, desperate, and frustrated, that I forget how disgusting I am. That is until the first pass of some stranger's washrag glides over my skin, revealing a different shade underneath. I've been sporting an apocalypse tan. Shades of dirt, grime, and maybe some blood mix to create a dull earthy color that collects on the rim of the tub.

I shiver, another pass of cool water running down my skin. Standing in the shallow bath I give myself a fourth pass with the soap. Head to toe I wash and recoil in disgust when I wring out the wash-cloth. All that's left is my hair, but when I look down at my feet, I can't see them. The water is so full of muck that I'll only deposit dirt into my scalp.

There are a few knocks at the door, and I instinctively cover my lady bits with my hands.

"Riley?"

"Who else would be…" he trails off.

Valid point.

"I made some food. If you're hungry."

"In what universe would I not be hungry right now?" I joke.

I also have a valid point.

"I meant when you're done. Just letting you know."

Why are we yelling through a door? This feels juvenile and that's the last thing I want. My mouth salivates with the idea of food, but when I step out of the bath, my reflection in the mirror catches me off guard.

"I'm Medusa," I mumble.

"What?" Riley asks.

My fingertips run through the mop on my head, and a leaf falls to the floor before I get caught in a tangle. I fail to remove my hand without ripping out some hair. Kicking around some of the products on the floor, I look for something that might help.

"Ouch. Ouch. Ouch," I mutter to myself.

No spray-in detangler but there is some overpriced shampoo and conditioner. For what these people paid for that brand, it should restore my hair to its original settings.

"Are you okay?" Riley asks.

He turns the doorknob which I did not lock. Instead of reaching to keep the door closed, I reach for a towel, haphazardly covering myself with one hand while the other is stuck in the bird's nest residing on my head.

He glances through the cracked door and seeing that I'm not completely nude, sighs and marches inside.

Is he relieved?

Shouldn't he want to see me naked?

It must be the hair.

"I need some help," I say.

"With your…"

He says, "Towel," and I say, "Hair," in unison.

"Maybe both," I shrug. Releasing my grip on the matted hair, I adjust the white terrycloth and secure it between my breasts. "My hair was braided. I must have lost my hairband running for my life for the tenth time this week."

"It hasn't been ten," Riley offers. "Maybe four."

"Ten if you count each cannibal as a separate threat."

Careful to hold the towel in place, I bend over and grab the hair products. They have gold embossing on all the cursive letters and I think there's a gemstone dotting the "I". This brand would sit behind glass at the store. A young, underpaid employee would need to be bothered to unlock it before carrying it straight to the register. I never had that kind of time or cash. Tonight I'm going to use this entire bottle.

"Is there any bottled water or, I don't know, any liquid to wash my hair? I'll take anything for some cleaner suds." I point to the tub, expecting Riley to be appalled. He shoves his hands in his pockets and asks if I feel better.

"Yes," I say. He looks remarkably cleaner, wearing fresh clothes that still have a line from where they were folded. I can only pray the woman in those family photos liked sweatpants. "Did you get washed up?" My heart sinks realizing my only option may be to shave my head.

"Sure did, but there's enough water for your hair." He reaches for the bottles, turning them over in his hands. There's a wide-tooth comb on the floor, and when I pick it up, I threaten it to work some magic or else. Riley doesn't respond to my antics. He turns on his heel and heads for the kitchen.

I pitter after him, still cold, goosebumps forming across my skin. Opening a hall closet along the way, he pulls out a floor-length sweater. "I don't think that will work for a trip to Canada."

"But it will work for the kitchen." His gaze slides down my body, and I realize I'm trembling.

"Oh, yes. That makes sense." I take the sweater, feeling sweet relief when I wrap it around my middle and secure it with a tie. "Thank you." Warmth washes over me, and I think about searching a bedroom for socks, but my desire to wash my hair takes precedence.

He grabs a chair from the kitchen table and drags it to the sink before setting a step stool in front of it. "Put your feet here so it's comfortable to lean back." The other 20-liter scratches across the floor with barely any water removed from the canister.

"How did you wash?" I ask pointing at the setup.

"There's a birdfeeder out front. I took the opportunity to use the rainwater and scope things out. Found some clean clothes." He pulls at the sweatpants that fit him all too well.

"I noticed." We stand there in silence for a moment and he taps the back of the chair. The scene clicks together, and I tighten the waist of the sweater. "Are you going to wash my hair? How do you even know how to do sink hair?"

"Maise," we both say in unison.

"She was utterly obsessed with her hair," he says ushering me to sit down. The water canister thuds onto the counter, and I oblige. I don't know how this will go, but it's got to be better than shaving my head. He collects my mass of hair in his hands and closes the sink drain while I sink into the seat.

"Here." A small plastic tube lands in my lap. "That should be easy to eat while we do this." It's difficult to lift my head in this position, so I raise the object to my line of sight, dangling it overhead.

I squeal and moan at the same time.

"Jerky! Sweet mother of this bloated wasteland. What a find." The wrapping proves tricky, but I manage to rip it open with my teeth, and the second the meaty goodness hits my tongue, I bounce in the seat.

"There's a whole box," Riley says. His voice is lighter somehow, pleased that I'm so satisfied with chemical-laden meat. "But we should only have a few here. It's light and easy to travel with. We can knock out some canned goods for dinner."

"Party pooper," I pout but don't mean it. I'm smiling too much to be serious.

"My mom used to wash my hair in the sink," I say. "We had a long counter I could lay on and she would let me do all these temporary colors when I was out of school. It was kitchen hair because we weren't paying for a salon, but she was so good at it. All my friends were jealous."

A stab of longing pierces my heart but mixed with the happy memory, it's bearable.

"I'm sorry I never got to meet her," Riley says. "You two had a special bond."

"We did," I agree. "When she died, I think I became sort of, mean, you know? I could blame it on the life's too short mantra. Why bother with niceties when you never know when your number's up? But I was just so mad. Really, really fucking mad."

"That's okay," he says. "Terrible things happened and you have a right to be upset about it."

I sniffle and take another bite of jerky while he rubs conditioner into my hair, using the comb at my ends before working his way up. He's done this a time or two.

"So, before nurse, did you consider hairdresser?" I ask, not entirely joking.

There's silence while he works a knot, steadily combing in the same spot until he can brush through the section. He places a kitchen towel under my neck, turning my head to the side. I'm staring at a toaster covered in dust, the same brand my mother owned. I bite my lip wondering how many pieces of bread this family shoved in that silver contraption. It's odd what I find depressing, but times are strange.

"One summer Maisie used this hair treatment to get blonder," Riley says. He's found another knot, and my head bobs while he combs. "She wanted to look like she had white hair or something. I don't know. Sounded ridiculous."

"Platinum," I offer. "She wanted to be platinum blonde. I bet it looked great on her."

"For about two days. Until swim practice for the week started."

My hand squeezes the jerky, and it almost pops out of the tube. "Oh, no."

"It wasn't good. Our parents said she had to experience the consequences of her actions. They didn't approve of all the bleaching and she did it behind their back."

"How green was it?"

Riley pauses combing. "How did you know?"

"It's in the girl handbook. I can't believe Maisie didn't get her copy. Chlorine makes it green. The warning even rhymes."

The comb glides through a large chunk of hair, and I smile with relief. If I'm going to die by the hands of a motorcyclist halfling, it should be with decent hair.

"Well, it's copper, not chlorine that makes it green. But chlorine is the catalyst."

"You know too much."

"I know I went to the chemistry teacher when she wouldn't stop crying. We had to put baking soda in it and mom made us do it in the kitchen so we didn't ruin the tub. I think she just wanted to watch and laugh a little."

Something tells me I would have liked Riley's parents as much as I like him. A part of me wants to ask what happened to them, but it's pointless. I know what happened. How it happened doesn't matter.

"The only problem was we didn't know that you had to keep washing it or wear a swim cap, so a week would go by and… well."

"She was the Grinch again," I say. "Speaking of, what day is it?"

He pauses and we both count nights. It's more difficult than I expect, all of our adventures meshing together into one long memory. "Is it… Christmas?"

"Eve," he says. "Christmas Eve."

I almost pop up from the sink, but the comb gets stuck again. Water pours over my scalp, and I toss the jerky wrapping, pulling at the sleeves of my sweater.

"I didn't get you anything," I say.

He reaches for the bottle of shampoo, and I scoot it closer to him. There's the sound of the product sliding between his hands and then his fingers run across my strands once more. It's divine. The best head massage of my life, and I close my eyes and take in the moment.

"You stayed alive," he whispers. His words are soft, almost pained. "That's gift enough."

CHAPTER
THIRTY-SEVEN

CAITLYN

I have clean hair that does not resemble a muppet. After finding a bottle of lotion that doesn't remind me of my grandmother's house, my skin smells like vanilla. I loved my grandmother, but there's an aesthetic we are going for, and it's *not* geriatric.

We eat canned food cold rather than removing every smoke detector. A hint of smoke and the batteries would roar those suckers to life and send the motorcycle halfling back to us in a flash.

Every bite energizes me, and sitting on the countertop, watching Riley scrape the last bit of green beans from a tin, I feel almost normal. We could be a couple on a Friday night, too tired from coitus to cook a meal, stopping only to find some calories before we go at it again.

Except we haven't kissed even when I stood in front of him bare ass naked.

"What was the best Christmas gift you ever got?" I ask. "And you can't say it's me staying alive. I mean before. When the world was normal."

He sets the green beans down, picks up the can opener, and opens some chicken noodle soup. "Tickets to the Superbowl."

"What!" I'm too loud, and cover my mouth, my eyes wide with shock.

"My dad got them from a vendor wanting his business. It's a long story, but he took me instead of someone at his company. All I had to do was pretend to work there. Fair trade, and after kickoff, no one talked about business."

I shake my head. "Wow. That is a good gift."

"What about you?" Riley asks.

I shrug. "My mom and I always did a craft together every year. She gave that as a gift. Honestly, they were all my favorite."

Missing her physically hurts, but I'm glad she missed all of this. Suffering is a spectrum, terrible no matter what when you're the person in pain. But there are levels of awful. This world would have destroyed everything she loved, everything she knew.

"I bet we can find some wrapping paper in the basement," Riley offers. "Find something in this house and do a gift exchange."

I can't tell if he's joking. Yes, tomorrow is Christmas, but aside from the jerky and a coat, I don't have a wishlist of stuff. We can't carry it north, anyway. Tampons, deodorant, hair ties. Those are the things on my list this year. A sleeping bag would be excellent, but from the photos we've seen, these people weren't campers.

"We need to go through and get things we need, not what we want," I sigh. "No need to wrap them."

"Come on, Caitlyn. Tell me what you want." There's something about the way he speaks, low and sultry, every word dripping with hidden meaning. It makes my insides tickle.

"What I want?" I can't hide the smile spreading across my lips.

"Yes. What could I give you for Christmas? What would be the perfect gift?"

He tosses back the last of the soup, setting the can on the counter and taking two big strides towards me.

My legs part. I blame it on instinct and toss the can I was eating into the sink. He stands between my thighs, his hands cupping under my knees and giving a slight tug. I scoot closer to him, placing my hands on his shoulders.

"What if I wanted to go sing Christmas Carols door to door?" I smile and bite my lip.

"If that's how you want me to use my mouth."

He waits for me to respond, his chest against mine, lips so close I could lift my chin and kiss them.

"I would like…" I trail off, unable to finish my thought. I'm out of breath, my voice cracking. I'm breaking under the pressure. This is it, and I can't make words and tell the man what I want.

I don't have to.

His lips are on mine, devouring me, telling me without words that the wait is over. I'm lifted from the counter, and I adjust my body against his, my legs wrapping around his middle.

We're desperate for each other, hands grabbing at clothing that we can't get off fast enough. I almost fall backward lifting his shirt over his head, and Riley drops to his knees, lowering me to the carpet. We've made it to the hallway, and that's good enough for me. I would have fucked him on the countertop. Who needs a damn bed?

My pants slip down my thighs, and I didn't bother trying to find panties in this place. He's far too dressed, and I sit up, reaching into his waistband with one hand, doing my best to yank the rest of his clothing off with the other.

I gasp when I wrap my fingers around his cock.

It feels amazing. Hot and hard. Thick and throbbing. My smile spreads, and it's infectious. The lopsided grin he returns sends me into overdrive. His imperfections make him sexier, and I palm his length until he tilts his head back and groans. His hand snakes behind my neck, grabbing my hair in a messy ponytail and pulling.

"Should I make a joke about unwrapping this Christmas present?" I say.

The grip on my strands tightens and I pump, slow at first. Root to tip I milk him, watching as his chest rises and falls with shaking breaths.

I am so glad I stayed alive for this.

He's about to lose control, and I'm teasing him, pulling his pants down to his knees so I can see everything.

"Do you ever shut up?" he says, but that smile is still on his lips. I feign offense, letting go of his cock for a moment and placing my palm on my chest.

I'm on my back in a second, Riley's face settling between my thighs. His arms capture my legs and spread them wide. With the first lick, I'm floating. His hot tongue knows exactly where to go and what to do. His fingertips dig into my skin, spreading me wider apart, bruising me, and I love every second of it.

"Finally!" I shout and run my fingers through his hair.

"I know. It's been a whole week," he says before his lips and tongue are back where they belong.

I laugh in between waves of pleasure and decide this is the best sexual experience I have ever had, and I haven't even come yet. The man lets me be mean to him, makes me laugh out loud, and licks my pussy into submission.

This might be love.

Every movement of his mouth sends me higher, and I feel him groan against me when he pauses a few times. He's holding back, doing everything he can not to climb on top of me and fuck me into oblivion.

I'd let him.

My fingers curl into his hair and pull when he finds a rhythm I like. Whimpers escape my lips, soft at first until I'm unable to control myself, my orgasm taking on a life of its own.

He's fused to my pussy while I shatter, my entire body trembling uncontrollably while he doesn't let up. It's only when I reach the peak, my back arching, nipples hard, nails scratching into his shoulders that he slows.

Everything in me relaxes, my body giving in to the release. I take in a large swallow of air, part of me wondering if I blacked out from the orgasm.

Riley's kissing the insides of my thighs, and I shudder a few more times, aftershocks of what this man has accomplished. It's better than I could do myself, a high compliment I don't think I can say to him, but I know it to be true. Every woman's goal is to find a man that is better than a vibrator, and dammit he's amazing.

He didn't even use his dick, and it's right there, bobbing for attention. I want him inside me even though I can barely move and I'm a pile of lifeless, well-orgasmed limbs.

There's the sound of soft humming, a tune I know too well, and I curl to the side and giggle.

"Are you singing Santa Claus is coming to town?" I ask.

He kisses down my leg until he's sitting up, looking at my spent body, and shrugs.

"Maybe," he admits.

I laugh, turning to him, my eyes casting over his cock that's still painfully erect.

"Bedroom?" he offers.

There's no response needed. I turn on my stomach and half crawl until I'm standing. He scoops me up and carries me over the threshold to the master.

My screams when he opens the door are not ones of pleasure.

CHAPTER
THIRTY-EIGHT

"What the fuck is this?" she spits.

I glance around the room, noticing there may be a small issue here but hoping she forgets about it and focuses on us. My cock needs to be inside her, and this might cause a delay.

"This is insane. These people are psychopaths," she carries on. "Do you see this?"

She picks up a figurine, a small child with tall eyes made of cold porcelain. The thing looks at her with innocence, and I notice a halo around its head.

That's not good.

"What does that thing say?" she asks, holding it up and shaking it in the air. "Baby's First Queef, or some ridiculous shit like that?"

I grab it from her, tossing it into a laundry basket. A pile of women's clothes softens the thud when it drops. Out of sight and hopefully out of mind.

"It doesn't matter. Ignore it," I plead.

Caitlyn doesn't listen, scurrying around the room, grabbing tiny human figures and tossing them aside.

There are hundreds of them.

Shelves upon shelves, lining the walls top to bottom.

When I checked this room earlier, I noticed there were some items, but didn't register the sheer quantity. Looking at it with fresh eyes, this is ridiculous.

One breaks after being thrown into a basket and I shake my head. "It's just someone's collectibles. Let's forget about it." I need this woman on the bed and around my cock. Her taste is still on my lips, the sweetness of her release fresh in my mouth.

"It's god dammed Precious Moments," she screams. She pauses her attack, realizing the religious sentiment behind these terrifying cherubs, and mouths a small, "I'm sorry," to whatever deity is up there.

I reach for her, my fingertip tracing her jaw until I take her mouth again. She kisses me, but I feel her pulling back.

"They bother you that much?" I ask.

Every molecule of my body wants her, and I can't believe that some bizarre collection is stalling this moment.

Her eyes narrow and she draws back, her soft skin slipping from my grasp.

"I know I sound crazy, but Riley, you have to get rid of them. This shit is sex kryptonite."

There's no getting around this, and as ordered, I lift one side of a shelf, figurines tumbling to the ground below. A few shatter, but it doesn't stop Caitlyn from scooping up mounds of them and tossing them into drawers, the laundry basket, and the closet.

"I cannot have sex with hundreds of angel baby eyes staring at me," she says slamming the door of the closet while I lift the end of another shelf. Her head whips in my direction. "Are you just going to leave them broken on the floor like that?"

"I'll cover them with a blanket."

It's then I realize that if every inch of these walls is covered with these ridiculous figurines, the floor will be too. "How about another room?" I offer.

We both pause, laughter bubbling up from my gut that I can't keep at bay. "There are…" I laugh. It's the first time in months I've heard the sound of my own laughter. Caitlyn appears utterly shocked by the noise. "There are other rooms in this place. What the fuck are we doing?"

"Not fucking!" she exclaims, her lips wide with a smile. "Which is ridiculous because that is all I want to do right now."

She strides toward me, and I pick her up, her legs wrapping around me as I back out of the room. We're back in the hallway, but I want to lay her in a bed. Her wet center rubs against my stomach and my dick bobs in response.

"You laughed," she says as I round the corner, bumping us both into a doorframe.

I mumble, "I'm sorry," as I crawl us onto another bed.

"Don't be sorry for laughing."

I kiss her, not wanting to explain what I meant. There isn't another second I want to waste between us.

She's soaked, and the moment her back hits the mattress, I line my cock up to her entrance, the tip hovering there while I run my tongue along her lips. Her hips rock, urging me inside, and I don't hesitate.

The first thrust makes the edges of my vision go dark. She's perfect, her walls pressing against every inch of my cock, taking me in and begging me to come. I can't help but growl into her skin, everything in me wanting to make this last as long as possible.

I'll be lucky if I slide out of her twice before exploding.

"Fuck," she whimpers into my chest. She rocks against me, begging me to keep going. My teeth clamp around her shoulder, and I bite down, enough to press into her skin but not enough to hurt.

A few more thrusts and she's moaning, soft cries that threaten to send me over the edge. I can't make it much longer, and I pull out completely, my soaked cock thudding down on the bed.

"No," she calls out. I release my mouth where dark pink teeth marks indent her collarbone.

"I'm about to come," I admit.

"That's the point," she says, taking my cock in her hand and directing it back inside her. I press forward, unable to stop myself. Everything about her feels perfect and good. I'm undeserving, but I'll take it. I'll take her. Every time she'll allow it, I'll fuck her like it could be our last moment together.

My cock begins to swell, and I reach back to grab her hair, tugging gently so her eyes meet mine. Our gazes lock and I see how perfect she is like this. Satisfied but still wanting me.

"Do you want me to fill you up?"

She tries to nod, but I'm holding too tight, her mouth slightly agape from the pull.

"Tell me," I order.

All the back and forth between us, every moment where her comments made me wonder if this was truly what she wanted - what she needed.

I have to hear her say it.

She needs to speak the words.

"I want you to come inside me. Please, Riley."

Her fingernails dig into my skin, her hard nipples press against my chest, and I push deeper, my throbbing cock filling her to the hilt. She lets out a soft cry trying to rock, needing the friction. I give her what she wants, deep slow thrusts until she's screaming as I empty inside of her.

She deserves everything, not just everything I can offer, but everything she could ever want or need.

Holding her against me, the steady pulse of my cock emptying the last of my cum into her, I see on her face that our first time was enough.

I am enough.

I can't change the world as it is today and give her something better, but I want to. I'll do everything I can to make our existence better every day she'll have me.

She reaches up and cups my scarred face. "I'm happy," she says.

"Me too."

I mean it. We both do.

Outside these walls are horror and death, but in this bed together, while both of us are one at this moment, things are perfect.

I smile, kiss her cheek, and force myself to separate from her. She turns to the side and faces me. My scar is visible like this, but I want her to see that it doesn't bother me. Caitlyn has all of me if she wants it.

I'm somewhat self-conscious that I didn't last as long as I wanted, but we've been in foreplay for too long. Not to mention I haven't had a release since the apocalypse.

Wait, no. Way before then.

I run my hand over her hip and realize it doesn't matter. I'll have her again before the sun goes down.

"I like you." She giggles and touches my scar with her fingertips. "You make things better somehow."

Her eyes are heavy and fluttering closed. That won't do. I need to show her how much I want her, and what I can do for her to make this terrible world worth living in.

"I love you." The words tumble out, but she doesn't react in shock.

"I think I love you, too," she whispers and buries her face in my chest. "I've just never loved a man. This is different."

"The world is different."

She curls around me, and I reach for the blankets we've kicked to the bottom of the bed.

"Don't go to sleep," I beg.

"Okay," she yawns. I've lost the battle, her body relaxing against mine despite how hard I'm getting again. Her touch is electric, but I'll have to wait and give her a chance to recharge. Her breaths slow, steady puffs of warm air against my skin before I too find myself getting drowsy.

The feeling of relief washes over me. Maisie's death still dances in the back of my mind, but Caitlyn soothes me. She makes the memories of my sister something I want to share. Her questions keep Maisie alive between us, and all the death and terror from then until now isn't as important as this moment.

This feeling between us is enough, even if that's all we will ever have.

Tomorrow is not promised, but this time when I close my eyes and feel her heartbeat against my chest is here, and I can live in that forever.

That is until dawn peeks through the curtains of our bedroom and the sound of a motorcycle thrums in the driveway outside.

CHAPTER
THIRTY-NINE

Caitlyn

"Just ignore it," I say. "He'll go away. Like a Jehovah's Witness." My voice shakes through the comment, giving away how afraid I am.

"You know it won't be like that," Riley responds. The same worry is in his words. He sits on the side of the bed, eyes narrowed at the crack of sunlight through the curtains. The rumble of a motorcycle doesn't move from outside the house. Halflings know we're in here.

We've been careless, leaving footprints or being too loud. Not to mention the mess of lawn furniture next to the basement window. Maybe we should have focused on cleaning up instead of fucking, but I think the orgasm was worth it. Riley's tongue and cock were my last meal.

"What are we going to do?" I ask. "I haven't been around a lot of halflings. Well, just the one I think. But this doesn't seem normal."

"The one?"

"When I told you about the woman at the grocery store, I mentioned she hadn't turned. Looking back, I think she was a halfling. She could sort of command the others. She held them back for a minute."

His eyes light up, the memory of my story returning.

"If what's outside wanted us dead, they would have eaten us in our sleep, right?" I ask.

That could be wishful thinking, but there wouldn't be a moment to sit here and wonder why they are revving their Harley in the driveway if they were fully turned.

I get up, open a dresser, and toss clothes from side to side before going to the closet where I find something that will work. I'm not sure if I'm dressing for my funeral, but I don't want to be naked unless I'm sitting on Riley's face. It's cold, and I have a feeling we might be running soon.

"You were right about it being halflings," Riley says.

A few seams pop when I pull a too-tight tank top over my torso. "Why would I lie about that? I know what I saw." I find a sweater that's too fancy for the apocalypse, but something camouflage catches my eye, and I decide that will do nicely.

"Thinking about it, we've seen them for the first time in the past few weeks. The bloats are popping left and right, so I don't know, the rule of large numbers," he adds.

This woman owned very few sweatpants, but I find what I think are pajama pants and hop into them. I'm fully dressed except for shoes when I turn around. "What's the rule of large numbers? Riley?"

He's gone.

Creaking wood comes from the front door before it slams shut.

"What the fuck," I mutter to myself and sprint out of the bedroom. Picture frames shake on the wall, threatening to fall from their hinges. I reach the front door and look through the rectangular pane of glass in its center. Riley is walking down the paved sidewalk, striding without a care in the world. My hand hovers over the lock, questioning what I should do next.

Two men, or what used to be men, wait for him to approach.

Maybe an orgasm was not worth this mess.

I lean back, take a breath, and turn around. Stopping at the hall closet, I grab the first pair of boots on the floor and shove my feet inside. How dare that asshole leave me in here after all of his lectures about staying alive. "No one dies tomorrow, Caitlyn," I mutter to myself, sarcasm dripping from every word. "I said stay quiet, Caitlyn. Are you sure they were halflings?"

I march toward the front door, mad as hell, and fling it open before I think about doing anything different.

The men turn to look at the haphazard camo-wearing angry woman standing in the doorway.

These are men, I decide. There's something wrong with them, probably that virus that has taken over the world, but seeing a halfling up close shows how human they truly are.

Their faces have grey lines that create spiderwebs under the skin, and they're weighty. Not fat, but not thin. There's a heftiness to them that's somewhat unnatural, but they still look like two people, not bloats.

It hits me that I don't have a gun or a weapon of any kind. The last thing I want is to turn back around, so I feign resilience and stride forward.

Narrowing my eyes, I do my best not to let my voice shake. "What the fuck do you think you're doing, Riley?"

"I'm going to talk with them," he says. "Go back inside."

Both bikes turn off, and the men dismount, standing at attention, hands clasped behind their backs.

How oddly polite.

"Merry Christmas," one of the halflings offers. He's so fucking sincere when he says it, that I burst into uncontrollable laughter.

Not the thing to do.

CHAPTER
FORTY

Riley

She's laughing.

A lot.

What's more surprising is so are these halflings. They are more human than bloat. Feelings and emotions, that's not something the infected keep.

It wasn't smart to walk out here, but I went with my gut. If they wanted us dead, we would be. Something else kept telling me that they weren't to be feared. A part of me, maybe Caitlyn's influence, encouraged me to accept fate.

They're here for a reason.

Halflings have only been seen venturing around with a pack of bloats, ready to lose all their humanity days after becoming infected. But what if they never do? What if they don't know where else to go?

When I looked through the curtains and saw these two, the possibility felt more like fact. They talked to one another using gestures and eye contact.

Not to mention they could operate motorcycles.

None of it fit, so before I could change my mind, I walked outside. Worst case scenario, Caitlyn could run while I was killed.

"Have we been turned?" she jokes. More giggles escape and she holds her middle, trying with all her might to stop laughing. "Did I miss it?"

"No," one of the halflings says. He's smiling, and relief washes over me. We're going to be okay.

The halflings introduce themselves as Kyle and Enzo. Neither of them knew each other before the apocalypse and both say they were infected within days of it happening.

I introduce us both, giving a high-level account of all we've been through. Caitlyn goes on a ten-minute monologue about cannibals. It's all very normal for an end-of-days meet and greet.

"It's a miracle you two survived," Enzo says.

"Well I can't seem to die no matter what I do," Caitlyn retorts. She's marching around in a most mismatched outfit without a care in the world.

"It's like when I try to get killed I can't. I'm not supposed to be here and neither…" she wags her finger up and down at the men, her face in pure disbelief. "Neither are you two. How are you still like this? And talking. And driving ridiculous motorcycles. Do you know that you are twenty-eight times more likely to die on a motorcycle than in a car?"

She frowns, lowering her finger and raising her hands to her hips.

"Is she serious?" Enzo says before he laughs.

Kyle nods and shrugs.

"I just heard how ridiculous that sounded," Caitlyn admits. "I'm a little wound up at the moment."

"This is a shock," Enzo says.

"So was the sex," Caitlyn mumbles to herself but we all hear her. Her cheeks flush, and she takes a step toward the men. They both back up, Enzo raising his palms to us.

"We don't know if we can infect people," he admits.

"Honestly, we don't know a lot about what's happening to the world and us," Kyle adds. "But we know replicants will be here tomorrow, and you'll have to leave."

"Bloats?" Caitlyn asks. "You call them replicants?"

"Death is gonna walk down this street tomorrow," Kyle responds.

"Call it whatever you want. You may think you're invincible, but if they spot you, you're gone."

Riley points to their motorcycles. There are supplies strapped to the back, items I didn't see when they left. They're scavenging and making their way through the world without being killed. "How have they not spotted you?"

"They do but we're infected," Enzo answers. "I could walk amongst them and nothing happens."

"Damn," Caitlyn says.

I stand there, slack-jawed.

"So you never turned all the way?" she asks. "You're still you but now protected from the bloats, um, er, replicants?"

They both nod.

"What's the capital of Kentucky?"

"Lexington," Enzo says.

"No, dumbass," Kyle corrects him. "Frankfort."

"I honestly don't know," Caitlyn admits. "That was a terrible test, but you pass. Do you eat?" She points to the bags on the bikes.

"We do, but not as much. We don't sleep as much either," Kyle says.

My medical mind wants to do a complete work-up, asking them every question to determine what factors made them this way. Except there are only two of them and any findings would be invalid. Not to mention all the differences in their medical history and genealogy would ruin any tests. One of them might have had mumps as a child or a genetic mutation for Parkinson's disease. It could all play a part.

"Can you talk to them?" Caitlyn asks. "The other infected."

Enzo pauses, his eyes shifting back and forth.

"Well, can you?" I ask.

"It's not exactly language," he admits. "When they're close, I can know what they're doing. There's been a time or two I wonder if they can hear me, but we mostly steer clear."

"It's like a signal," Kyle adds. "We're afraid of it honestly, but we've seen others like us living amongst them."

I cross my arms and nod. "Understandable. Who knows what too much exposure could do."

"I know what it would do to you all," Enzo replies. "You need to leave."

"We're going north. I heard that replicants, bloats, whatever we call them, don't do well in the cold."

They both shake their heads and sigh, unsure of the validity of the theory. "I guess that's as good a plan as any," Kyle says. "But if I were you, I would take the boat."

The four of us stare at each other for a moment.

"The one that comes every few weeks," he adds.

It's still crickets, and we all wait, befuddled about what he's talking about.

"What boat?" I finally ask.

"There's a boat of survivors," Enzo explains. "We've talked to them. They know of other halflings like us. We sometimes go west to check ahead on things for them."

"Yeah, they aren't going North," Kyle adds. "Replicants can't swim, so the boats are the best way to travel as long as you are careful when the river narrows."

My head spins, and Caitlyn's eyes are as wide as saucers. "Survivors," she manages to get out.

The men nod, and I can't get out all the questions I want to ask them. I'm lightheaded, the knowledge that there's a real safe haven somewhere feels too good to be true.

"Are they cannibals?" Caitlyn asks. "It could be a trap leading people to slaughter."

Now I'm laughing.

Enzo shakes his head. "No, these are good people. My mother is with them."

"Your mom," Caitlyn exclaims and presses a palm to her chest. "Oh, that's so nice."

They could still be leading us to a human oven, but it doesn't seem likely. What do they have to gain by lying?

"I don't like her going out on the boats, but she says she's old and lived her life. She wants to help others," he adds. "Are you sure you want to try and get North on your own? A lot can go wrong from here to there, and I know they'll help you."

"They haven't seen a survivor in close to a month," Kyle admits. "But they're committed to going out, and we promised we would talk to ones we find. Or, try to. Lots of folks are skittish."

"You know that could get you killed," I tell them.

Enzo laughs. "Hard to kill." He raises his shirt and displays what I surmise are healed bullet holes. Black rings of scarred flesh indent his body, but he's here, looking healthy-ish and talking with us. "I might be undead. Not sure what I am, but I'm still me."

"I think I might pass out," Caitlyn says.

"Better than screaming. She's a screamer," I tell the men.

"Oh, we heard," Kyle quips. Caitlyn's jaw drops, and I laugh again. This is becoming a habit.

My heart leaps in my chest from excitement. Everything has changed in the last thirty minutes, and I'm so grateful.

Months of wandering, hoping to stay alive, and hating my past all led to this.

A future.

I turn to Caitlyn, reaching for her hands and kissing her cheek. "I think we should go for the boat," I whisper in her ear.

"Oh, definitely," she agrees. "Far less cold, and I estimate the chance for cannibalism is low."

Enzo takes some of the bags off his bike and sets them down on the ground between us. "For your journey."

I look to Caitlyn and all the possibilities for our future swarm my thoughts.

She grabs the bags and holds them to her chest. "So, boys," she proclaims. "When's the next boat coming?"

CHAPTER
FORTY-ONE

I was never a huge fan of caves.

They are dark, darker than anyone's eyes can perceive when no light finds its way inside. Cold and dank, with echoes and shadows around every corner, I didn't understand the appeal.

But this cave, our cave, it doesn't suck.

It's full of people I care about and one that I love. Yes, it is very dark and quite cold, but not Canada-cold.

We make do.

Together.

A huge plus is the giant board in the mess hall of our little cave system.

Written in chalk is the number fifty-seven. That's how many days it's been since the halflings have seen a bloat. Presumably, they've popped themselves into extinction, but Riley and I aren't taking any chances.

Enzo's mother left for the surface permanently the moment the number thirty was scribbled on the wall. She was a hoot, and I miss her.

"I'm older than these, caves, Caitlyn," she would say. "If I kick the bucket up there, so be it. I'm done with living in the dark."

True, the darkness of the caves is beyond imagination. It's terrifying if I don't have Riley next to me after lights out.

When we got here, and I saw the massive number of makeshift beds in the cold underground with water dripping everywhere, I thought there might be an adjustment period, but no problem.

I quickly discovered why we huddled together in one space to sleep. When the darkness takes over, I focus on the breaths around me and remember that I'm not alone and I'm safe.

Riley's hands wrap around me from behind, both of us staring at the wall.

"Sixty," I say.

"One-hundred twenty," he counters.

The discussion of when to go above ground continues. In the twenty-seven days since the seniors packed up, none of them have found themselves face to face with a bloat. It's not enough for Riley who keeps pushing our time here further out.

I debate him a little, but it's all in fun. What's another few months when I plan on loving this man forever?

"Think of how loud I could be during sex," I tell him and turn. We face each other, our lips almost touching. "I could scream as loud as I want without worrying who is around."

He grins, a common occurrence these days, and reminds me I never really care who hears me, which is true.

"Guess what I have," he says, waving a radio just above our heads. I kiss him until he lowers the device and turns the dial.

"Jim!" I shout through the speaker.

"Hey, there Caitlyn. Guess who wants to talk to you."

There's some rustling from his side while Lana grabs at the radio and the babbling commences. I listen as Jim goes on about how she had fruit for the first time this week. Missy felt comfortable enough to let some of our people bring it to an agreed-upon location. They haven't seen bloats in a while either, and after growing the most pathetic clementines I've ever seen, Lana got a taste.

Jim's laughing at her in the background, and we talk while I pace the cave, imagining the day when we will visit.

"We can't wait to see you," Jim says when Lana begins to yawn.

It's nap time and she chooses a grandmother to sleep with in what they call "the big chair". It's a recliner decked out with some stuffed animals, blankets, and handwritten books. That child is living her best life.

How can you miss someone you only knew for a day? I'm not sure but it's possible.

I'm reassured that everyone is clothed each time we speak which is nice, but reminds me of all the old penises. Some memories never go away, no matter how much we want them to.

We say our goodbyes, and when I give Riley back the radio, his hand wraps around my wrist.

"Let's go somewhere," he says.

Oh, hell yes.

I'm almost jogging to keep up with him as we make our way through a passage. It's one we've walked a hundred times before with and without light.

He passes a friend, telling him to keep the hall clear. The guy chuckles and agrees as we keep walking, darkness creeping in around us.

"This is a dead end," I tell him.

The walls close in on us, but I know there is an opening to a storage room just ahead. It leads to nowhere, but Riley keeps all the medical equipment inside. It's his place really, but it's missing an important addition.

A door.

We reach the room, and I hear Riley's hands slipping along the dirt wall before a snap, and a flashlight casts shadows across the space.

"What are you-" but I'm cut off before I can ask the question. My breasts are pressed against the cold wall, his body trapping me from behind. There's another snap, and the flashlight turns off, darkness so black, that my mind can't perceive the color.

"Lights on or off?" he asks.

His warm hand slides underneath my sweater leaving a trail of heat in its wake. He unsnaps my bra, and I feel it loosen before the other hand reaches inside the front of my pants. His mouth presses against the nape of my neck and he asks again. "On? Or off?"

I lean back as he lifts my shirt over my head, cupping my breasts when it hits the ground.

"Off," I whisper.

I'm not afraid of the dark.

All fear disappears with Riley.

I feel his grin against my cheek, and he plucks at my hard nipples, his erection growing thick across my back.

His lips press against my ear. "I want you to be loud in here."

That perfect cock escapes, hard and long, searing my bare skin. My pants slide down my legs, and I feel how Riley is just as naked. When your vision is gone, every other sense is heightened.

The sound of his breath growing faster — sharper — and the touch of his throbbing cock, every vein pumping blood through the shaft, is sometimes better than seeing.

I'm lifted, unsure of where he's taking me as my feet rise from the ground. He knows every inch of this place, memorizing it days after we came here. When I'm set down, he bends me over, and I reach forward, feeling his desk and placing both hands palms down.

"Tell me what you want," he orders.

There's movement behind me, and then the feel of his hands running up and down my legs, massaging my thighs until he reaches my ass and spreads me open.

"You know what I like, Riley." I'm breathy, struggling to make words because I'm so fucking desperate for his mouth and cock.

"Louder," he orders before placing a kiss on the top of my thigh. "Couldn't hear you."

I giggle in response. He's too perfect, too affectionate, and too good at giving me orgasms.

There's not a lot to do down here in these close quarters, but we find a way to fill the time.

"I want you to lick me," I say. It's not loud enough, but I'm teasing him.

"What was that?" I can feel him smiling against my skin and then his hot breath hits my center, close enough to reach with his tongue. My fingernails scratch into the desk, and he smacks my right ass cheek. "Bend over more and tell me, Caitlyn."

"Please lick my clit," I beg while I lean down on the desk, my forehead flush against the wood. "I need it."

He's satisfied with that answer, and the moment his mouth is on me, I cry out. His tongue runs along my dripping pussy, focusing on my clit. Fingers press into my opening. One at first until I'm pushing back against him, begging him with my body.

"Say it," he orders.

"Deeper," I tell him. "More." I'm struggling to speak, my voice trembling from his movements. Riley knows how to press my buttons, and he's pressing them all tonight with perfect force and in the right order. I'm already trembling against this desk, my legs threatening to buckle.

He brings me to the edge, only to pull away, using his fingers and tongue to taunt me, delaying the gratification I'm begging him for.

"Please, Riley. Fuck, I'm close."

"Deeper?" he asks, plunging two fingers inside.

I rear back against him, feeling how swollen my pussy is against his palm. "Your cock. Please. Oh, yes."

I'm a begging mess, pathetically desperate when he has me like this.

And Riley has me like this a lot.

He's fucked me in every corner of this cave, in every way, every day. I thank whatever deity kept me alive this long that my copper IUD is still going strong because nothing stops us from the non-stop fuck fest that is us in these caves.

I've come so much I swear I orgasm in my sleep just from dreaming of his mouth and thick cock.

I scream when he plunges inside me, stretching me to my limits.

"Deep enough?" he taunts, slamming me against the desk.

It doesn't take long, my walls thrumming against his length. His hand reaches for the back of my head, grabbing a fist full of hair and gently pulling my chin up.

"Come loud for me," he orders.

I whine and moan while he slams into me, loving the pricks of pain when he pulls my hair. He pulls out, flips me around, my ass barely seated before he's back inside, his cock stretching me while my ankles are on his shoulders.

When his thumb rubs circles around my clit, I lose control, clawing at the desk and screaming so loud it echoes until we're both spent. His muscles tense as he releases, and in this moment, I wish I could see the sheen of sweat across his chest and the look of pure pleasure on his face.

My legs fall off his shoulders, and he takes me in his arms and kisses me. It's soft and slow, kisses full of promises and love. I rest my hand on his scar, planting a peck there before hopping down from the table.

"Do you think anyone heard?" Riley jokes. I give him a wink but he can't see me.

"We heard," his friend yells from down the hallway.

"How many days until we can leave, again?" I ask Riley.

There's the sound of him feeling around and looking for our clothes.

"Maybe it's up for debate," he offers.

CHAPTER
FORTY-TWO

"Morning," I say with a smile. My mood is exceptional after yesterday.

"Hey, Caitlyn." Myra's greeting is always genuine. She's kind and beautiful, a little too sweet for apocalyptic times.

She isn't exactly a survivor either.

Considering how things have gone for her, Myra's squeaked by due to a series of fortunate events. She's too nice. Giving her food away to anyone she thinks might be hungrier. I caught her about to cut her hair for a stranger, a woman convincing her that she needed a wig.

"A wig of your hair, Myra!" I screeched at her.

She shrugged. "I don't need hair, I guess."

"Yeah and neither does she."

I'd pulled her into a makeshift closet and scolded her again, explaining that this way of life meant she needed to toughen up.

"I just think if it matters that much to them, and not so much to me, why not," she had explained. It's difficult staying angry at someone so generous, but her hair is too nice to cut off.

People take advantage of Myra, but she has Cade looking out for her. He's at her side this morning, doting over her when I walk over.

Riley stands close by, holding a plate of food and talking with another nurse. He catches my eye and gives me that wonderful lopsided smile.

"Are you volunteering?" Cade asks.

My blank expression gives him the answer. I take a seat next to Myra who pokes around at her oatmeal concoction.

"For the scouting south?" he continues. "Still too cold for a northern adventure."

"Ah, no. Not us," I tell him.

This morning, a group of elders announced that some of them wanted to venture further south to look for survivors. They need some younger adventurers to come with. I knew Riley wouldn't be for it, so I didn't bring it up.

"Riley's set on four months with no sighting," I explain.

"And here's the man, the myth, the legend," Cade says, waving for Riley to come over.

The lights flicker today, which has been happening more and more frequently. I'm glad he's by my side if things go dark.

"We are thinking of heading South," Cade says.

Riley nods to him. "You should."

"You're encouraging this?" I ask. "Well, maybe we should join them."

"It's a little more complicated than that," Myra pipes up. "You two should stay, and I think Cade and I are in perfect condition to leave."

I drop my fork and clasp my hands together. I'm missing a piece of this puzzle. "Condition? What are you talking about? Also, I happen to think my condition is fabulous."

Riley wraps an arm around my shoulders and kisses me on the cheek. "Yes, it is. We're having a cave meeting tonight."

"I really think we should have come up with a group name," I interrupt. "The caverners. Cavetown. Cave-o-rama."

"Oh, I like Cave-o-rama," Myra says while the men chuckle.

"The ask from the elders brings up something I've been thinking about for a long time," Riley explains. "We're outgrowing this area. The generators are having a hard time keeping up, and all signs point to minimal bloats above."

I'm confused, and it's written all over my face. Riley's kicking everyone else out, but I have to stay in Caveville?

"There are vulnerable people that should stay here, and that should be sent here," Riley explains. "New mothers. Those that have an illness. And I could use your help."

Riley's been showing me the ropes of nursing, and I've been useful. There's nothing like going through an apocalypse to make you realize a little blood and guts isn't a big deal. I'm numb to it at this point.

"So make this like a hospital?" Myra asks. "I love that."

"Let's see how the others like it," Cade adds.

We look around at the groups eating and talking. They're happy enough, but there's non-stop chatter about going above. We've grown restless in the dark, and fifty-eight days is a long time to go without seeing a bloat. Our hybrid friends travel everywhere we can't, and their reports are the same.

"What about people like Enzo?" I ask. "Are you planning on… seeing what made him that way?"

"I'd thought about it," Riley admits. "They feel very isolated. We are fairly certain they can't infect anyone, but it would be great to do more testing and be sure. Maybe even see if we can find a vaccine."

"Wow, big dreams," Myra says. "I love it. How would you test the vaccine? Would you need volunteers?"

"For the love, Myra," I berate her. "You are not volunteering."

"I wasn't saying me, it's just, you know kids should have a whole life and, you know," she trails off, knowing she's caught. "What if it comes back?"

"It's very kind of you to think of that, Myra," Riley adds. "But any vaccine is decades away."

We finish eating under the flickering lights. They go out for a full minute once, and Riley holds me close, easing any fears. There couldn't be a better time to bring this idea to the masses. No one wants to be left in the dark.

The day goes on as it normally does down here. I help Riley with the inventory the elders have brought. We extract a bad tooth which is fascinating and gross. People come and get some condoms that are dangerously close to expiration. There may be some expectant mothers down here soon at this rate.

Riley and a few elders who came below for the announcement give a convincing speech.

"We aren't asking anyone to leave," he insists. "This is a discussion and then a choice. It's something to consider for the good of everyone left."

Everyone left.

It's a sobering thought. A few more survivors trickled down after us, but until we venture further out, I don't know if we'll find anyone else.

It doesn't take much convincing. The sign-up sheet barely hit the table before people lined up to leave.

When the day is done, which is sometimes hard to tell down here, I'm yawning on a cot in Riley's arms. Soft snores from others around us lull me to sleep. Our apocalyptic lullaby.

"Guess what I made you in the storage room?" he asks.

"Our favorite sex spot? Is it a swing? A Saint Andrews Cross?"

He laughs into the mattress trying to keep the noise down. "No," he tells me. "A wall of tampons, just for you."

"I love you," I say. It's not just the tampons, and he knows it. Even though I do very much love having a stash of absorbent cotton material.

He tilts my chin up, kissing me before saying my favorite words. "I love you, too."

I curl into his chest, finding the spot that keeps me safe and close.

"Do you wish we were going above ground?" he asks. "It's different now. You have choices. If you want to go, I understand."

I think about his words. How that undercurrent between us still swells at times. Riley will always wonder if I'm with him because that's the option the universe gave me, and all I can do is show him with actions and time how that's not why I'm here.

I'm here because I want to be. I want the man who showed me that love is worth living for, and I'm the woman who taught him surviving isn't living.

We are meant to be together. Most fairy tales are horror stories, anyway. A little doom and gloom won't ruin our tale of true love.

"I want to be where you are. Even if that's in a dreary cave pulling out an abscessed tooth."

I can tell he's smiling in the dark. "That's the most romantic thing you've ever said to me."

He might be right, but there's still time for me to find more ways to show my love. We could deliver a baby together. That's gross.

Maybe even our own.

At some point, this IUD won't be pumping out whatever baby proofs my uterus, and I'm okay with that.

Someone coughs, and it echoes through the cave. I frown and whisper in his ear. "But maybe a little re-decorating in your underground hospital. Like a sick and well wing. Maybe a door somewhere. What do you think?"

"Anything for you, Caitlyn."

He kisses me once more and pulls me closer. Our legs wrap together, finding warmth in the perpetual cold of the underground.

I drift off to sleep happy, fulfilled, and alive.

At least for one more day.

Tips for surviving the apocalypse.

Find someone you love, and live. Don't just survive.

TO CONTINUE READING...

Our Serial Survivors keep on living! Up next is Myra Might Survive, another story in the apocalyptic world alongside Caitlyn. Myra's too kind for the end of times. She'll need Cade's help to make it, and he's all too willing to stand by her side.

For other works and signed paperback copies, visit www. lizhambletonbooks.com and read below.

The Storm Series is a completed trilogy. It follows Rowan as she navigates a post-apocalyptic future with her twin nephews. She stumbles across an unconscious man, and they create a family together in the chaos of this new world.

The first book in the series is The Third Storm.

The Fate and Flame duet is a completed series set in a future where fated mates are real—and revealed through touch. Emry and Sebastian have built a happy life together, convinced they'll never find their destined matches. But when Emry unexpectedly brushes against Theo, everything changes.

The first book is Twisted Fate.

The Center Duet is a romance set in a dystopian future where marriage is only promised for ten years at a time before you are forced to renew or find a new partner.

The first book in the Duet is The Discovery Center.

Affluence is a dark romance standalone about a woman who comes back to her island job ten years later to seek revenge and come face to face with the man she still loves.

Keep in Touch is a contemporary second-chance romance standalone about a woman who moves to another country. She wants to connect with a pen pal she's kept since childhood, but an unexpected romance blossoms along the way.